MURDER OF A MARTIAN

A Bernie Fazakerley Mystery

JUDY FORD

MURDER OF A MARTIAN.

Published by Bernie Fazakerley Publications

ISBN-10: 1-911083-10-4
ISBN-13: 978-1-911083-10-8

DEDICATION

To my mother, Beryl Rodd, who has been assiduously
pointing out typographical errors in my previous books, in
the hope that I may have eliminated them all *before* she
reads it this time!

APOLOGY AND DISCLAIMER

I would like to apologise to the University of Oxford for inventing a totally implausible committee (The Intercollegiate Widening Participation Committee) and peopling it with members who are totally unrepresentative of the staff at that illustrious organisation. This committee is completely fictitious and bears no resemblance to any real body at that, or any other, university.

The opinions about the university and its members, expressed by characters within this story, are their own and are included for the purposes of the plot. They should not be assumed to be shared by the author or to have any basis in fact.

This book is a work of fiction. Any references to real people, events, establishments, organisations or locales are intended only to provide a sense of authenticity and are used fictitiously. All of the characters and events are entirely invented by the author. Any resemblances to persons living or dead are purely coincidental.

CONTENTS

ACKNOWLEDGMENTS

I would like to thank the authors of a wide range of internet resources, which have been invaluable for researching the background to this book. These include (among others):

- Wikipedia (https://en.wikipedia.org/)
- Google Maps (https://www.google.co.uk/maps)
- The University of Oxford (http://www.ox.ac.uk/)

Hogwarts School of Witchcraft and Wizardry and the Whomping Willow (which feature in Chapter 11) may be found in the Harry Potter books by JK Rowling, published by Bloomsbury.

Every effort has been made to trace copyright holders. The publishers will be glad to rectify in future editions any errors or omissions brought to their attention.

CHAPTER 1

'I'm sorry to disturb you at home, sir,' Detective Sergeant Anna Davenport said apologetically when Detective Inspector Johns answered his mobile phone. 'But I thought you would want to know about this body we've got. It looks like foul play to me.'

'Yes, you did the right thing,' Peter Johns answered, trying to keep the resignation that he felt out of his voice. He looked at his watch: eight forty-five. By the time he had viewed the scene and made sure that it was secure from being tampered with, it would be well after the time that he usually retired to bed. 'Where are you?'

'The canal. It's in one of those boats moored at the back of Worcester College.'

'OK. Right. I know the place. Just give me twenty minutes or so and I'll be there.'

He put the phone in his pocket and went upstairs to let his wife know that he was going out.

'I'm sorry, Bernie,' he said, putting his head round the door of her study. 'There's a body turned up in a boat on the canal. I'll have to go out and see what's what.'

'Not to worry,' she answered calmly. Bernie had been a policeman's wife for a number of years, on and off, and was used to the demands of the job interfering with normal family life. 'I've got plenty to occupy myself here.'

'Don't wait up,' Peter told her. 'I could be some time.'

When he reached the towpath, Peter saw a bustle of activity centred about a traditional-style narrow boat, one of several moored along the southernmost section of the Oxford Canal. Its name was painted on its prow: *Maid of Saxony*. Anna Davenport hurried over to meet him. She was thirty years old, taller than average, with blond hair secured behind her head in a black 'scrunchy'. Peter had great respect for her professionalism and was convinced that she would have been promoted to inspector before now if her career had not been interrupted by two spells of maternity leave.

'The body was found by two students,' she explained to Peter. 'They're over there on that bench. I think they'd like to go, so maybe you could interview them first?'

'Very well. Take me to them.'

Anna introduced Olivia Best and James Pickering. They were both first-year history students. They had been walking together along the towpath. It was getting dark and there was a light on in the *Maid of Saxony*. Olivia happened to glance in and saw the body quite clearly. They had thought he might still be alive, so they had gone aboard and had a closer look, but he seemed quite lifeless. That prompted them to phone for the police, and now, here they were.

Peter thanked them for reporting the incident and then took down details of the time that they had found the body and asked if they remembered anything else about it.

'Did you see anyone else around, for example,' he asked. 'Particularly anyone who might have just got off the boat.'

'No,' Pickering said, shaking his head. 'It was getting dark, like I said. There was no one else about.'

'Well,' his companion said cautiously, 'there was that man we passed a bit further back. He seemed in a tearing hurry and wasn't looking where he was going.'

'Tell me more,' Peter said, encouragingly.

'It was just this man,' Pickering answered. 'He looked like he was a rough sleeper, maybe. Like Ollie said, he was in a hurry and he pushed past us and nearly tipped Ollie in the water. But that was before we got to the boats, so there's no reason to think he had anything to do with it.'

'But he was coming away from where the boats are moored? Is that right?'

'Yes,' both students nodded.

'So he might have seen something, which means we'd like to find him. Can you describe him to me? And do you think you'd recognise him if you saw him again?'

The description that they eventually agreed on was sufficiently bland as to be virtually worthless, but it was a start. They were both clear that the man had grey hair and a long, dark-coloured coat. Best thought he was rather short, but Pickering, who was a towering six-foot three, said he had not noticed anything unusual about the man's height. Anna carefully noted everything down and hoped that the forensic evidence would give them some better leads than this. It would be hard to convict a man on the basis of having grey hair and being of somewhat less than average height.

Peter finished his questions and told the students that they could go, but that he might need to speak to them again. Then he turned to Anna.

'So, now tell me,' he said. 'Who exactly *is* our body in the boat?'

'We haven't been able to identify him yet,' she answered, 'but the boat is registered in the name of a Martin Riess – that's R-I-E-S-S. I've got his address from the company that owns the moorings.'

Peter climbed down into the boat and looked into the living quarters. Pathologist Mike Carson was there, bending over a figure slumped across a small table. He looked up when he heard Peter arriving.

'Now then, Peter,' he said in his soft brogue, 'come and have a look at this head wound, why don't you?'

Peter pushed past the photographer, who was engaged in capturing a record of the scene, and looked down at the body. Its face was resting on the table, making it easy to see the damage that had been inflicted on the back of the skull. The black hair was matted with blood and there were splinters of bone visible amongst it.

'Is that what killed him?' Peter asked.

'Well, as you know, I never like to commit myself this early on,' Mike said, smiling, 'but I think that's probably a fair assumption.'

'There doesn't appear to be any cash around,' Anna commented, peering in through the hatch. 'And we searched through all his pockets for credit cards, in the hope that they might tell us who he is, and didn't find any. Do you think it was a robbery that went wrong?'

'I suppose it could have been,' Peter murmured, looking round the interior of the boat. 'But it somehow doesn't feel right. This fellow appears to have been caught off guard and hit over the head while he was sitting at the table. If he'd interrupted a robbery and been attacked as the intruders ran away, he'd be on the floor near the door or even out on deck – wherever he was when they realised he'd discovered them.'

'And there's no sign of forced entry, either, sir,' piped up Andrew Lepage, a young, very earnest, trainee detective constable who was keen to make a good impression. 'It looks like he knew his attacker and let him in.'

'Or he may have left the hatch open,' Peter observed. 'I'm not sure we can read too much into the boat being unlocked. I think the residents of narrow boats take a rather different attitude to such things from the average householder.'

'Yes, sir,' the constable agreed, sounding rather deflated.

'But it was a good idea,' Peter added kindly. 'Now, you

say you've got the name of the owner of the boat. Is there any reason not to assume that this is him?'

'No. In fact, I was really assuming that it must be,' Anna replied. 'I mean, that would make sense of him being sat there at the table, wouldn't it?'

'I agree,' Peter concurred. 'So I think we ought to pay a visit to his house next and see if any of his nearest and dearest are around to give us a positive identification. You say you already have the address?'

'That's right, sir,' Anna said. 'I've got it written down here.'

Peter took the piece of paper that she offered him and read the address.

'Headington,' he commented. 'I know that road. It's not far from where I live. Maybe I *will* get to go to bed tonight after all! Right, let's get a move on.'

'Before we go, sir,' Anna said, 'there was one other thing.'

She fished in her pocket and drew out a plastic bag containing a sheet of pale lilac writing paper. Peter read it rapidly. It was addressed to 'Dear Martin' and signed 'Ed'. 'Martin' was presumably Martin Riess, which provided confirmation that the corpse was indeed the owner of the boat where it had been found. The message it contained was short and to the point.

Dear Martin,

Your attitude is quite intolerable. I want you out of my house and out of my life. You will find your things in these boxes. Kindly remove them at your earliest convenience. I never want to see you again.

Ed.

'This was in the deceased's pocket,' Anna said. 'I found it when I was looking for his credit cards – oh! And there's this too.' She held out another bag, containing a small scrap of paper with some characters written on it.

'3 – d – w – 1 – n – 6 – 9 – 1 – 6 – d – y – 5 – C – 1 – 6 – r – 4 – 5 – 0 – n,' Peter read out. 'Any idea what that could mean?'

'Search me,' Anna said, shrugging her shoulders. 'Could it be in some sort of code?'

'Sir!' constable Lepage called out suddenly. 'Look what I've found!'

While they were talking, Lepage had been continuing to search the boat for any clue that might help with the investigation. He held up a laptop computer, which he had found in the storage space beneath one of the bunk beds.

'Now that certainly is interesting,' Peter agreed. 'Bag it up and get it checked for fingerprints, and tomorrow we'll see if we can find out what's on it.'

'Yes sir,' Andy said, pleased that he seemed to have redeemed himself in the inspector's eyes, 'and sir?'

'Yes?'

'Those characters on the piece of paper, sir? I'd say it was a password, sir. It's what some people do. They change some of the letters in a word to be numbers instead, so that it's more difficult to guess.'

'Well, well, well, you don't say,' Peter Johns smiled. 'Do you know something, Lepage? I think you may be right. Tell you what: you can have a go with it on that laptop tomorrow morning. Now, carry on with the search. Anna and I had better get off to Headington.'

As they walked together along the towpath, Peter turned over in his mind the facts of the case so far.

'What do you make of that note?' he asked Anna.

'I don't know, sir. The handwriting looked like a woman's to me – and that notepaper too. I don't know quite how to explain, but the whole thing looked sort of feminine. But the name – Ed – that looks like a man. So could it be a gay relationship? Perhaps a gay man would choose mauve paper and write like a girl. I don't really have any experience of what they're like.'

'One thing I've learned over all my years in this job,'

Peter observed drily, 'is not to generalise about people. They don't all fit nice and neatly into little boxes labelled "gay man", "black teenager", "middle-aged woman" and so on.'

He paused for a moment, before continuing.

'Anyway,' he resumed, 'I think we can safely assume that Martin and Ed, whatever their relationship, had been sharing a house together and had fallen out.'

'I wonder if that was why Martin was in the boat,' Anna suggested. 'Perhaps he was living on the boat after being chucked out of the house.'

'In which case,' Peter agreed, 'presumably we may be about to encounter Ed.'

CHAPTER 2

Martin Riess lived in a semi-detached house in the part of Headington situated outside the Oxford ring road. It was not as old as the Edwardian villa a few streets away that Peter Johns shared with his wife and stepdaughter, being part of the 'new' developments built in the middle of the twentieth century. Peter and Anna drew up outside and walked up the drive to the front door. Peter noted the tidy display of bedding plants and neatly mown lawn in the front of the house. The front door looked freshly painted and the brass knocker was highly polished. Evidently, someone in this house liked to keep things looking nice. He could see a narrow slit of light shining through the heavy, lined curtains that were drawn across the bay window. It looked as if there must be someone in.

The door was answered by a small woman with white hair and blue eyes, who looked up at Peter anxiously. He introduced himself and Anna. She looked enquiringly back, clearly wondering what this visit was all about.

'Am I right,' Peter asked, 'in thinking that a Mr Martin Riess lives here?'

'Yes. Well, it's Doctor Riess,' the woman answered. 'He's my son. But he's out at the moment. What is it? Is there anything wrong?'

She spoke in perfect English, but with a marked German accent and with a touch of anxiety in her voice. She looked from Peter to Anna and back again.

'He is the owner of the narrow boat *Maid of Saxony*. Is that right?' Peter asked.

'Yes, that is correct. Why do you ask?'

'There's been an incident on the boat,' Peter told her, trying to explain why they had come without immediately revealing the true enormity of what had occurred. He always found it hard to break bad news to the relatives of victims and it was particularly difficult in these circumstances, where he was still unsure whether or not it was her son who had been found brutally murdered.

'Vandalism, I suppose,' Mrs Riess said, nodding. 'Well, I am expecting him back any moment, so you will be able to speak to him about it then. He has been dining at his college.'

'His college?' Peter asked. 'He's a member of the university, then?'

'Oh yes!' she replied with a note of pride in her voice. 'He holds a tutorial fellowship at Lichfield College and a university lectureship. The Master expects the fellows to dine on high table least once each term. Martin will not be long – in fact, I was expecting him back before now. Would you like to come in and wait?'

'Did he say anything about calling in at the boat, either before or after the dinner?' Anna asked, hoping to bring the conversation round to a point where they could break it to Mrs Riess that it was possible that her son would not be coming home after all.

'No. He had only just come back from the boat shortly before he set out for college.' Mrs Riess looked somewhat puzzled at the question. 'There cannot have been anything wrong with it then or he would have told me. But look! There he is! You can ask him all about it yourself now.'

Peter and Anna turned to see a man on a bicycle

turning in at the drive. He wore a blue cycling helmet and a hi-vis cycling jacket over black trousers. When he saw Peter and Anna, he dismounted and walked towards them, pushing his bike.

'Can I help you?' he asked, looking up at Peter with an air of mild belligerence and taking off his helmet to reveal a shock of yellow-blond hair. He was a small man – much shorter than Peter and even shorter than Anna – with pale blue eyes, like his mother's, and an expression on his face that made it clear that he would not stand for anyone doing anything to upset her. He looked young for a tutorial fellow – in his thirties, Peter judged – but then, Peter's own wife must have been less than that when she gained her fellowship, so perhaps he was wrong in thinking that dons were normally not appointed until they were approaching middle-age.

'Are you Martin Riess?' Peter asked calmly, 'the owner of the *Maid of Saxony*?'

'Yes,' the man answered in a puzzled tone. 'What of it? And who are you?'

'I'm Detective Inspector Johns,' Peter answered, holding up his warrant card, 'and this is Detective Sergeant Davenport. We need to talk to you about an incident that has taken place on your boat.'

'An incident?' Riess repeated. 'What do you mean?'

'Some passers-by found a dead man aboard,' Peter said bluntly, after a moment's hesitation. 'We had assumed it must be you.'

Mrs Riess gave a small intake of breath at the mention of a dead man, and her son looked up at her anxiously.

'Go inside, Mutti,' he said with gentle authority. 'And take these officers with you.'

He turned to Peter.

'If you can just give me a minute to put my bike away I'll be with you directly.'

'They followed Mrs Riess into the front room and sat down on a three piece suite, upholstered in green velvet that matched the curtains. There was a piano standing against one wall, with sheet music piled up on top of it. The small bookcase standing next to it held a mixture of books in English and German. On top, there stood several photographs. Peter recognised a younger Martin Riess dressed in gown and mortarboard and carrying a degree certificate. Was the young woman in the next photograph, pictured sitting at a grand piano in a long evening dress, Mrs Riess? He could not make up his mind.

'Can I get you anything to drink?' Mrs Riess began, but she was interrupted by the arrival of her son, who guided her firmly to take a seat on the sofa and then turned to speak to Peter and Anna.

'Might I suggest, officers, that we go elsewhere to talk about this? My mother is not in any way involved and there is no need for her to take part in your enquiries.'

'Very well,' Peter agreed readily, sharing the desire to avoid distressing Mrs Riess unnecessarily. 'We need you to come down to the boat in any case, so that you can tell us if anything has been stolen. I suggest that you come down there with us now and we can talk on the way.'

He got up and Anna followed suit. They said brief good-byes to Mrs Riess and headed for the door. Martin followed them, after speaking in a low voice to his mother, urging her to go to bed and not to worry.

'I am sure that it will turn out to be an accident of some kind,' Peter heard him saying to her. 'Just put it out of your mind and I'll tell you about it in the morning.'

Then he said something more in German and placed his hand on her shoulder briefly before turning to go.

'You drive,' Peter ordered Anna, when they got outside. 'I'll go in the back with Dr Riess.'

As they drove down Headington Hill, back towards the city centre, Peter handed Riess the letter that had been in the dead man's jacket pocket.

'Can you tell me why a man might have turned up dead on board your boat with this letter in his pocket?'

Riess looked at the letter and then turned in his seat so that he could look Peter in the eye.

'The man was an old friend. He came to me asking for a bed for the night and I let him stay on the boat.'

'But this letter,' Peter insisted. 'Why did he have it? It's addressed to you.'

'No. On the contrary, it is addressed to him. His name is Martin Fellowes. It is from his wife, Edwina. You may perhaps have heard of her. She is a politician – not a particularly famous one, but a Member of the European Parliament. She uses her maiden name: Edwina Clarkson.'

'So, let me get this straight,' Peter said. 'You're telling me that this Martin Fellowes had fallen out with his wife and she'd chucked him out and he came to you?'

'That's right. He came to me in my college room and asked if I could put him up until he found somewhere more permanent to live. I said that I could not have him at home because it would not be fair on my mother, but that he could stay in the boat if he liked.'

'And when was this?'

'Last Thursday.'

'So he'd been staying there for five days.'

'This would have been the sixth night, yes.'

'Did he tell you what it was that he and his wife had quarrelled about?'

'No. I didn't ask.'

'So you've no idea what she meant by his intolerable attitude?'

'No.'

'When did you see him last?'

'Just this afternoon. I called in at the boat at around about four and stayed until half-past five. Then I came home to dress for dinner, because I was dining on high table.'

'And how did he seem when you left him?'

'Just as usual.'

'Not upset or anxious in any way?'

'No.'

'Did he have any enemies?'

'Someone who might want to kill him, do you mean?'

'Anyone at all who might wish him ill.'

'I don't know any names,' Martin answered with a shrug. 'He was a journalist. He specialised in exposing people's failings. I imagine that might make him enemies, but whether they would …'

'What about his wife? That letter said she wanted him out of her life. Do you think she could have wanted him dead?'

'I don't know. I would not have thought so. It would be so risky for a public person to do such a thing.'

Peter noted silently that Riess had not suggested that the man's wife were incapable of murder, only that her position made it unlikely that she would attempt it. Was this the frank observation that it appeared, or a clever ploy to sow seeds in the minds of the police that Edwina Clarkson could have wanted her husband dead?

'You say this Martin Fellowes was a friend of yours. How did you know him?' Peter asked, deciding to try a different line of questioning.

'We met while I was studying for my PhD at Cambridge. He had just graduated from that university and, at that time, he had a job with a local newspaper there.'

'Did you know his wife too?'

'They were not married then; but, yes – I knew her. She was in her last year of a law degree when I went there and then she went on to become an articled clerk with a firm of Cambridge solicitors.'

'And then, after you left Cambridge, you stayed in touch?'

'Martin and I used to correspond occasionally. I was working in America for several years, so we rarely met, but we sent cards at Christmas – that sort of thing.'

'And yet, you were the person that he chose to come to

when his wife turned him out of their house?'

'I suppose his more recent acquaintances will have been his wife's friends too,' Riess said, with a shrug. 'Perhaps he was afraid that they would take her side. I did not ask. He came to me and I felt obliged to do something. It was no problem allowing him to use the boat, and he said he would make other arrangements in a few days' time.'

They left the car in the large car park in Worcester Street and walked the short distance to the towpath. As they approached the *Maid of Saxony*, two men climbed out of her, bearing the body of Martin Fellowes concealed in a body bag. Behind them came Mike Carson, pulling off his latex gloves and loosening his protective clothing.

Peter accosted them and asked them to unzip the bag to reveal the victim's face. He and Anna gazed down with interest. Up to now, the dead man had been face down on the table and they had not been able to see what he looked like. They saw a handsome face with even features, a bronzed complexion and black hair. He looked much older than Martin Riess, although, from what Riess had said, they must be almost exact contemporaries.

'Dr Riess?' Peter said, looking up again. 'I wonder if you would mind taking a look and telling us whether this is Martin Fellowes.'

Riess stepped forward and looked down at the dead man. His already pale face turned even whiter and, for a moment, Peter thought he might be about to faint. Then he recovered himself and took a step backwards.

'Yes,' he said quietly. 'That is Martin Fellowes. What happened to him? I mean how did he die?'

'We can't be sure yet,' Peter explained, 'not until after the post mortem. But it looks as if he must have been hit from behind.'

'So, you think someone killed him? You don't think it could have been an accident?'

'It certainly doesn't look that way,' Peter said

cautiously.

'We'll have a much better idea once we get him back to the mortuary,' Mike added cheerfully. 'Just give me a chance to put him on the slab and open him up, and we'll soon know what's what!'

'Yes, thank you. Mike,' Peter said firmly, seeing that Riess had paled again at the mention of a post mortem. 'I don't think we need all the gory details, do we?'

He took Riess by the elbow and ushered him aboard the boat.

'We think it's possible that the killer entered the boat intent on robbery, thinking it was deserted, and hit your friend to stop him raising the alarm. So we'd like to you check whether anything has been stolen.'

'Well, I'm not sure how much help I'm going to be to you in that respect,' Riess said tentatively. 'I mean – I don't know exactly what Martin brought with him.'

'But there must be lots of things that come with the boat – furnishings and equipment. You'd be able to tell if any of them were missing, wouldn't you.'

'Yes, I suppose so – but there wasn't much that would be worth stealing.'

'If you wouldn't mind taking a look anyway …' Peter suggested.

They climbed down the steps into the cabin. Riess looked around. Then he started systematically going through the cupboards and drawers. After making a thorough search, he turned to Peter.

'The only thing I can say for certain that is gone is Martin's laptop. He kept it in that drawer there,' he said, pointing towards the drawer from which constable Lepage had taken it. 'The laptop and the power cable are both gone.'

'Thank you. We have the laptop. We need to go through it to see if Mr Fellowes left any messages on it that might help us work out who killed him. So, you're saying that, as far as you can tell, nothing has been stolen?'

'Yes. That is correct.'

'Alright,' Peter said slowly. 'Now sit down for a minute and tell us about your movements, from when you left the boat this afternoon to when you came home after dinner – just for the record, so we can be sure of the timings.'

Riess looked back at him thoughtfully. Peter was sure that he was completely aware that he was the prime – if not the only – suspect at present.

'As I told you,' Riess began, 'I left the boat at half past five. I know that was the time because I checked my watch. I had fixed with myself that I must get away at five-thirty in order to be in time for dinner in hall.'

'And you got home, when?' Peter prompted him.

'It must have been just after six. I dressed for dinner and set out again at about twenty past, reaching Lichfield at about quarter to seven. I chained up my bike and went to the Senior Common Room for drinks before dinner. Dinner is at seven thirty. I was hoping to get away by nine, but the Master delayed me with some questions about the university strategy for widening participation. I'm not sure what time I eventually left, but it's about half an hour by bicycle, so you will be able to work it out by subtracting thirty minutes from the time I arrived home – which I expect you will have noted down.'

'Thank you. That's all very clear and precise. Now, I have to ask: were you and Martin Fellowes still on good terms when you left him? You didn't quarrel about anything?'

'No. Everything was just as previously. We parted completely amicably.'

'Good. Now, do you have contact details for Mrs Fellowes?'

'You mean Edwina? I can find you the address and telephone number of their London flat, but she may well not be there. As I said, she's an MEP so she's constantly travelling between London, Strasbourg and Brussels. It's a wonder,' Riess added, with the first sign of humour that he had shown that evening, 'that they met frequently enough to have time to fall out about anything. Would tomorrow do? I'm not sure if I left it at home or in my college room.'

Peter looked at his watch. There would be little point in trying to contact the widow tonight. It was not as if she were anxiously awaiting her husband's return. He might just as well wait until the morning when, if she were not in the flat, she might be traceable through her constituency office. He nodded.

'Very well, I think that's all for now then,' he concluded, closing his notebook. 'You can go home now, but I will need to speak to you again tomorrow and I need you to have those contact details ready for me.'

'I quite understand, but please could we meet in my room in college – or at the police station, if you prefer – rather than at home. I do not want to have my mother upset.'

'Very well. How will we find you in college?'

'Just give my name at the Porters' lodge and they'll direct you.'

Anna made her own way home, while Peter drove Martin Riess back, dropping him off in front of his house and then continuing the short distance on to his own house. Peter pondered to himself as he turned in at the drive and prepared to park the car. He had been favourably impressed by Martin Riess, who gave every appearance of being honest and straightforward, and who showed a touching concern for his mother. On the other hand, his reluctance to involve his mother could be prompted, not so much by a desire to keep her from unpleasant realities, as to prevent her learning about the killing and perhaps telling the police things that Martin did not wish them to know. He was, after all, the obvious murder suspect, being the last person to see the victim alive, and having known both the victim and his wife. Could it be that he was more on the wife's side than he was admitting to?

Peter tried his best to avoid waking his wife, as he changed into his pyjamas and climbed carefully into bed beside her. As soon as he lay down, however, she turned over and put her arm around him demonstrating that he had failed miserably in his efforts not to disturb her.

'How's your body in the boat?' she asked conversationally.

'Difficult to say. It's almost certainly murder, but by whom or why – well, as I will tell the press in the morning, we are still in the very early stages of our investigation and we are keeping an open mind and ruling nothing out.'

'And who is he – or she – or it?'

'Some journalist by the name of Martin Fellowes. According to his bosom friend and the owner of the boat – who is a Dr Martin Riess of Lichfield College – he'd fallen out with his wife and was staying in the boat until he found somewhere more permanent to live.'

'Did you say, Martin Riess?' Bernie asked, suddenly alert.

'Yes. Do you know him?'

'Only very slightly. He and I share the dubious distinction of having been nominated by our respective colleges to serve on a particularly boring university committee. So, once a month we sit around a table discussing proposals that hardly anyone is interested in and passing resolutions that never get implemented and then we go away again and nothing happens until the same time next month.'

'So what's is all in aid of?'

'Getting more students from state schools and working class backgrounds into Oxford. The trouble is, most of the members are dinosaurs who've only been put on the committee by their respective colleges because they can't be trusted with anything really important, and who think that admitting a couple of boys from Manchester Grammar constitutes making real inroads into the inner cities of The North.'

'Would that be called, "widening participation" by any chance?'

'It would indeed – where did you pick up the jargon from?'

'Martin Riess told me that the Master of his college engaged him in conversation about it after dinner and thus prevented him from getting home to his doting mother on time. Of course, my suspicious mind tells me that it could be camouflage to conceal a trip back to his boat after dinner for a spot of murder.'

'So old Martin's on your suspect list?'

'Currently, he's not only on the top of the list, but it's a list with no other names on it – with the possible exception of the victim's wife. So, now tell me about this Martin. What's he like?'

'I already told you – I hardly know the man.'

'But you must have some ideas.'

'What do you want to know? When it comes to the refreshments, he always chooses the brown liquid that the catering staff euphemistically refer to as "coffee" rather than the equally vile liquid purporting to be tea. He takes it without milk and with three sugars. You can tell when he's really fed up with the proceedings because he keeps his head down and pretends to be very busy reading the meeting papers. He's a useful ally when it comes to pushing through new ideas, because, unlike most of the members, he doesn't accept that "but the university has done it that way for the last four hundred years" is a valid argument.'

'But what is he *really like*?' Peter asked, smiling at Bernie's description of the attitudes of her more conservative colleagues.

'Well, I'm not prepared to commit myself on the subject of whether or not he would be capable of murder, if that's what you're hoping for. All I can say is, if he is guilty, could you please put off making an arrest until after a week next Thursday, because I'm relying on him to support me in a bid for funding for a programme of outreach projects to try to raise the academic aspirations of children in care.'

'OK,' Peter said, keeping his voice deadpan, despite being highly amused at his wife's response. 'I'll bear that in mind – provided he doesn't turn out to be a serial killer. I don't think the Chief Super will be much impressed if I admit to having allowed a murderer to kill again just so as to keep him in circulation for long enough to get your plans through the committee!'

CHAPTER 3

Wednesday dawned cold and bright. As he ate his breakfast, hardly any time, or so it seemed, after arriving home in the early hours, Peter considered the priorities for the day. He must try to contact the victim's widow. He had better do that himself, so that she would not think that she had been palmed off with some junior officer. Did he have any other family who ought to be informed, he wondered. He had forgotten to ask Martin Riess about that – he must add it to the list of things to include in his interview that morning.

Then there was the laptop. He had told young Andy Lepage that he could look into that, but perhaps he ought to ask Anna to keep an eye on Andy to make sure he did not miss anything. Andy was keen as mustard, but inexperienced and might easily overlook something important. He was one of the new breed of graduate trainees, with a first class degree in criminology from the University of Leicester but rather little in the way of life-experience.

Peter did not like to admit it, but he knew that he was in danger of favouring Lepage, due to his racial origins (about which Peter would never dream of asking him) being apparently very similar to those of Peter's own children. His skin was a smooth caramel brown – paler now than when Peter had first met him, fresh from his initial training at the tail end of last summer – and his hair was the familiar frizzy Afro that Peter had loved in his first wife and struggled to keep under control in his two children. Of course, it was because his superiors knew that Peter could be relied upon to be sympathetic towards a mixed-race trainee that Lepage had been allocated to him. Peter hoped fervently that Andy was not aware of this. His approach was to ignore all racial and other differences, and he made a conscious effort to treat Andy exactly the same as if he had shared Peter's fair skin and red hair.

He must brief a team of officers to do house-to-house visits in the hope that someone would have seen something suspicious – and that had better be done first thing, so as to get out there while people's memories were still fresh. What time would Mike be starting the post mortem? Peter would like to be there, but perhaps this was something else to give to Anna.

'Penny for your thoughts?' Bernie said, gently guiding Peter's hand, in which he held the teapot, so that it was positioned over his cup, rather than his bowl of breakfast cereal, which he seemed about to drown in tea.

'Sorry,' he replied, pouring his tea and replacing the pot on the table. 'I was just trying to decide the running order for today. There seem to be too many things that all need to be done first.'

'Can't you delegate?'

'Yes but it's not just a matter of me not being able to do everything at once. It's things like: I could do with knowing what's on Fellowes' laptop before I talk to Riess; but I have to talk to Riess before anything else, because he's the only person who can tell me how to find Fellowes' wife.'

'I thought you said she was an MEP. Surely that means she'll be easy to track down. You just have to pretend that you're a constituent and there must be plenty of ways of getting to talk to her.'

'That's a point,' Peter agreed. 'You're right. We can trace her and talk to her first before getting back to Riess. We really must find her ASAP, because she's his next-of-kin, even if they have fallen out, and she has a right to know.'

'Assuming she isn't the murderer and hence all too well aware of what's gone on.'

'Riess thought she wasn't likely to have done it,' Peter recalled. 'He reckoned she knew it would be too dangerous, with her being in the limelight so to speak.'

'She could have paid someone else to do it for her, I suppose,' Bernie suggested. 'Isn't that what politicians do? They just provide the window-dressing and get other people to do all the work in the background.'

'That's a very cynical attitude.'

'I know. It's sad to see it in one so young, isn't it?'

'It certainly is,' Peter agreed with a smile. At fifty-six, he was a mere seven years older than his wife and he was well-aware that she had no real pretensions to youth.

'What does cynical mean?' demanded Lucy, Bernie's seven-year-old daughter, looking up from her bowl.

'It means, assuming the worst of people, I suppose,' Bernie answered. 'So, for example, suppose I went up to your room and found you'd tidied it without me nagging at you. If I was a cynical person, I might put it down to you trying to get on the right side of me so that I wouldn't mention the grubby finger marks you've left all over the wallpaper on the stairs.'

'How did you know it was me?'

'Elementary my dear Lucy,' her mother answered with a grin. 'Nobody else in this family has hands that size or positioned at that distance off the floor.'

'And nobody else manages to get their hands so filthy before breakfast,' Peter added. 'And those marks weren't there last night.'

'Sorry,' Lucy said contritely. While she exhibited little respect for her mother, she was always very concerned not to lose the good opinion of her stepfather, who was also her favourite person.

'Well I can't hang around here all day,' Peter declared, getting up. He picked Lucy up off her chair and gave her a hug. 'See you later, sunshine. Have a good day at school.'

When he got to work, Peter found that Anna had already assembled a team of officers ready for his briefing. Andy Lepage was sitting eagerly in the front row, evidently keen to be involved in this exciting case. The room fell silent as Peter walked in and he experienced a moment of self-doubt as he realised that everyone was relying on him to bring the investigation to a successful conclusion.

He briefly outlined what they knew so far and sent the majority of the group off in pairs to conduct the house-to-house enquiries.

'Don't forget to call at the boats on the canal, he reminded them. 'A lot of them have people living in them permanently. They are the most likely to have seen something useful last night.'

There was a clattering of chairs as the officers organised themselves into pairs and left the room. Then Peter turned to Anna and Andy.

'I assume the laptop is with the forensics people?' he asked.

'I told them to get it back as soon as they can,' Andy nodded.

'So, while we're waiting, I'd like you to do the rounds of the homeless shelters – take PC Hughes with you – looking for anyone answering the description that those two students gave us of the man who pushed past them on the canal bank. Don't mention the murder, just say we're looking for witnesses to an incident on the canal. Hughes knows a lot of them and I think they'll trust him.'

'Yes sir,' Andy said, looking pleased but a little anxious. 'I'll get on to that right away.'

Don't worry,' Peter added, noting the anxiety and correctly deducing that Andy was concerned that he might not be given the promised task of searching the victim's computer for clues. 'We'll give you a buzz when the laptop comes back.'

Peter turned to Anna.

'Can I leave you to get an incident room set up, with plenty of staff to receive phone calls? I'm going to set one of the secretaries on to tracking down Edwina Clarkson MEP and then get on to the local radio stations to put out an appeal for witnesses.'

'Yes sir. And then will we be going to see Dr Riess again?'

'Not just yet. I must try to get hold of the widow before the radio broadcasts go out – and before rumours start circulating. Those two students won't have been able to keep what they saw to themselves, I'm quite sure, and you never know who Dr Riess may have been talking to, either. The other thing is that it may be better to see what we can find on that laptop before talking to Riess, in case there's anything there that we need him to explain. At the moment he's the only person we've got who knows anything at all about this Martin Fellowes. Tell you what – if you get a moment, after you've sorted out the room, try Googling him and see what you can find. If he's a journalist he's likely to have some sort of presence on the web.'

Peter's morning was frustrating, with much activity but little to show for it. Edwina Clarkson's London office told the secretary who rang them that she was in Strasbourg and was not expected back until the weekend. The Strasbourg office reported that she had flown to London on Monday evening and they had heard nothing from her since. There was no reply on her mobile number or the landlines at her flat in Canary Wharf and her house in Beaconsfield. Peter told the secretary to keep on trying and turned his attention to the press conference that his superiors had decided must be held at once. Something must be done, they told him, to keep at bay the growing crowd of journalists and TV crews assembling at the entrance to the towpath and blocking the A4144, with resultant chaos for traffic attempting to enter the city from the west.

Peter hated speaking in front of the camera, but he recognised that there was no better way of appealing for witnesses to come forward. It was also essential to keep the press on his side – all the more so when it was one of their number who had been killed. Not that he was at liberty to confirm the identity of the victim until he had made contact with the widow and any other family that there might be. He ordered a press conference to be arranged for eleven a.m. and sent a contingent of uniformed officers to inform the waiting press and persuade them to go back to their homes and offices meanwhile to leave the roadway clear for travellers.

At ten forty-five, a call came through from Strasbourg to say that Edwina Clarkson had returned there the day before and was now in her office. Peter spoke to her briefly on the phone – something that he usually tried to avoid when imparting bad news to relatives – and gained the impression that she had much better things to do with her time than to discuss the death of her estranged husband. She gave permission for his name to be made public and referred Peter to her own press agent in case any journalists asked for a statement from her. As far as she knew, Martin's only living relative was a brother in Canada. She would get her secretary to email Peter his contact details. She would be returning to London on Friday, to spend some time in her constituency. If it was necessary, Peter could interview her then, but she was sure that she had nothing to tell him that would be of any help in finding Martin's killer. No, it would not be possible for her to come back to the UK any sooner. She had a busy programme of work to complete in Strasbourg.

Peter put down the telephone receiver and sat for several minutes contemplating what he had just heard. He could not understand the attitude of this woman, who seemed to see her husband's sudden death as merely an inconvenient interruption to her own important work. His own first wife had been killed in a racist attack four years previously and he still held vivid memories of the moment when he had looked up from his desk to see Chief Superintendent Fuller standing there, looking very uncomfortable and struggling to find the words to tell him that Angie was dead. Nothing in the world could have kept Peter from going straight away to the scene of the crime to see for himself the hideous reality. There must be something seriously wrong with Edwina Clarkson's marriage if she could carry on calmly as if nothing had happened, after being informed that her husband had been bludgeoned to death.

But perhaps he was wrong. Could it be that this was her way of coping with an unbearable situation? Was she continuing in a familiar routine in order to avoid having to face up to an unthinkable event and an uncertain future?

On the other hand, quite apart from their recent rift, Mr and Mrs Fellowes clearly had a very different relationship from what Peter saw as normal married life. Although he loved his work, he was always glad at the end of the day to return to the bosom of his family and he always missed Bernie acutely when she went off to conferences or on collaborative visits to other universities. What sort of marriage was it where one of the couple was constantly flitting between England, Strasbourg and Brussels? They must have seen very little of one another, which perhaps made it all the more significant that Edwina had thrown Martin out so peremptorily. If she simply did not wish to see him anymore, it would surely have been easy enough to avoid him, what with her job and their two homes.

Peter shook his head in puzzlement. Then he looked at his watch and realised that he was late for the press conference. He pulled on his jacket, straightened his tie and headed for the door. Better get it over with.

As Peter had anticipated, several of the attendees at the press conference appeared to be friends of the deceased. Even among those who did not know him personally, there were many who were vocal in calling for justice for a fellow-journalist and in demanding to know whether the police thought that his murder had been prompted by his work as an investigative reporter. Peter had positioned Anna at the back of the room, near the entrance doors, and he had primed her to make a note of anyone who might be worth interviewing to gain information on Fellowes' background, and he had a team of officers waiting outside the room to intercept them as they departed. Meanwhile, he answered their questions as briefly as possible, emphasising how early it was in the investigation and assuring them that they were in the process of following a number of lines of enquiry. Of course, these were experienced reporters who would be well aware that this form of words simply meant that they did not know what had happened and would not have told the press if they did.

Peter concluded with an appeal for anyone who had been on the towpath the previous day to come forward. Then he got up and made what he hoped was a dignified exit, accompanied by the Chief Superintendent, who was in attendance to add gravitas to the occasion and to make it clear that this case was being taken extremely seriously. Then, the moment the door closed behind them, he ran down the corridor to the other end of the room in order to watch the audience dispersing through the main doors.

Anna was there, watching the departing crowd and, every so often, drawing one aside and handing them over to be interviewed by one of the police team. Peter admired her quiet efficiency. It was a shame that she was still a mere detective sergeant: she deserved better. But perhaps Jessica, aged six, and Marcus, aged five, preferred that their mother did not have to shoulder the added responsibility of an inspector's role. Family life was so complicated these days.

After a hurried lunch, Peter convened a meeting with Anna and Andy to review progress so far. Andy arrived clutching the laptop, which had been released with a report that the only fingerprints that could be distinguished on it belonged to the corpse himself. He was clearly desperate to try out his password on it, so Peter allowed him to set it up on the desk and power it up.

While they waited for the machine to boot up, Peter asked him about his morning's work among the homeless community. Andy got out his notebook and flicked through it.

'We found a couple of people who answered the description of the man on the towpath,' he reported, 'but neither of them admitted to having been there last night. They both claim to have alibis, but I haven't had time to follow up on them yet.'

'Don't worry about that,' Peter interjected. 'Just write down the details and we can get someone to check them out later.'

'There's also a rough sleeper that Constable Hughes reckons might be our man,' Andy went on. 'Apparently he prefers to sleep out under one of the canal bridges, rather than in a hostel. Gavin says he doesn't have a record for violence but he's a petty thief and might have lashed out if he was cornered.'

'That's interesting. Any idea where he is now?'

'No. Gavin's going to ask around. He knows some of his mates and he thinks he may be able to get them to talk to him if he can get them on his own. He seems to know them all, so I thought maybe it was best to leave it to him,' Andy finished, sounding a little dissatisfied.

'Quite right,' Peter agreed. 'They're a tight-lipped bunch, but if anyone can get them to open up, it's Gavin Hughes. Did he have a name for this potential suspect?'

'Dave Gillis. Have you come across him?'

'I have,' Anna broke in. 'Gav's right. He's been convicted of theft quite a few times, but only very small, opportunistic stuff. I'd say he might well have gone aboard the *Maid of Saxony* to see what he could find, and then panicked when he discovered that Martin Fellowes was there.'

'Except,' Peter objected, 'and I keep coming back to this: if Fellowes was sitting down at the table, the way it looks as if he was, why didn't Dave Gillis, or whoever it may have been, simply run away when they saw him? Why bother hitting him over the head?'

'Perhaps he thought Fellowes would be able to identify him?' Andy suggested.

'I'm not convinced,' Peter argued. 'Why risk a murder conviction for the sake of a minor theft? In fact, he hadn't even taken anything!'

'His plastic cards and wallet were gone,' Andy pointed out, reluctant to give up the idea that he might have discovered the perpetrator of the crime through his efforts that morning.

'But those would most likely have been in the pocket of his jacket, which he was wearing when we found him,' Peter pointed out. 'So the thief could hardly have already taken them when he came across Fellowes sitting at the table.'

'So, maybe he hit him over the head in order to rob him,' Anna suggested. 'He may not have intended to kill him, just to knock him senseless. Maybe he was desperate for money to feed a drug habit – a lot of rough sleepers do have drug or alcohol problems.'

'I'm still not convinced,' Peter said sceptically. 'I can't help thinking this attack was more personal and that we need to be looking for the killer among the victim's family and friends.'

Then, seeing the disappointment on Andy Lepage's face, he added, 'but it was good work identifying this Dave Gillis. If he is the man on the towpath he could well be a valuable witness.'

'Would you like me to go out with Gavin this afternoon and try to find him, sir?' Andy asked, brightening up.

'No. You've got a more important job to do,' Peter answered, pointing towards the laptop, which by now was displaying a login screen. 'Sit down and let's see how you get on trying out that password you're so proud of.'

Andy immediately sat down in front of the computer and moved the cursor to the appropriate place. They all stood round, waiting eagerly, as he carefully keyed in the sequence of characters from the slip of paper in the victim's pocket. There was a moment of anxious anticipation while they waited to see whether it would be accepted, and then a feeling of relief when the word "welcome" appeared on the screen.

'Well done, Andy!' Peter said warmly. 'I'll leave you and Anna to browse around to see if there's anything here that might help us. You can stay here in my office out of the way. I'd better get back to the incident room and see if we've had any useful calls from the public or anything turning up from the house-to-house.'

Some twenty minutes later, an excited Andy Lepage arrived in the incident room, looking for Inspector Johns. Peter looked up from the statement he was reading from the occupant of a neighbouring boat, who claimed to have heard noises coming from the *Maid of Saxony* at about eight fifteen the previous evening.

'Yes, Andy,' he said mildly, 'what is it?'

'We've found something that we think you ought to see, sir. It's an email that Fellowes sent the night before he was killed.'

Peter followed Andy back to his office, where Anna was seated in front of the computer, gazing intently at the screen. She looked up when Peter entered.

'Look at this, sir,' she said, moving aside so that Peter could sit down at the desk, and pointing at a window on the screen where an email message was displayed.

'Martin came round after dinner,' he read aloud, 'and we shared a bottle of scotch – or it may have been two. He got rather maudlin and started going on about how he'd killed his father. Rather an interesting idea, don't you think? I couldn't get him to go into details but I'm thinking it could make rather a good story if we can get it out of him.'

He looked round at Andy and Anna.

'What do you think that's all about?' he asked.

'If Riess really did kill his own father,' Anna said tentatively, 'and then told Fellowes, that might give him a motive for getting Fellowes out of the way before he could spill the beans.'

'It's addressed to an Arthur Finch,' Andy put in. 'Shall I Google him and see if I can find out who he is?'

'Yes. Go ahead,' Peter answered, smiling at the young trainee's enthusiasm.

Andy sat down at another computer and got to work. Peter re-read the email on the laptop screen. 'He refers to Riess by his first name, which suggests that this Finch character already knew about the situation and didn't need to be told who he was – I mean, he doesn't say anything to explain which Martin he's talking about or why he might call round. The date stamp is last Sunday morning, which suggests that the drunken orgy took place on Saturday night. Have we got a reply to this at all?'

'Yes.' Anna took the mouse from Peter's hand and selected another message. 'Here you are.'

'Sounds interesting. See what you can find out. If it isn't big enough to run on its own, we might be able to combine it with Ben's "dirty dons" story.'

'Here you are!' Andy exclaimed. 'He's got a Wikipedia entry. Just listen to this: born Arthur Edward Finch on 4th June 1967; residence Didcot; education Winchester; alma mater Magdalene College Cambridge; occupation magazine editor, journalist; spouse Coralie Thornton;

children Louise (2004) and Agnes (2006).'

'So he's a forty-year-old married man with two young kids,' Peter said.

'And he's another journalist,' Anna pointed out, 'who was probably at Cambridge at the same time as our victim.'

'Yes,' Peter mused. 'And, like Fellowes, he must have graduated at about the time that Riess went there to start his PhD. They probably all knew each other. Well done, Andy. It looks as if we may be getting somewhere here.'

'Shall I see if I can find out how Riess's father died?' Andy asked, feeling intensely proud of the praise and trying to think of a way of following up on his success.

'Yes, you might as well – but I may possibly have a shortcut on that front.'

Peter got out his mobile phone and selected Bernie's number. After a short delay she answered.

'Peter! What can I do for you?'

'Just a quick question. You probably won't be able to answer, but I just wondered if you knew whether Martin Riess's father had died recently. I thought you might have heard through that committee of yours.'

'Why do you want to know?' Bernie asked, with an unexpected tone of suspicion.

'It's just some random email we've come across,' Peter answered, trying to avoid giving away evidence but recognising from Bernie's voice that she did not intend to give him any information without knowing what it was to be used for. 'The victim in our murder enquiry appears to think that your Martin Riess may have killed his father.'

He gave a little laugh to imply that he was not taking this accusation seriously. There was a pause and then Bernie replied, sounding rather cold and serious.

'Well, I can tell you for a fact that Martin's father has been dead these past thirty years. You'd better come round to my room and I'll Reveal All – as the actress said to the bishop.'

'OK, I'll be right over.' Peter turned to the others.

'Right, Anna, you come with me. Andy: carry on the good work finding out whatever there is to know about Finch and his family and about Fellowes and his wife. Find out where Finch works and then ring his office and see if you can make an appointment for us to see him. We'll be back in … well, in less than an hour, anyway.'

A few minutes later, Peter was ushering Anna up a narrow staircase in St Luke's College. On the first floor landing, she saw a heavy oak door, standing open against the wall. As is common in Oxford colleges, the doorway had a second inner door, which was closed. It bore the inscription 'Dr Bernadette Fazakerley, Fellow in Applied Mathematics'. Peter rapped on the door with his knuckles and then entered without waiting for an answer.

Anna followed him into a large room with three windows along one side, through which the spring sun was shining, making the whole room bright with yellowish light. At one end there were two enormous desks standing against the wall: one set up as a computer workstation, the other covered with piles of papers and books. Near the other end there was what looked like a round meeting table with four chairs arranged around it. Under the central window, opposite the door through which they had entered, was a long sofa with loose covers in a floral design. Two matching easy chairs stood on either side of it, arranged around a coffee table.

They were greeted by a woman, whom Anna judged to be a few years younger than Peter. She had very short grey hair, no makeup and wore glasses – very much the studious don, Anna thought until, to her great surprise, the woman greeted them in a strong Liverpool accent, which seemed very out of keeping with her surroundings. Peter introduced her as 'my wife, Bernie'.

As Peter knew that she would, Bernie already had the kettle boiling, ready to 'make a brew'. Anna looked down slightly dubiously at the dark brown liquid in the mug that Bernie offered her and wondered what it was likely to do to her insides. Peter saw her expression and reached for the teapot.

'I think Anna would like hers a bit weaker,' he said, pouring a new mug of tea and topping it up generously from the kettle. 'She's a cop, not a builder!'

Grinning, Bernie swapped the mugs and sat down on the sofa, cradling her own mug in her hands as if keeping them warm on it. Peter sat down next to her and motioned to Anna to take one of the easy chairs.

'Now,' Bernie demanded, 'what's all this about someone accusing Martin of patricide?'

'It's not so much someone accusing him as him having confessed,' Peter explained. 'His friend, Martin Fellowes – the one who has now turned up dead in his boat – sent an email to another friend, in which he describes how Riess got drunk one night last week and told him that he'd killed his father.'

'I see.' Bernie sat in thought for a moment. 'OK then. I'd better tell you all about it. For a start, Helmut Riess – that's Martin's father – died on the twenty-second of July 1977, three days before Martin's tenth birthday. And he was shot as he was trying to get across the border to West Germany from the East. So, as you can see, there is absolutely no question of Martin having killed him.'

'I thought you said you hardly knew the man,' Peter said, taken aback by this detailed account. 'How come you have all these facts and figures at your fingertips?'

'It's perfectly true!' Bernie protested indignantly. 'Martin and I have probably only exchanged a dozen words over the three years since he came back to Oxford. What I didn't mention – because it was gone midnight and you didn't ask – was that I *do* know his mother rather well. Or rather, I – or it would be more accurate to say, Richard – used to know her very well. Martin was away in America during the period when Eva Riess was a regular guest at our house, so I never met him until he took up his fellowship at Lichfield.'

'And how come you know the date of his father's death off pat like that?' Peter asked.

'I got married on the twentieth anniversary of the day,' Bernie answered, smiling at Peter and glancing towards Anna to see how see was taking all this. 'I thought you might have remembered – after all, you were there!'

'In my capacity as Best Man,' Peter explained, seeing Anna's amused expression and realising that she evidently thought she had caught her boss out in the archetypal married man's blunder of being unable to remember the date of his own wedding anniversary. 'Richard was Our Bernie's first husband.'

'We invited Eva to come,' Bernie went on. 'But she couldn't because she was off to America to celebrate Martin's thirtieth, which is how I know his date of birth. Eva commented on the fact that we were getting married on the anniversary of Helmut's death. I almost think she felt it was bad taste on Richard's part. I gather they'd been very close at one time.'

'So Martin Riess must be forty,' Peter commented, 'if he was thirty when you and Richard got married. 'I'd put him down as younger than that.'

'It's because he's small,' Bernie opined. 'Your brain is subconsciously making you confuse diminutiveness with youth. Mind you, I'd have thought a lot of people seem small to you. I only notice because it's so unusual for me to be able to look a man in the eye without craning my neck!'

'If this Martin's father was shot dead by the East Germans,' Anna said slowly, 'why on earth did he tell Fellowes that he'd killed him?'

'I think I may know the answer to that,' Bernie answered. 'Eva always reckoned that Martin blamed himself for the family getting split up. You see, what happened was that Eva and he managed to escape to the West, leaving his father behind. Helmut was arrested and interrogated by the Stasi. Then, a few months later he was released and not long after that he made an attempt to get across the border and was gunned down. Martin thought that his parents only wanted to get to the West in order to give him a better life.'

'But why?' Anna asked in a tone of puzzlement. 'I mean, it was their decision.'

'He was only eight at the time,' Bernie tried to explain, 'and, from what I can gather, a sensitive child. These days you'd say that he suffered post-traumatic stress. I think he brooded on it all over the years and came up with his own version of what had gone on – and why. His father was a physics professor, so not the sort of person who was ever likely to be allowed out of the DDR.'

'East Germany,' Peter interjected, seeing that Anna did not recognise the acronym. 'I don't suppose you remember what it was like before the Berlin wall came down. A physicist would have been too valuable to allow out to the West – and may even have known secrets about the government's nuclear programme and things.'

'I do remember seeing pictures on the TV news of the wall coming down,' Anna said, 'but I didn't really know what it was all about at the time. I've learnt more about it since, though.'

'Anyway,' Bernie continued, 'Eva, on the other hand, was a concert pianist and she managed to get permission to go on a tour with an orchestra that she used to play with. Somehow or other she managed to smuggle Martin out with her. I don't know exactly what happened, but I reckon it must have been pretty dramatic, so it's not surprising it made a deep impression on him. One version is that she hid him inside a kettledrum; another was that she bribed an official to give him an exit visa – or maybe used her charms to seduce him. Whatever it was, they arrived in Britain and, almost immediately after that, Helmut Riess was arrested for selling secrets to the Americans. Eva immediately claimed political asylum and the two of them have been living in the West ever since.

There was some retired music professor in Oxford who supported her application and that's what made her choose to settle here. From what I gather, Richard got to know her through having been involved in some sort of police protection operation when there were concerns that the Stasi might try to kill them, even in England, to make an example of them.'

'But I still don't see why Martin Riess should think he was responsible for his father's death,' Anna persisted.

'What Eva told us,' Bernie explained, 'is that he believed – and this was probably true – that Eva and Helmut would probably not have considered escaping to the West if it hadn't been that they wanted Martin to have a better life than they could imagine for him in the East. And he also believed that his father deliberately contrived his arrest the moment they arrived in England as a way of forcing Eva's hand. Apparently they were a very close family and she might not have gone through with it, if it hadn't looked as if there was no going back.'

'Hmm,' Peter murmured. 'I think I can see how, when he was drunk and feeling sorry for himself, he might have said something that made Fellowes think he meant that he had actually killed his father – assuming that Fellowes didn't know the real story.'

'The main thing,' Bernie said decisively, 'is that you can give up any ideas you may have had that Martin killed his friend in order to prevent him telling people that he'd murdered his father.'

'Yes,' agreed Peter, 'I suppose this does rather put the kybosh on that theory. OK then,' he added, putting down his mug and getting to his feet, 'we'd better make tracks. I want to go back and pick up Lepage and then we'd better see Dr Riess again. I'd like to know what he thinks Fellowes meant when he said that he and Finch might be able to make something of that business of Riess killing his father.'

CHAPTER 4

When they got back to Peter's office, Andy looked up eagerly from the computer screen and Peter, smiling at the young man's enthusiasm, invited him to tell them what he had found out.

'I've got a bit more background on Arthur Finch, and it may be significant,' Andy began. 'He's the editor of *Revelations* magazine, which specialises in exposing the hypocrisy of people in power, and showing up anyone who might be considered part of any sort of élite group. I guess Fellowes was suggesting that Finch might want to publish a story about an Oxford don killing his father.'

'Yes,' Peter agreed. 'Just for the record, we now know that that story has no basis in fact, which means that it doesn't provide a motive for Riess killing Fellowes.'

'But he's still the last person to see Fellowes alive,' Anna added, 'and there may have been another motive that we don't know about yet.'

'I've also found some more about Mrs Fellowes,' Andy continued. 'Or rather, Ms Edwina Clarkson MEP. Her twin sister is Martina Plant.'

'You say that as if it ought to mean something to me,' Peter said.

'The TV presenter,' Andy replied with a slightly surprised tone in his voice.

'I know who you mean,' Anna broke in. 'She presents a lunchtime news and current affairs programme. I remember now. She's one of these women who are cited as "having it all": brilliant career, stable marriage, a string of children and, with all that going on, still managing to look as glamorous as the day she graduated with her first class degree from Oxbridge!'

'Both sisters left Cambridge with law degrees in 1989,' Andy went on. 'Martina initially started training to become a barrister, but then she got a break in regional television and gave up law to become a presenter. She got married in 1992 to a Geoffrey Plant. They had a double wedding with Edwina and Martin Fellowes. They have five children and now live in High Wycombe. Oh! And they both have form – sort of.'

'What do you mean?'

'The two Clarkson girls, together with Martin Fellowes, were arrested in Cambridge in 1987 in connection with a disturbance during a student protest march – something to do with global warming or conserving wildlife or something like that. They belonged to some sort of green activist group.'

'But Edwina Clarkson is a *Tory* MEP!' Anna exclaimed. In her mind, green activism and conservative politics were incompatible.

'Dunno,' Andy shrugged. 'I suppose you might want to conserve wildlife in order to have more of it to shoot!'

'Anyway,' Peter intervened. 'Well done for hunting all this out. It'll be useful background for when we interview them. I think it's now about time we paid a call on Dr Riess and asked him about Fellowes and Finch and how well he knows the Clarkson sisters. Andy – I want you to come along with us and take notes. Riess is still a suspect, but we don't have anything definite on him at present, so as far as he's concerned, we're interviewing him simply as a witness. It will be good for you to see how we go about it, so listen and learn.'

'Yes, sir,' Andy replied, gratified to have been included, but feeling that he had been put very much in his place as the trainee who would not be participating actively in the interview. He resolved to produce a set of notes to be proud of.

A short while later, the three officers found themselves outside another thick oak door on another narrow staircase. This one bore the legend, 'Dr Martin Riess, Fellow in Geology'. Peter knocked on the inner door and they all stood waiting on the small landing. A moment or two later, the door opened and Martin Riess looked out. When he saw who it was, he stepped back into the room and held the door open for them to enter.

This room was smaller and darker than Bernie's had been. The two narrow windows faced north and looked out into a narrow street with buildings opposite. The walls were lined with bookcases, all crammed full, with books laid on their sides on top of the rows of upright volumes. More books lay on one of the three desks arrayed along the side of the room containing the windows. In one corner stood what looked to Anna like a miniature grand piano, but which Peter later told her was a spinet.

Dr Riess ushered them in and they sat down on easy chairs around a large rectangular coffee table, piled high with copies of "Nature" and "Terra Nova" magazines. He bent down, picked up a large pile of journals and moved them to the floor to make some space on the table in front of his guests.

'Can I get you a drink?' he asked. 'Tea? Coffee?'

'No thank you,' Peter answered for all of them, 'we'd just like to ask you a few questions and then we'll be on our way.'

Martin Riess sat down and looked at Peter expectantly.

'To get straight to the point,' Peter began, getting out a piece of computer-printout from his pocket, unfolding it and handing it to Riess. 'Can you tell me what you make of this?'

The don looked down at the piece of paper. After studying it for a few moments he looked up again with a wry smile on his face.

'It looks as if Martin and Arthur were hoping to cash in on my indiscretions,' he answered. 'In case you're wondering, I have no case to answer as far as murdering my father is concerned. I can give you the details if you like, but basically all Martin had to go on was the drunken outpouring of my personal neuroses.'

'How does it make you feel, to know that your supposed friend was planning to take advantage of your confidence and perhaps to get you convicted?' Anna asked.

'Disappointed, I suppose, but not that surprised really. That's what Arthur's magazine is all about: finding out people's dark secrets and shining a light on them for everyone to see. You do know that he edits *Revelations*?'

'Yes. We are aware of that,' Peter said. 'And were you aware that Fellowes had sent him this email?'

'No,' Riess said shortly. 'And it wouldn't have made any difference if I had. It certainly didn't make me want to hit him over the head with a blunt instrument, or whatever it was made that mess of his skull.'

'I take it you knew Arthur Finch personally?' Peter resumed.

'That's right,' Riess confirmed. 'We were all in Cambridge together. Arthur and Martin had been friends while they were undergraduates. When I arrived, Martin had just got a job with a local paper and Arthur was in his final year of a languages course.'

'And you knew Edwina Clarkson, who became Mrs Fellowes. Did you know her twin sister, Martina, as well?'

'Yes. In fact, it was Martina who introduced me to Martin.'

'So the five of you: Martin, Arthur, Edwina, Martina

and yourself, were all friends together.'

'Yes. And then later there was Coralie as well.'

'Coralie?'

'Arthur's wife. She was younger than the rest of us. She did a teacher training course at Homerton. When she started going out with Arthur, she joined our group.'

'You make it sound like a club or a society,' Anna commented.

'It was. Only a small, quite informal one, but we were very much in earnest. We wanted to save the planet from the excesses of mankind.'

'And you campaigned for green issues, I suppose,' Peter suggested. 'Like Fellowes and the Clarkson sisters had done previously?'

'You know about that then? Yes, we were a very small, select green pressure group. We called ourselves the Martians.'

'Why, Martians?' Anna asked.

'Because everyone knows that Martians are little green men,' Riess answered, with a grin. 'It all started out with me and Martin and Martina, you see. When Edwina met us all for the first time, we were talking about what to call ourselves and she said, looking at the membership, we ought to be the Martins. Then Arthur suggested changing it to Martians. None of us could think of a better name, so we stuck with that.'

'And the Martians were you, Martin Fellowes, Arthur Finch, Edwina and Martina Clarkson and Coralie – Coralie what?'

'Coralie Thornton. She came along in … nineteen eighty-nine, I think. And there was one other: Geoffrey Plant joined in nineteen ninety-one, just before I left Cambridge. He married Martina the following year.'

'OK. I think I'm getting the picture,' Peter said, glancing across at Andy Lepage to check that he was writing all the names down. 'Now, tell me, how many of these Martians do you still keep up with?'

'As I told you before, Martin and I used to exchange Christmas cards. The same goes for the Finches – at least, Coralie used to send a card and a round-robin letter and I sent a card, because I didn't like not to. I never really knew Coralie, and Arthur was ... well, Arthur.'

'Meaning?'

'That he wasn't really much interested in anyone except Arthur Finch and making Arthur Finch richer and more influential.'

'Oh?'

'I mean, I was never really convinced that he cared much about the environment. I think he took up green politics as a way of making friends with people at the university who were better connected than he was.'

'Such as?'

'Principally Edwina and Martina. They were very much part of the establishment élite: been to a good school, an uncle in the House of Lords, Daddy was something big in the City, as far as I remember, with a big country house as well, where they went huntin', shootin' and fishin'. I think Arthur was hoping to get off with one of them.'

'But in the end they both married someone else.'

'That's right. And Arthur was left with Coralie as the booby prize.'

'What about you?' Anna asked sharply. 'Were you hoping any of them would choose you?'

'Me?' Riess laughed. 'In retrospect, I think probably I was the one member of the Martians who really did care passionately for the environment.'

'And what about Martina Plant?' Peter asked. 'Do you ever see anything of her or her husband?'

'Again, we exchange Christmas cards, but I don't think we've met since two thousand and four. That was the year I came back from America – I suppose you will have checked out my biography and know that I spent some time teaching over there. The Plants invited me over to their house for a reunion – and to show off their kids.

They'd just had their fifth and were feeling very pleased with themselves. I didn't bother mentioning that the Martians had campaigned for a limit of two children per woman in the interests of reducing over-population.'

'Thank you,' Peter said, bringing the interview to an end and getting to his feet. 'This is all very helpful background information. Now, can you give me addresses for the Finches and the Plants? And then we'll be off.'

'Martin went over to his desk and consulted the contacts list on his computer. He wrote down two addresses on a pad of paper and tore off the top sheet.

'Here you are. I assume you've already found Edwina?' he added casually. 'How is she?'

'Perhaps I'm being harsh,' Peter answered, 'but I'd say, *unaffected* sums up her reaction. Is that what you'd have expected?'

'I don't know,' Martin said slowly. 'I always thought … at least … well, I suppose I assumed she must have been in love with Martin, but I'd never noticed it before I left for America and I wasn't expecting it when they announced they were getting married.'

Peter shepherded Anna and Andy ahead of him towards the door. Just before following them through it, he turned to address Martin again.

'I will have to speak to your mother,' he said apologetically. 'I need her to confirm the time you got home on Tuesday afternoon. Would tomorrow morning be OK?'

'Is it alright for me to be there?' Martin asked. 'She's not used to being questioned by the police.'

'Yes. So long as you let her answer for herself. I'll try not to alarm her.'

'Thanks. Of course,' Martin went on, smiling wryly again, 'being my mother, she's unlikely to contradict anything I've told you, is she?'

'Perhaps,' Peter agreed, 'and that means that, if you are guilty of anything, her testimony is unlikely to carry much weight in court unless she does disagree with your version of events.'

'Which makes it a very good thing for me that I don't need to ask her to lie for me, doesn't it?'

Peter smiled and made his exit. He could not help liking this small, rather unprepossessing man with his wry sense of humour. Usually Peter felt ill at ease in the company of the Oxford intelligentsia, whom he always suspected of looking down on him – although they rarely showed this openly. This Martin Riess seemed very open and straightforward and appeared genuinely concerned for his mother – perhaps not surprisingly, given their family history. Nevertheless, it would not do to allow his personal feelings towards the man to cloud his judgement. Dr Riess was still the only definite suspect they had.

CHAPTER 5

They headed back to the office where they left Lepage to type up his notes.

'We've just got time to make a visit to Didcot to see the Finches,' Peter said, looking at his watch. Andy had rung the *Revelations* magazine office earlier and found out that the editor was working at home that day. 'If you have time after you've finished those notes, see what else you can dig up about this magazine that Finch edits. In particular, has Fellowes written any articles recently that might have upset someone enough to make them want to kill him? Oh – and get on to Mike Carson and see if he's done the PM yet. Tell him from me that we need an estimate of time of death ASAP. We probably won't be back before knocking off time, so mind you get off home at the end of your shift. I want you bright and bushy-tailed in the morning, so no burning the midnight oil.'

There should have been plenty of time to make the short journey to Didcot and back in what remained of the afternoon, but Peter had reckoned without the lorry which shed its load of sand and stones across the southbound carriageway of the A34 shortly before they joined it. Not long after passing the first exit to Abingdon, they saw a queue ahead. Anna, who was driving, slowed down to a crawl. As they sat in stationary traffic, waiting for the road to be cleared, Peter looked anxiously at the clock on the dashboard. What should they do? If they came off at the next junction, they could make their way back through Abingdon, abandoning any attempt to interview Arthur Finch and his wife until the following day. Peter was reluctant to give up the chance of speaking to Finch that day, but he was conscious that Bernie would be expecting him home and that Anna had a husband and two young children who would be anxiously awaiting her return.

'The kids are staying with my mum,' Anna said, as if reading his mind, 'and Phil is away at a conference; so I'm not bothered if we're late getting back.'

'Are you sure?' Peter asked solicitously, mindful that he ought not to exploit his junior officers' goodwill.

'Sure thing,' Anna nodded.

'Right you are then. In that case, I'll just give Our Bernie a ring to let her know I'll be late,'

Shortly after 6pm, Peter and Anna turned into the short cul-de-sac where the Finch family lived. An unexpected scene greeted them. The road was crowded with parked vehicles. There was an ambulance and two police cars drawn up on to the pavement in front of a spacious detached bungalow on the right-hand side of the road. Peter saw a uniformed police officer standing outside the house, in front of a cordon of blue-and-white police tape. He checked his notes and then peered at the numbers on the houses.

'That's the one,' he said. 'Number eleven. It looks as if there's something going on in there.'

With some difficulty, Anna found a space in which to park the car and they both got out and walked towards what was evidently a crime scene. Peter showed his warrant card to the young police officer stationed on the pavement outside.

'I'm DI Peter Johns and this is DS Anna Davenport,'

he said. 'Can you tell me what's going on here?'

'The SOCOs are going over the place, sir, and the doctor has just arrived.'

'But what are they here for?' Peter asked. 'What exactly has happened?'

'I'm sorry, sir, I don't understand,' the young man looked from Peter to Anna and back again with an expression of confusion on his face. 'Isn't that what you're here for? To investigate the murder, I mean.'

'No, constable, we are here to interview Mr Arthur Finch in connection with the death of a man on a canal boat in Oxford. Is he here?'

'Well, he *is* here,' the officer replied, 'but I'm afraid you're too late to interview him. He's in there, dead, with his head smashed in.'

Peter and Anna looked at one another. The description sounded all too familiar to them.

'Would you like me to send for DCI Porter, sir? He's the officer in charge.'

'Yes, you do that,' Peter answered, recognising the name with mixed feelings. He and Jonah Porter had been part of the same team for several years, starting from when Porter first joined CID as a raw detective constable and Peter was a detective sergeant. Porter had excelled in his work, gaining promotion to inspector rank, and in the process moving to another division and out of Peter's immediate circle, ahead of him. Peter, who was not an ambitious man, did not resent Porter's success, but in his presence, he always felt somehow inadequate, as if he were in the shadow of the younger man.

'If you don't mind waiting here, sir,' the constable began, turning to go and then turning back to address Peter again. 'Here he is!'

Peter looked up and saw a familiar figure rounding the side of the house, striding energetically.

'Where's that photographer got to?' Porter called out, addressing the world in general. 'I need her round the back. There are marks on one of the windows suggestive of a break-in.'

'I think she's still inside, photographing the blood stains you asked for,' answered one of the scenes of crime officers, looking up from where he was engaged in a minute study of the front door frame.

'Well tell her to get round the back the moment she's done with that.'

Peter stepped over the tape and started up the drive. Anna hesitated for a moment and then followed.

'Jonah!' Peter called.

'If it isn't old Peter!' Porter replied, noticing the new arrivals for the first time. 'Long time, no see. What brings you to this neck of the woods?'

Anna watched as the two men greeted one another. DCI Porter was a little shorter than Peter and a few years younger. His hair was mousey-brown, greying a little at the temples. His blue eyes shone with the thrill of the chase.

'We were hoping to have a little chat with Arthur Finch,' Peter explained, 'but I gather we've missed the boat.'

'You have indeed. May I ask what it was you wanted to talk to him about? And could it possibly provide an explanation of why someone might have hit him over the head with a blunt instrument?'

'We have our own corpse,' Peter explained. 'And we had been hoping Finch might have been able to give us an idea who might have wanted him dead. Apparently it was a friend of his.'

'Really? How fascinating. D'you want to have a look? The pathologist is just giving him a once-over at the moment, but I'm sure she won't mind.'

'Yes please,' Peter said eagerly. Jonah's enthusiasm was infectious. Peter had forgotten how much energy his colleague always put into an investigation and how effectively he got everyone around him working with a passion rarely exhibited when he was not present.

Jonah led the way into the house and through to a rather dark room with a window facing on to the side passageway. This was evidently Arthur Finch's home office. There was a desk under the window and two filing cabinets against one wall. The small room seemed to be crowded with people in protective clothing all intent on examining it for possible evidence. Central to the scene was the body of Arthur Finch, lying sprawled, face down across the desk, in much the same position as Martin Fellowes had been the day before. A woman looked up from where she was studying the wound on the back of Finch's head and gazed enquiringly at Jonah.

'These two officers are hotfoot from another murder scene,' he told her with relish. 'They'd like to see how the two corpses compare.'

He introduced Peter and Anna to Dr Christine Patterson. To Peter, she looked too young to be a fully qualified pathologist, but he supposed that was just a sign that he was himself getting old. Whatever her age, she seemed competent at her job and just as reticent about making any definite statements as every other pathologist he had come across.

'The head wound looks to have been inflicted from behind,' she said, 'by something heavy – a large hammer, for example. It's quite a distinctive shape; so, if you find the weapon, we might be able to match it up.'

Peter peered down with interest, beckoning Anna to look closer.

'What do you think?' he asked her. 'Does that look to you like the wound on the back of Fellowes' head?'

'I think so,' she said cautiously, 'but I'm no expert.'

'We'll need you to liaise with Mike Carson,' Peter told the doctor. 'Do you know him? He's the pathologist who's doing the PM on our murder victim.'

'Yes,' she smiled. 'I was his registrar, back in the day. I'll arrange for us to exchange notes. I might even go over and have a look at your corpse for myself.'

'Good man!' Jonah said, slapping her on the back. 'Now, come back outside, Peter, and I'll fill you in on what we know.'

They went and sat on wooden chairs on the patio at the back of the bungalow. As they basked in the late April sunshine, Jonah told Peter and Anna what had happened.

Mrs Finch had arrived home from the primary school where she worked, at about four o'clock that afternoon, to find her husband lying dead in his study, just as he was now. She had immediately called 999 and the officers who attended a few minutes later had called for CID. Jonah had only been on the scene for about half an hour before Peter and Anna arrived. His next task was to interview Mrs Finch; presumably, Peter would like to be in on that?

Peter acquiesced readily and they went back indoors and into the living room, where Coralie Finch was sitting hunched up on the sofa. She was an unprepossessing woman, but perhaps it was unfair to judge her appearance under the current difficult circumstances. Her shoulder-length hair was a nondescript brown colour; her eyes, red with weeping, were a dull grey and the area around them was puffy. She wore a long, full, brown skirt and a brown turtleneck jumper. A policewoman in uniform was sitting in an easy chair close by, holding a box of tissues.

'Do you feel up to answering a few questions?' Jonah asked kindly. 'I'm sorry to have to ask you, but the more you can tell us, the more likely it is that we'll be able to find whoever did this to your husband.'

'Yes. I'm ready,' Coralie answered, sitting up straighter and looking round at the three police officers standing before her. Jonah briefly explained who Peter and Anna were and why they were there. She opened her eyes wide and gave a little cry when she heard that Martin Fellowes had been killed in a similar way to her husband.

'I heard the report on the radio this morning,' she said, 'but I didn't realise who it was. 'It just said a man, believed to be a journalist.'

'We had to wait until we'd spoken to his wife,' Peter explained. 'Just as we won't release your husband's name until you tell us that all his immediate family know about it.'

'And do you think it's the same person?' Coralie asked, nodding to indicate that she understood. 'Why would anyone want to kill both Martin and Arthur?'

'We were wondering if it could be something to do with their work,' Peter said. 'Martin used to write articles for your husband's magazine, didn't he?'

'Did he?' Coralie asked vaguely. 'I never got involved in Arthur's work, but I suppose it would have been natural for him to publish things that Martin wrote. Why do you think that would make someone want to kill them?'

'We thought something they wrote might have upset someone – someone who thought they were being unfair to them, for example, or who didn't want other people to know about something they'd done.'

'D'you think you could take us through what you and your husband did today?' Jonah intervened. 'Start with this morning. What time did you get up?'

'About half seven, as usual,' Coralie answered, frowning in concentration as she tried to remember the events of only a few hours before. 'Agnes woke us at five and I brought her into our bed to get her back off. Then, when the alarm went, I got up first and then I got the children up. I took them downstairs for breakfast. Arthur always waits until we've gone down before he gets up. He doesn't like getting dressed with the kids running round the bedroom.'

'And how did he seem this morning?' Jonah asked. 'I mean, did he appear anxious or agitated at all?'

'No,' Coralie looked round as if she hardly understood the question. 'No, he was just the same as usual.'

'So, you all had breakfast,' Jonah prompted. 'What did you talk about? Did your husband say anything about what he was planning to do today?'

'No. We just talked about the children – about needing to get new shoes for Louise – that sort of thing.'

'So, he didn't mention that he was expecting anyone to call round to see him – about his work, for example?'

'No. He always had meetings at the office. He didn't invite people to the house.'

'I see. Now, go on, what did you do next?'

'I took the children round to my Mum's – she looks after them while I'm at work – and then I went to school.'

'And did you speak to your husband at all while you were at work? Did he ring you during the lunch break, for example, or send a text?'

'No. I was on dinner duty, so I had my phone switched off all day. Anyway, he wouldn't phone me at work – not unless it was an emergency.'

'Alright,' Jonah continued gently. 'So, let's move on to the end of the school day. You left – when?'

'About twenty to four. Mrs Brookes was on duty at the gate, so I got off as soon as school finished. I came straight home and went in to tell Arthur I was back and – and – there he was!' Coralie collapsed in sobs. The policewoman pressed a tissue into her hand and placed an arm round her shoulder. Peter, Jonah and Anna waited patiently for the weeping to subside.

Eventually Coralie composed herself and looked up at them.

'If it's alright with you,' Peter began carefully, anxious not to upset her further, 'I'd like to ask you about some old friends of yours – from your time in Cambridge.'

Coralie said nothing, but looked towards him and nodded, so he continued.

'We've spoken to Martin Riess. You remember him? He said you still exchange cards at Christmas.'

'Yes. That's right,' Coralie agreed, nodding again.

'Martin Fellowes was living on his boat when he was killed,' Peter explained. 'He told us that there were a group of you at Cambridge. You called yourselves the Martians.

Do you remember about that?'

'Yes,' Coralie smiled a weak smile. 'We were very young and idealistic and thought we could change the world. Martin – Martin Riess I mean – was very earnest about it all.'

'There were seven of you – is that right? You and your husband, Martin Fellowes and Edwina Clarkson, Geoffrey Plant and Martina Clarkson, and Martin Riess.'

'Well, yes,' Coralie hesitated, 'but that wasn't how it started. I mean, when I joined – that is when Martina invited me – Martin Riess was going out with Edwina and Geoffrey wasn't even part of the group. He only came along much later.'

'That's interesting,' Anna said thoughtfully. 'What happened to make Edwina switch to Martin Fellowes? Did she and Riess fall out?'

'No. I don't think so. He went off to America on some sort of scholarship and a few months later – or so it seemed – both the Clarkson girls announced they were getting married.'

'And that was Martina marrying Geoffrey – the newcomer to the group – and Edwina marrying Martin Fellowes?' Peter asked, wanting to make sure he had everything clear in his mind.

'That's right. Of course, we soon realised why Martina had to marry Geoffrey in such a hurry,' Coralie continued, a little vindictively, 'when little Amber arrived only four months after the wedding. I suspect their rich Daddy had something to do with it. I can't see him being happy with a grandchild born out of wedlock – and he was a dab hand with a shotgun by all accounts,' she added with grim humour.

'And how did Martin Riess feel about all that?' Anna asked. 'I mean how did he react to finding his girlfriend was marrying another man?'

'Well he was over in America, wasn't he? He didn't come back for the wedding – I do remember that. But then that might just have been because of the cost or because he couldn't spare the time from his job over there. He still used to keep in touch with Martin and Edwina – and with Martina too as far as I know, so he can't have been that upset, can he?'

'Now, can we come back to this afternoon, when you came home from work?' Jonah said gently. 'You said that you found your husband – was that immediately you got in or did you do anything before you went in to see him?'

'No. I went straight in to his study to let him know I was back.'

'Good. And then you rang 999. Did you do anything first? Did you try to help your husband in any way, for example? Or touch him to check that he was dead?'

'No. I just saw all that blood and his head all smashed in and went straight back into the hall and rang for help.'

'So you didn't touch anything in that room where you found him?'

'No. I closed the door. I didn't want to see ... to see ...' Coralie tailed off into renewed sobbing.

'Alright, Mrs Finch,' Jonah said kindly. 'I think we'll leave it at that for the time being. I'm afraid we may need to speak to you again later, but our other questions can wait. Now, tell me: is there anyone you could go to stay with for a few days?'

'My Mum,' Coralie gulped. 'I rang her to say I'd be late picking up the girls, but I didn't tell her ... about this!'

'That sounds like an excellent idea. Sergeant Meadows will take you there and help to explain the situation to your mother.' Jonah turned to the policewoman, who had sat down on the sofa next to Mrs Finch and was plying her with more tissues. 'Can leave that with you, sergeant?'

'Yes sir,' she answered promptly. 'Mrs Finch has already given me the address. I'll help her get a few things together and then we'll go – if that's OK with you, sir.'

'Yes, yes – the sooner the better,' Jonah murmured dismissively, his mind already on the next step in his investigation.

He left the room, followed closely by Peter and Anna. Peter looked at his watch.

'I think we ought to go now,' he said, looking towards Anna. 'I promised Lucy I'd read her bedtime story.'

They went out of the front door and started walking towards Anna's car.

'How's Lucy doing?' Jonah asked suddenly, briefly taking his mind off the murder case at the mention of Peter's stepdaughter. 'Looking forward to her birthday on Sunday?'

'Lucy's fine,' Peter answered tersely, fighting down the resentment that he always felt when Jonah took an interest in the little girl who had started out life as his goddaughter and for whom he was now "Daddy". 'She's growing up fast,' he added, forcing himself to say something more, to cover up his feelings and appear gratified at Jonah's interest. 'The latest is that she wants to be a forensic pathologist when she grows up!'

'An excellent ambition,' Jonah declared. 'What brought that on?'

'It was Mike – you know Mike Carson, don't you? Lucy found this injured squirrel in the garden and tried to nurse it back to health. After it died, Mike jokingly offered to do a post mortem on it to find out cause of death. I think he probably regretted it when Lucy took him seriously and insisted that he went through with it. Anyway the two of them did the autopsy together on the kitchen table and afterwards Lucy said she wanted to be a pathologist and cut up dead people to see how they'd died.'

'Good for Lucy!' Jonah laughed. 'Maybe that'll teach Mike not to say things he doesn't mean. I bet Bernie's pleased. She always wanted Lucy to go in for the sciences.'

'I don't know about that,' Peter allowed himself to be drawn into a conversation that he had intended to keep to the minimum demanded by politeness. 'I think she rather liked Lucy's previous plan to be a police officer.'

'And what do you think?' Jonah asked as Peter opened the passenger door and climbed into the car.

'I think I like the idea of Lucy staying safe in the mortuary and the lab better than her being out on the streets dealing with drunks and muggers.'

To save time, Anna drove Peter straight home, dropping him outside his house with an agreement that she would pick him up from there in the morning, since his own car was still parked at the police station. He said a hasty goodbye to her and hurried inside. He was immediately greeted by a cry of joy from above, followed by a pattering of bare feet on the landing.

'Daddy!' Lucy called over the bannister rail at the top of the long staircase. 'Come up and finish my story!'

'I'm on my way!' Peter called back, flinging off his jacket and hurrying up the stairs. 'Just you go back to bed like a good girl.'

'I told Mam you'd be here, but she wouldn't wait,' Lucy continued in an aggrieved voice, turning to go.

When Peter reached Lucy's room, she was sitting up in bed holding a paperback book and watching eagerly for Peter to arrive. Bernie was standing next to the bed also looking towards the door.

Peter sat down on the bed and took the book from Lucy's hands. Bernie headed for the door.

'I'll go down and sort out your tea,' she said over her shoulder. 'Don't be long.'

About half an hour later, Peter was sitting at the large kitchen table eating pie and chips while Bernie busied herself with washing up after her own meal with Lucy.

'Have you made any progress with that body you found on Martin's boat?' she enquired.

'I don't know whether you'd call it progress,' Peter answered. 'We've now got a second body that looks to have been killed in much the same way.'

'A serial killer, you mean? And was this on a canal boat too?'

'No. In a house in Didcot.'

'So what makes you think the deaths are linked?'

'The second victim was a friend of the first – it was the recipient of that email I told you about: the one that accused Martin Riess of killing his father. We were wanting to interview him about it, but when we got there we found a police investigation already going on, because he was dead – hit over the head just like our man in the boat.'

Bernie said nothing, so Peter continued.

'And who do you think is in charge of the investigation?' he asked.

'Surprise me.'

'It's your friend Jonah Porter.'

'*My* friend?' Bernie said, raising her eyebrows. 'You're the one who worked with him for – what? – ten years?'

'Eight: from seventy-nine to eighty seven.'

'Eight then,' Bernie conceded. 'Whereas I've only met him eight times in total, on most occasions for less than an hour. So if he's anyone's friend it must be yours rather than mine.'

'Well, anyway, Jonah's running the show in Didcot, so I imagine it's only a matter to time before he takes over this end of the investigation as well – just as soon as we establish for sure that the two cases are linked.'

'Why should he take over from you?' Bernie asked, detecting a tone of resentment in Peter's voice. 'The Oxford murder is on your patch. You know the area better than Jonah.'

'He's more senior than me,' Peter answered, resignedly, 'and, now that we've got a TV celebrity and an MEP involved, someone's bound to decide that the case can't be left in the hands of a mere DI.'

'But surely they won't take you off the case,' Bernie argued, sitting down at the table opposite Peter. 'If it's such an important one, they'll need someone with your experience.'

'To do the donkey work, yes,' Peter answered, getting

to the nub of his problem. 'But someone has to be in overall charge and that's bound to be Jonah.'

'And you don't want to be working for Jonah, is that it? He doesn't strike me as someone who would be a difficult boss.'

'No, I don't suppose he is. It's just …'

'It's just that you were already Richard's favourite sergeant when Jonah was just a humble PC,' Bernie finished for him, suddenly realising where the difficulty lay. 'And, after you'd trained him up to be a detective, he goes off and gets promoted to inspector – and now to chief inspector – ahead of you and you don't want him to be in a position to tell you what to do.'

'It sounds awfully petty when you put it like that.'

'No – not really. It's only natural – especially when I know Richard thought so very highly of you, and your slow promotion was quite probably partly due to him holding you back so that he could keep you as his side-kick instead of letting you go off and make a glittering career for yourself.'

'Don't talk rubbish,' Peter said loyally. 'Richard supported me all the way. He was the one who pushed for me to be made up to sergeant and he encouraged me to go for inspector as soon as he thought I was ready.'

'OK, tell it your own way,' Bernie shrugged, pleased at least to have shaken Peter out of his brooding on the injustice of his junior colleague having achieved promotion ahead of him. 'Now tell me how you're getting on. Is poor Martin Riess still your prime suspect?'

''Well, he's our only definite suspect – unless you count some rough-sleeper who may or may not have been out on the towpath at round about the time Fellowes was killed. But it looks as if Fellowes and his friend – the one who was killed in Didcot – could well have upset all sorts of people by writing unpleasant, and possibly untrue, things about them in their magazine. It's called *Revelations*. Have you come across it?'

'I don't think so,' Bernie began, 'at least – I wonder ... I think maybe that was where the original article appeared that sparked off the allegations of rich parents buying places for their offspring at Oxford colleges by making donations. I don't suppose you took much interest, but it caused a lot of trouble a few years back.'

'That sounds like the sort of story they might run,' Peter agreed. 'Apparently they specialise in knocking the establishment – especially anyone with money or privilege.'

'Is that where the TV star and the MEP come in? Are they aggrieved parties who've suffered at the hands of *Revelations* magazine?'

'No. They're the wife and sister-in-law of the first victim and old university chums of the second – not to mention one of them apparently having gone out with Martin Riess when he was in Cambridge.'

'Really? Eva told us that she thought he'd been pretty serious about some girl in Cambridge, but it never came to anything. Richard and I assumed she must have got fed up with waiting for him to come back from America.'

'So you *do* know more about Riess than you've been letting on,' Peter pounced on this new snippet of information. 'What else haven't you told me about him? I need to build up a picture of what he's like.'

'So you can build a case against him?' Bernie asked, smiling but with a note of concern in her voice.'

'So that I can establish whether or not he killed two people. I can see you've got a soft spot for the fellow – however much you protest that you hardly know the man – but you've also told me that he's traumatised from losing his father at a young age and now you're saying that his girlfriend jilted him. So, on the face of it, he might well be sufficiently unstable mentally to kill if he felt threatened.'

'Oh dear! You really think he might have done it, don't you?'

'At the moment I can't rule it out – which is why I'm asking you to tell me everything you know about him.'

'Well,' Bernie said slowly, thinking hard, 'I really *don't* know him very well. As I said, we've only met in big meetings and only talked about items on the agenda. He always seemed to be genuinely concerned about the students and genuinely interested in improving the educational opportunities of disadvantaged youngsters. When I said he was suffering from post-traumatic stress, I didn't mean that he was jumpy or got panic attacks or anything like that – I was just trying to explain why he might have felt guilty about his father's death.'

They sat for a few minutes in silence.

'Well,' Bernie said at last, 'I do hope, for his mother's sake, Martin isn't guilty. She's all alone apart from him. They left all their friends and family behind when they came here and she never seemed to make many new ones in Oxford. She went to live with Martin in America when Richard died.'

'You make it sound as if the two events were connected,' Peter commented.

'Oh, I think they were – definitely. I think Richard was probably the only person she really felt she could talk to after Martin went to America. Neither she nor Richard ever said anything, but I got the impression that they'd been rather more than just friends. My theory is that Richard asked her to marry him and she turned him down. Probably she couldn't bring herself to be unfaithful to the memory of Martin's father. It's rather sad, really – she'd have made Richard a far better wife than I ever did.'

'Bernie!' Peter protested reproachfully.

'No, but it's true. I never could understand what Richard saw in me – I'm not his sort of woman at all – whereas he and Eva used to play piano duets together and all sorts.'

'If you knew his mother so well,' Peter said, keen to get off the subject of Bernie's suitability, or otherwise, as a wife for his old boss, 'I can't understand how it is that you claim to have hardly spoken to Martin over the last –

what? – three years?'

'It's not that easy,' Bernie explained, 'especially when you're in a room full of people. I mean, I could hardly go up to him and say, "Hi there! My late husband used to go out with your mother." And, if he's put the past behind him, he might not want me raking up painful memories of their escape from East Germany and his father's death and all that. I keep meaning to introduce myself – because, of course, with me not using my married name he won't have any idea who I am – but the longer it goes on the more difficult it is to find a natural way of getting round to the subject.'

She sat pondering for a few moments.

'I suppose,' she went on thoughtfully, 'what I ought to do is to ring Eva and invite her over. I should have done it before. I haven't seen her since Richard's funeral. She must have been quite lonely after he died. Before that, she was round our place almost every week.'

'Well, if you really think you ought to be renewing the acquaintance, you'd better wait until the current investigation is over,' Peter advised. 'I can do without giving anyone an excuse for claiming that I've got a conflict of interest. Anyway, I don't see why you should be the one to make the first move,' he went on, seeing that Bernie had started to blame herself for neglecting Richard's old friend. 'I would have thought it was up to her to call round on the grieving widow, not your responsibility to think of her.'

CHAPTER 6

The next morning, Peter and Anna called at the Riess family home at half past eight. Martin had asked them to pay their visit to his mother early, because she gave piano lessons and her first pupil was due to arrive at ten. Eva Riess led them into the bay-fronted living room where they had waited for Martin on the night that the body had been discovered. It was bright with sunshine now. The heavy velvet curtains were drawn back and held in loops of cord, revealing a cluster of photographs standing on the windowsill.

Just as they were sitting down, Martin appeared, looking rather anxious.

'Is it alright if I come in?' he asked. 'Or did you want to speak to my mother alone?'

'No, it's OK,' Peter assured him, motioning him to come in and close the door. He wondered to himself whether Martin wanted to be there to make sure that he knew what his mother had told the police – or even to ensure that she told them whatever story he had rehearsed with her – or out of a genuine concern that she might be upset by the encounter. He reflected that Eva's experience of growing up behind the iron curtain might well have made her nervous of anyone in authority. 'We need to talk to you as well in any case. There have been some developments, but I'll come to that later.'

When they were all seated, Peter turned to Eva.

'We won't keep you long, Mrs Riess,' he began. 'I just need you to tell me, as exactly as you can, what time your son Martin came home on Tuesday evening – you remember he came home to get dressed for dinner at his college?'

'I cannot be very exact,' Eva said, speaking slowly and carefully. 'I know that it was before six, because my last pupil – I teach the piano,' she explained, gesturing towards the instrument that stood against the wall opposite the window, '– was still there. I heard Martin coming in through the back door and going upstairs. Then, after the lesson finished, I went with my pupil to the front door, and Martin came downstairs to let me know he was home.'

'I see. This pupil – would he or she have seen Martin, do you think?'

'I am not sure,' Mrs Riess looked rather confused. 'I suppose she may have done – before I closed the door.'

'Could you give me her name?' Peter asked. 'I don't expect we'll need to speak to her, but you never know.'

'I am not sure if she would like me to-,' Eva began.

'I can help you there,' Martin broke into the conversation. 'Her name is Dr Diane Matheson and she's recently been appointed to a fellowship at St Luke's College. If you need to speak to her, you can find her via the college, but I'm afraid she's unlikely to be able to help.'

'Thank you,' Peter noted down the name and then turned to Eva again. 'Now the other thing we need from you, Mrs Riess, is the time that your son went out again that evening. Can you remember?'

'Let me see … as I said, it was about six when he came downstairs, and he had to get changed after that ... I suppose it must have been at least quarter past six by the time he left. It could have been later.'

'Thank you Mrs Riess,' Peter said, nodding, 'I think that's all we need from you. I have a few more questions for your son, but I'm sure you have things to do around the house, so don't let us detain you.'

Martin sprang to his feet to open the door for his mother. As she left, he murmured something to her in German as if reassuring her that she had acquitted herself well in the interview and perhaps also trying to impress upon her that there was nothing sinister about his having been asked to stay behind for more questions. He closed the door firmly and then turned to Peter with a slightly amused expression on his face.

'You're welcome to speak to Diane,' he said, returning to his seat, 'but I doubt she'll be able to confirm my alibi – if that's what this is all about. I made quite certain that I didn't come downstairs until she was safely outside the front door.'

Peter looked at him enquiringly.

'Was there any particular reason for that?' Anna asked. She was not sure what to make of this smiling don who, apart from the possible impact on his mother, did not seem to be taking the investigation very seriously.

'My mother has decided,' Martin explained, 'that it is high time I provided her with some grandchildren, and she has identified Diane Matheson as a suitable person to be their mother. That's why she scheduled Diane's lesson as the last one of the day and that's why she allowed it to over-run by a few minutes. If you ask Diane, I'm sure she'll agree that it was after six by the time I got home. I don't know whether that makes me more or less likely to have killed Martin, but those are the facts.'

'I'm afraid we don't know that either,' Peter confessed, feeling a growing affinity for this small man who clearly understood that he was the prime suspect and yet continued to treat the investigation as some sort of game or puzzle. Perhaps it was his scientific background that made him view everything with a degree of objectivity.

'Until we get the post mortem report we won't know the time of death so, as you suggest, we'll just note down the facts and see what they tell us later.'

'You said that there had been developments,' Martin pointed out. 'Are you permitted to tell me what they are?'

'I dare say you'll hear them soon enough on the news,' Peter replied. 'That is, if you haven't already. We went round to interview your old friend Arthur Finch yesterday.'

'And was he able to throw any light on what happened to Martin?'

'Unfortunately not. Someone had been there before us and knocked a hole in the back of his head, so he wasn't in any position to answer our questions.'

'You mean he's been killed too?' Martin asked in a rather shocked voice.

'That's right,' Peter confirmed, 'and killed in very much the same way, as far as we can tell.'

'So you think it's the same person responsible?'

'Now that I can't say.'

'It could have been someone else trying to make it look as if it was the same person,' Anna added.

'That would have to be someone who knew how Martin was killed,' Martin suggested with the wry smile that Peter was starting to recognise as indicating that he realised that he was under suspicion and that the evidence might be against him. 'Someone who had seen the body on board the boat, perhaps?'

'That's all speculation,' Peter said firmly, 'but I do need to ask you about your movements yesterday. So let's start at the beginning: what time did you get up?'

'The alarm is set for seven. I switched it off and got up straight away. I got dressed – which probably took about ten minutes, I suppose – and went downstairs. My mother was already in the kitchen – she's an early riser – warming some brötchen (that's bread rolls) in the oven. We ate breakfast together and then I went to college. I got there about half past eight – the porter may remember me calling in to check my pigeonhole – and went to my room. I had tutorials all day until two-thirty pm – that is apart from going down to hall for lunch at twelve. Then you came round and found me still working in my room at about three.'

Martin paused for breath and looked towards Peter, who nodded briefly and smiled encouragingly.

'After that,' Martin went on, 'I couldn't settle to any more work, so I went home. I don't know what time it was, but I met one of my mother's pupils in the hallway, waiting for her lesson to start. That means it was probably just before four, because lessons usually start on the hour. I stayed in my room until the lesson was over and then I came down and my mother and I spent the evening together.'

'Thank you, that's a very comprehensive account,' Peter said, immediately regretting having said this in a tone that suggested that he thought that it was, therefore, a manufactured account. 'Have you got all that down, sergeant?'

Anna nodded.

'We'll need the names of the students that you were tutoring,' Peter added, handing Martin his notebook and a pen. 'If you could just write them all down there for me.'

Martin obediently wrote down a list of names and times and returned the book to Peter.

'Of course,' he said with a twinkle in his eye, 'since their degrees depend to a certain extent on me, they too may be tempted to perjure themselves on my behalf.'

'I'll just have to hope that, with ten of them to choose from, I'll be able to find at least one who lacks that special loyalty to their tutor,' Peter said solemnly.

'Mrs Finch told us something rather interesting,' Anna said, anxious that Peter appeared not to be planning to tackle Martin on the subject of his relationship with the victim's wife. 'According to her, you and Mrs Fellowes went out together while you were in Cambridge.'

'Yes. That's right,' Martin confirmed, apparently unfazed by this statement. 'The original Martians were me, Martin and Martina – I think I told you that – and then Martina got Edwina involved and that's when we thought up the name. Martina was the driving force behind the group. She was determined to make a name for herself somehow. Presumably that's why she ended up going into television. She found Arthur, and soon he and Martin were thick as thieves, dreaming up ways of getting publicity for the cause. Edwina was quieter and more serious than Martina. I liked her better and she seemed to like me. We went out, as you say, for about two and a half years – right up until I left for America.'

'So what happened to change things?' Anna asked.

'I'll come to that, but let me finish telling you about how things were when we were in Cambridge. Martin and Martina were an item for a while – about six months I suppose – and then she seemed to go off him, I don't know why. A bit later, she – that's Martina – introduced Coralie to the group. She always seemed a bit lightweight to me, but Martina thought she helped to make us look less like a lot of public school toffs trying to impose our ideas on ordinary people. I got the impression that Coralie fancied Martin Fellowes, but he only had eyes for the Clarkson sisters. I suppose after Martina ditched him, he thought that Edwina would do just as well.'

'And, once you were off the scene, he moved in to take her?' Anna suggested.

'I suppose you could put it like that, but there was more to it, I think. Shortly before I left for America, Martina found Geoffrey and introduced him to the group. I never got to know him properly, but I got the impression that he only joined the group in order to be with Martina. I think he was rather overwhelmed by her glamour, which was very different from anything he'd seen in his life up until then – with him being an accountant, and from a family of accountants, by all accounts. When Martina and he announced that they were getting married, my theory is that Edwina decided that *she* had to find a husband too, to avoid being upstaged by her sister. I was three thousand miles away and Martin was right there, pining to be invited to take her up the aisle, so she fixed on him.'

'That's a very cynical view,' Anna observed a little coldly.

'Or perhaps I'm just trying to cover up the deep hurt inflicted on me by her rejection,' Martin replied, smiling pleasantly at her.

'And yet,' Peter put in, reluctantly taking up the inquisition, 'you were the friend to whom he came when his wife grew tired of him and told him to leave. Doesn't that strike you as odd?'

'Not particularly. That was all a long time ago and I'm not much good at harbouring grudges. Edwina didn't have time to wait for me to come back from America and was happy to throw herself into Martin's arms. I can hardly blame him for being willing to catch her, can I?'

'So you felt no resentment towards Martin Fellowes at all?' Anna asked sceptically.

'I certainly didn't feel strongly enough to smash his head in, if that's what you mean,' Martin replied calmly, with the now-familiar wry smile.

'Very well,' Peter cut in before Anna could respond. 'I think that's all for now. Thank you for being so open with us.'

He got up to go and then something stopped him in his tracks. He stood for a moment looking at one of the photographs on the windowsill.

'This is Detective Superintendent Richard Paige, isn't it?' he asked at last.

'That's right. At least, I think he was just Chief Inspector when that was taken. Did you know him?'

'Very well indeed. He was my boss for getting on for thirty years.'

'Of course! It's *Peter* Johns, isn't it? I should have

recognised the name. He thought very highly of you.'

'So, how do you come to know him?' Peter asked innocently.

'He was very good to me and my mother when we first arrived here from East Germany. That was back in the seventies when the Cold War was at its height and it was a very difficult time for her. I think he was the only real friend she had. In fact, there was a time when …,' he paused briefly before resuming. 'I did think at one time that he might become my stepfather, but nothing came of it. She wrote to me while I was in America to say that he was marrying a don from St Luke's College. It was a tragedy, what happened to him. I was still in America when it happened. I never got the chance to thank him for everything he did for my mother.'

'I suppose you'll have been able to thank his widow,' Peter suggested. 'With you both being at the university, I mean.'

'The university is a big place,' Martin answered, smiling at the idea that every don would automatically be on familiar terms with every other. 'But, by an amazing coincidence our paths do happen to cross quite regularly. I don't suppose she has any idea that I knew Richard, though.'

'Really?' Peter said encouragingly. 'How's that then?'

'We both have the misfortune not to have been quick enough off the mark with our excuses when people were being selected for an exceptionally tedious university committee,' Martin explained. 'So, once a month, we sit round a table with a whole lot of other unfortunate tutors and drink abominable coffee and read pointless reports and then we go back to our respective colleges until the next month. That is why I said our paths cross regularly, but we never get much opportunity for personal conversation, only business matters.'

'And what do you make of her?' Peter asked bluntly.

'That's a rather odd question, if you don't mind my

saying so.'

'I know. It's just, well, Mrs Paige never struck me as quite your average Oxford don and I was curious to know how her peers viewed her.'

'I see you've met Our Bernie,' Martin said, laughing. 'You're right, there are a good few of the older ones who think she's not quite People Like Us.'

'And what about you,' Peter pressed him. 'What do *you* think of her?'

'I think she cares passionately about improving the opportunities for working-class kids. And I know she doesn't have a lot of patience for some of the old codgers on that committee who are more interested in keeping their colleges at the top of the Norrington table and keeping in with their old friends from their respective public schools. You can always tell when she's getting frustrated with them,' Martin smiled broadly, as he pictured the scene in his mind's eye, 'because her accent becomes stronger and stronger until it's almost incomprehensible – to me at any rate. I just keep my head down and pretend to be deeply engrossed in the meeting papers when she's on a roll like that, because I know that, if I caught her eye, I'd never be able to stop myself laughing.'

He paused again, looking more sombre now.

'I wish I'd had the courage to get to know her properly,' he continued wistfully. 'The difficulty was always finding the right moment to tell her who I was. I knew, from the minutes of the meetings, that she was on the committee – Fazakerley is such a distinctive name – but she wasn't there at the first meeting I went to, when it would have been easy to say something while I was being introduced to everyone. Her name came up in the list of apologies and someone said that she couldn't be there because her daughter was ill. That was the first I knew that she and Richard had any children.'

'The child was born after he died,' Peter explained.

'Yes, the secretary who was minuting the meeting mentioned that. One of the old buffers said something about that being the trouble with having women on the staff: when they weren't on maternity leave they seemed to expect to take time off all the time because their children needed them. She, the secretary, said how much she admired Bernie for managing so well under the circumstances and then the whole story came out about her husband having been a policeman and having been killed falling from the roof of one of the colleges. I knew at once it must be Richard they were talking about. Anyway the old fellow wasn't to be put off: he described Bernie as "a ghastly woman" and said something along the lines of how, while he wouldn't wish such a death on anyone it must, in many ways, have come as a blessed relief to her husband compared with being yoked to her for life.' Martin paused in this unexpectedly long narrative and looked up at Peter with a grin on his face, 'Of course, after that I was absolutely determined to like her, just to spite him!'

'So how come you never got to know her properly?'

'I made up my mind to tell her who I was at the next meeting, but somehow I didn't get the opportunity. And then, every month it became more difficult. She's always very focussed on the business in hand. She never gossips about her home life the way some of the committee members do, so there haven't been any natural opportunities to broach the subject. Somehow, it just never seems to be the right moment, and I'm afraid of opening old wounds by reminding her …'

Martin sighed and sat for a few moments apparently deep in thought.

'I did hear,' he went on, 'that she'd married again – to another policeman. Do you know whether that's true?'

'Yes,' Peter told him, 'I believe it is.'

Anna opened her mouth as if to speak, but then caught Peter's eye and changed her mind.

'Well, anyway,' Peter said, heading for the door, 'I think that's all for now. It's been good speaking to you.'

Once the front door was safely closed behind them, Anna turned to Peter and addressed him in a tone that managed to be both incredulous and accusatory.

'You *believe* that Superintendent Paige's widow has remarried?'

'Certainly I do,' Peter answered, his voice serious but with a twinkle in his eye. 'It's a subject on which I have particularly strongly-held beliefs.'

'You don't think that's a rather misleading thing to have said to Dr Riess – sir?' Anna added hastily.

'Don't you think I have a right to a bit of harmless fun at the expense of a man who has so patently taken a shine to my wife?' Peter asked, grinning openly now.

Anna did not know what to say to this. She had never seen Peter in this mood before. Usually he took life – and his job in particular – extremely seriously. She would never have imagined that he might adopt this facetious attitude towards a witness, particularly one who might turn out to be a murder suspect.

'And to make things worse,' Peter continued cheerfully, 'I have every reason to believe that the sentiment is reciprocated.'

'In that case,' Anna suggested, trying to adapt to this new whimsical side of her boss by responding in a similar vein, 'you seem to be remarkably laid back about it.'

'As our Dr Riess claims to have been over the loss of the fair Edwina. I could see you weren't convinced by his protestations that he didn't hold it against Fellowes.'

'Well, don't you think it would be only natural for him to resent the way Fellowes went off with her while Riess was out of the country?'

'He might have thought the fault lay more with Edwina. The way he talked just now, it was as if he thought that she didn't care much for Fellowes; it was more that she needed a husband – any husband – in order to keep up with Martina.'

'In that case,' Anna suggested, the thought only just having occurred to her, 'might he not be hoping that the rift between them provided him with an opportunity to re-kindle his own relationship with her?'

'Possibly, but what are you suggesting?'

'That he might have thought his chances would be improved if Fellowes was removed from the scene altogether.'

'I'm not so sure about that,' Peter argued. 'It could easily have had completely the opposite effect and made her realise how much she missed the husband that she'd just rejected, after all.'

'Or Edwina may have confided in him what it was that Fellowes had done to upset her and he could have been so incensed about it that he killed him in her defence,' Anna suggested, unwilling to give up completely on her theory that Martin Riess was by far the most likely killer.

'Now that sounds considerably more likely,' Peter agreed, 'and it's something that we must remember to check out with Edwina when we finally get an audience with her.'

CHAPTER 7

'I think I'll set Lepage checking out those tutorial students,' Peter said, as they parked up outside the police station and made their way to the incident room. 'It's very straightforward, but it will involve him interviewing each of them to check that those tutorials really did take place when Riess says they did. It's a good opportunity for him to get experience of working on his own without any risk that he could mess it up.'

'If you think a trainee ought to be questioning members of the public alone,' Anna said dubiously, remembering her own early days in CID when she had felt that none of the established team trusted her to do anything more than making the tea or ordering a takeaway.

'He can take one of the uniformed officers with him if you think he needs support,' Peter conceded, conscious that he might be allowing his desire to advance the career of a mixed-race officer to lead him into showing favouritism. He did not believe in positive discrimination and would have said, if asked, that he treated everyone equally regardless of ethnicity or gender, but it was difficult for him not to feel a paternal interest in a young man who reminded him so strongly of his own two children.

'Hughes might be a good choice – if he can be spared from his other duties. He's dependable and not likely to interfere or to be offended by being asked to be backup for a trainee.'

There were several reports waiting for Peter when they got back to the incident room. The house-to-house interviews had produced a large number of statements, but nothing of any consequence. The hunt for Dave Gillis continued, having been fruitless so far. Several sets of fingerprints had been found on various parts of the boat but, so far, the only ones that had been identified belonged to Martin Fellowes and Martin Riess.

The post mortem report on Martin Fellowes put time of death at between six and eight-thirty on Tuesday evening, with the balance of likelihood tending towards the later time. The cause of death was a single blow to the head, inflicted from behind by some sort of heavy metal object. The wound had a distinctive shape that suggested that the weapon might be a claw hammer of a sort widely available in hardware shops and DIY stores.

'Assuming that Riess and his mother are telling the truth about him arriving home at six, that puts him out of the frame for the first murder,' Peter observed to Anna as they studied the report together.

'I don't know about that, sir. He could still have gone back to the boat on the way to dinner at Lichfield,' Anna objected. 'I think we ought to get his clothes examined for traces of blood.'

'Hmm. That's a good point,' Peter admitted, 'but I don't want him to think he's under suspicion just yet. He's already had time to remove any obvious bloodstains, so the chances are it won't make any difference leaving it for a few days longer while we check out his alibi for the other murder and talk to the other members of the SCR about what time he really arrived at the college for dinner. If he did get there at six forty-five, as he claims, it's hard to see how he could have got back to the boat from Headington, killed Fellowes and then gone on to the college all within about half an hour.'

'He could have set out earlier than he said – or perhaps he didn't really go home at all. You admitted yourself that his mother can't be treated as a reliable witness, if it's a matter of keeping her son out of the dock.'

'OK.' Peter accepted the validity of Anna's argument and realised that he was in danger of allowing his liking for the little don, and his wife's anxiety for the peace of mind of Eva Riess, to cloud his judgement. 'I'll send Andrews to collect the suit Riess wore to the dinner and the clothes he wore earlier when he went down to the boat to see Fellowes. I can trust him to understand about being tactful and not upsetting Mrs Riess.'

'I could do all that, sir,' Anna volunteered. 'Mrs Riess might be more reassured by a woman approaching her to take away her son's things.'

'No. I want you to come with me to High Wycombe to see the Plants,' Peter answered firmly. 'I've made arrangements to interview them there this afternoon, so we'll just get a bite to eat and then set off. Unless you need to get home early this afternoon,' he added, remembering that Anna had a young family to consider.

'It's OK,' she assured him, 'Philip doesn't get back until tomorrow evening and I'm not picking the kids up from Mum until Saturday morning.'

'Good. Andrews!' Peter called across the room to where a tall detective sergeant with a mop of untidy black hair was bending over the shoulder of a young constable who was pointing at something on her computer screen. 'I've got a job for you.'

Peter explained to Sergeant Andrews what he wanted, putting great emphasis on the need to take care not to alarm Mrs Riess.

'And while you're there,' he added as an afterthought, 'I suppose you'd better take Mrs Riess's fingerprints. The chances are she'll have been on that boat at some time and some of those unidentified prints may be hers.'

'Right you are, sir,' Rupert Andrews answered. 'I'll go right away – and I'll be tactful.'

Peter looked round the room again and called another of the officers across to him.

'Philipson,' he said, addressing a slim young woman in a smart trouser suit, 'I'd like you to go over to Lichfield College and talk to as many of the fellows as you can who dined on high table on Tuesday night. All I want to know is what time Dr Martin Riess got there. Make a note if anyone volunteers any information about his demeanour – if he seemed agitated or upset at all – but don't ask about that explicitly. I don't want to start them all thinking he's under suspicion.'

'Yes sir,' Monica Philipson answered promptly. 'I'll make an appointment to see the college principal – or whatever they call them at Lichfield – and get them to give me permission to speak to the dons. And, how about the college servants? There may have been someone handing out sherry in the SCR who would have been the most likely to be watching for people arriving.'

'That's a good idea,' Peter acknowledged, reflecting to himself that here was another officer who deserved to have been promoted by now. What was an Oxford graduate with seven years' police service doing still only at constable rank? 'I knew I could rely on you to know how to deal with those academics. It wouldn't do any harm to drop into the conversation the fact that you went to Keble. It'll make them feel that they can trust you.'

'I'll do my best,' Monica answered, smiling with pleasure at receiving praise from a man for whom she had great respect. Peter Johns had none of the academic qualifications of many of his younger colleagues, but his knack for empathy and his genuine concern for the officers beneath him made him more highly regarded than he would ever realise.

A little over an hour later, Peter and Anna drew up outside the Plant family's spacious home on the outskirts of High Wycombe. Husband and wife would be expecting them, since Peter had made the arrangements the previous evening, after deciding that he needed to press on with contacting the remaining Martians before Jonah Porter had a chance to take over that side of the investigation. He already had an appointment booked to interview Edwina Clarkson at her constituency office on Saturday. (Her secretary had managed to squeeze him in between a meeting with her political advisor and a working lunch with a group of farmers anxious about their EU subsidies.)

Anna rang the bell and they both stepped back off the step, waiting for a response. It was not long before the door opened and a large man with a small grey moustache looked out at them. His hair, what little was left of it, was grey also, but looked as if it might once have been black, to match his bushy eyebrows which dominated his face. He looked at them with dark brown eyes, appearing to size them up. Peter stepped forward holding up his warrant card and introduced himself.

'And this is Detective Sergeant Davenport,' he added, gesturing towards Anna. 'Are you Mr Geoffrey Plant?'

'Yes. You'd better come in.'

Geoffrey stood back to allow them into the house. He led them down a long hallway and into a room at the back.

'Martina, darling,' he said as they entered, 'the police are here.'

Peter could not help staring at the tall, slim woman who came forward to greet them. Her hair, which curled luxuriantly round her face and rested lightly on her shoulders, was an attractive shade of red – rather like Peter's own hair in days before the ravishes of time had changed it to a sandy grey. Her complexion was flawless and her features symmetric and well-proportioned. She looked much younger than her husband, although Peter knew that he was, in fact, only a few months her senior.

She smiled rather sadly at him and held out her hand.

'Good afternoon, Inspector,' she said calmly, but with a slight air of pathos in her voice, as if she were bravely fighting back her emotions. 'Such a dreadful thing to have happened to poor Martin – and now to Arthur as well. Of course, we want to do anything we can to help you find out who did it. Do you really think it has something to do with when we were all in Cambridge together?'

'That's one of the things that we're trying to find out,' Peter answered, taking the seat that Geoffrey offered him and indicating that everyone else should also sit down. In the silence that followed, while Peter gathered his thoughts and decided where to begin, he became aware of sounds coming from a room above. Someone appeared to be pacing the floor; then there was a banging sound as if that someone were beating his or her fists against a wooden partition. As he listened, Peter heard the keening of a woman's voice, sounding distressed, although he could not make out any words. He noticed that Martina was sitting rigid in her chair, clearly also listening to the sounds. Then she got up abruptly and turned to address Peter.

'I'm sorry,' she said, still outwardly calm but with increasing anxiety showing on her face, 'you'll have to excuse me for a few minutes.'

She left the room and Peter could hear her hurrying upstairs.

'You'll have to forgive my wife,' Geoffrey said apologetically. 'It's our daughter, Amber. She has had some mental health issues and tried to commit suicide earlier this week. Naturally, we're both very worried about her. We warned her that you would be calling, and I think she's afraid that you could be planning to take her away. She's been sectioned once before and she hated every minute of her time in the mental hospital.'

'I'm sorry,' Peter said, feeling that this was a very inadequate expression to use and also feeling guilty at having, by his mere presence, added to the troubles of a family already going through great difficulties. As so often happened in the course of his work, he felt that he was intruding upon this family's private grief. 'We'll be as quick as we can. Perhaps, while your wife's away, you could give us some basic facts?'

'Certainly. What do you want to know?'

'For the record, we need to know where you both were on Tuesday and Wednesday of this week – that's yesterday and the day before.'

'That's easy. We spent Monday night at the hospital, waiting to see that Amber was going to pull through. We were there all day Tuesday as well. At least, Martina was there all day, and I was there until about one in the afternoon, when I gave Martina's sister a lift to the station. She's an MEP and had to get back to Strasbourg – but I suppose you know all about that.'

'Not as much as we'd like to know,' Peter admitted. 'Mrs Fellowes hasn't had time to talk with us about her husband's death yet.'

'How like Edwina!' Geoffrey said with a brief smile. 'Her political career comes before everything else with her, I'm afraid. No – that's not fair, she did fly back straight away when she heard about Amber's suicide attempt and she stayed with us at the hospital all night, even though she'd already had a long day in Strasbourg.'

'Presumably your wife and she are close?' Anna asked.

'Very. They are identical twins, after all.'

'So, if there was a problem in Mrs Fellowes' marriage you would have expected her to talk to your wife about it?'

'If you mean, did Edwina tell us she'd thrown Martin out, yes. She rang Martina to say that she'd given him an ultimatum and then a few days later she let us know that she'd sent him packing.'

'But did she tell you exactly what the disagreement was about?' Anna persisted.

'You'd have to ask her about that. I know there were various things she wasn't happy with. I think he found it hard to cope with her being a public figure. He was more used to being on the other end of press revelations.'

'You mean the sort of thing that Arthur Finch publishes?' Peter asked, picking up on Plant's use of the word *revelations*.

'I suppose so. Martin was happy to make money out of publishing details of other people's private lives, but I don't think he was so pleased when other people commented on his wife's.'

'Anyone in particular?' Anna asked. 'Did Finch, for example, ever publish anything about Fellowes or his wife?'

'Not that I know of,' Geoffrey Plant backtracked quickly. 'I was just speaking generally.'

'To get back to your movements on Tuesday and Wednesday,' Peter resumed. 'You say that you left your wife at the hospital at one p.m. and took Mrs Fellowes to the station. What did you do after that?'

'I went home. Someone needed to feed the cat. We'd packed the younger children – we have four in addition to Amber – off to my parents' house, but we'd completely forgotten about the cat until about lunchtime on Tuesday.'

'I see,' Peter said encouragingly, 'and can you remember what time it was when you got home?'

'Let me see … I suppose it must have been between half past two and three o'clock. I'm afraid I'm really not sure.'

'And then what?' Peter asked mildly.

'How d'you mean?'

'What happened next? Did you go back to the hospital, once you'd fed the cat?'

'No, no. I stayed at home. I rang Martina and she said that Amber was sleeping and the hospital said that the sedative they'd given her would probably make her stay that way until the following morning. There didn't seem much point both of us having another sleepless night and we were worried about leaving the kids with my parents for too long.'

'So, are you saying you brought your other four children back to be with you at home for Tuesday night?'

'Yes – no – well, I rang my parents and they picked up Harry and Zoe from school and brought them over. Jake – he's the oldest, apart from Amber – had arranged to sleep over with one of his mates and didn't want to come home. It suited me to have him out of the house until after Amber was settled back in, because he tends to tease her and make things worse. Aaron – the youngest – stayed with his grandparents. My mum likes him and I didn't feel I could cope with his demands right then.'

'Can I get this straight?' asked Anna, who had been taking notes. 'You got home between half past two and three o'clock; you fed the cat and then rang your parents and this friend of your son's and then your parents brought two of your children home here. At about what time would that have been?'

''Five past five,' Geoffrey Plant answered promptly. 'I know that because Zoe was upset that she'd missed five minutes of some television programme she likes to watch which started at five. I'd been expecting them to come straight from school, but they went back to my parents' house to collect their things, so it was after five by the time they got here.'

'So,' Peter said, 'from five past five on Tuesday evening, presumably until they went to school on Wednesday morning, you were here at home with Harry and Zoe? How old are your children, by the way?'

'Fifteen, thirteen, ten, eight and three. And yes – we all stayed at home until I did the school run in the morning. After that, Martina rang to say that they were discharging Amber. So, you see, she's only been home since yesterday morning. That's why she's so terrified that she might be taken back in.'

The door opened and Martina Plant returned. She walked across the room and resumed her seat.

'I'm sorry about that,' she apologised. 'I suppose Geoffrey will have explained about our daughter, Amber?'

'Yes,' Peter confirmed. 'I'm sorry she's not well. We'll try to keep this as short as we can so that we can leave you in peace.'

'I'm afraid we need to know where you both were on Tuesday and Wednesday,' Anna added. 'Your husband has told us that you were at the hospital from Monday evening to Wednesday morning. Would you be able to tell us what you did after that?'

'I stayed here with Amber,' Martina replied. 'I ought to have been doing the show, but I couldn't leave her on her own and anyway I couldn't have faced the cameras with so much on my mind.'

'Did you both stay home all day then?' Peter asked, turning to Geoffrey.

'No, I went back to work for the afternoon,' he replied. 'I had some rather important clients who I didn't want to lose. I'd cancelled their appointments when I got the news about Amber and I'd promised I'd see them as soon as I could.'

'So you went in to your office – at what time?' Anna asked.

'No. These were visits to the clients' own businesses. I can give you the names and addresses.' Geoffrey Plant reached into his pocket and pulled out an electronic organiser. 'Here you are.'

He held it out so that Anna could read the diary entries and note down the details.

'Wallingford and Abingdon,' she said aloud. 'That must have brought you quite close to Didcot.'

'Yes, I suppose so, but I didn't go through Didcot. I cut across to the north along the A415.'

'I see,' Peter said, with a finality in his voice that indicated to Anna that she should not press the Plants any further on their movements. 'Now, I'm sorry to have to ask more questions, but I need you to tell me as much as you can about Martin Fellowes and Arthur Finch and in particular if you can think of anyone who might have had a grudge against either of them. I gather you knew them both well when you were together in Cambridge, and I presume,' he added, addressing Martina, 'that you will have continued to see quite a lot of your brother-in-law more recently.'

'Beaconsfield is only just down the road, after all,' Anna added.

'Yes, you're right,' Martina Plant agreed. 'We used to see them most weekends, but it's dropped off since Eddie got elected to the European Parliament. She spends a lot of time in Strasbourg and Brussels or else on the road between meetings.'

'She left her husband a note,' Peter said, pulling out from his jacket a copy of the letter that Anna had found in Martin Fellowes' pocket. 'Do you know what she meant by his intolerable attitude?'

'You'd better ask her about that. I know they had stopped seeing eye-to-eye on a lot of things.'

'I *will* ask her when I meet her on Saturday,' Peter said patiently, 'but I'd like to know what *you* think too. Do I gather that you were not very surprised when she told him she wanted him to leave?'

'I suppose so,' Martina appeared to be thinking. 'Looking back, I think that for a long time Eddie was only sticking with Martin for the sake of her political career. She thought that separation or divorce might make her less electable in the eyes of grass-roots Conservatives. Even in this day and age, there are a lot of them who think that a stable marriage is the only really respectable way of life, and she was hoping to be chosen for a safe seat in the next UK election.'

'So what changed her mind?' Anna asked sharply.

'I think she came to realise that divorce was inevitable and she thought it would be better to get it over with well in advance of the election.'

'You make your sister sound very calculating,' Peter observed mildly, wondering whether the twins were really as close as Geoffrey had indicated. To Peter's way of thinking, Martina's words smacked more of sibling rivalry than of a close sisterly bond.

'Oh, she was,' Martina assured him. 'Why do you think she switched her politics away from the Green party? For her, power is more important than principles.'

'I don't think that's quite fair,' Geoffrey protested weakly. 'You have to admit that some of the ideas we had back in the Cambridge days were a bit unrealistic.'

'Perhaps we could talk about Arthur Finch now,' Peter suggested in the hope of diverting the couple away from what looked as if it might develop into a family row. 'How well do you know him and his wife?'

'Arthur was always more Eddie's friend than mine,' Martina said, 'but lately Coralie has made quite an effort to get to know us better. I always liked her, but she became a bit distant after I got my TV job. I think maybe she was a bit over-awed by the idea that I might consider myself to be some sort of celebrity now.'

She gave a little nervous laugh before going on.

'When their kids were born, Coralie suddenly became much more outgoing and confident in herself,' she said, her eyebrows curving attractively in concentration as she thought through what she wanted to say. 'You know, I think she felt she was a failure not having any children and then when she finally managed to get pregnant she suddenly got her confidence back.'

'I'm not so sure Arthur saw it that way,' Geoffrey said darkly. 'I think he liked being the centre of attention at home and wasn't that enamoured of having a couple of kids taking up Coralie's time and energy.'

Peter thought back to Martin Riess' description of Arthur Finch, and reflected that he had yet to find anyone who thought that he cared for anyone apart from himself. Was this a true reflection of his character or was there some other reason why his friends wanted him to appear selfish and unlikeable?

'What was Arthur Finch like?' he asked. 'Can you think of anyone who might have borne him a grudge?'

'How long have you got?' Martina asked grimly. 'His business was publishing half-truths dressed up as news and always skewed to make the people he was writing about appear in the worst possible light. I would have thought that almost anyone in the public eye and quite a number of ordinary people who just happened to be in one of the groups that he didn't think much of – civil servants, the police, bank managers, the intelligentsia, you name it – may well have slept easier in their beds last night having heard that he wouldn't be peddling any more of his so-called revelations!'

There was silence after this long speech. Then Geoffrey cleared his throat, looked round at everyone and suggested that perhaps it was now late enough for them all to have a drink.

Peter declined the offer and got up to go, having decided that the Plants had told him all that they could and that it was time they were left to care for their daughter. He judged that their younger children would be home from school soon and he had no desire to disrupt family life any further.

CHAPTER 8

Peter arrived at work early the following day and was annoyed to discover Jonah Porter already there, waiting for him. He was sitting in the incident room, holding a mug of coffee and chatting with one of the officers who had been on duty overnight in case any calls came through in response to the appeal for witnesses. He got up when Peter entered and greeted him cheerfully.

'I've brought over the PM report on Finch,' he explained, holding out a manila folder, 'and I was hoping to sit in on your briefing this morning, if you don't mind, just to bring myself fully up to speed with this end of the investigation. You'll see from the PM that it's pretty likely the two murders are linked. The weapon is either the same one or two identical hammers and the pathologists even seem to think that the way that the wound was inflicted is similar in both cases – something about the angle of the blow, I gather.'

'Thanks,' Peter said shortly, taking the folder. 'Would you like to address the team, when they get in? To fill them in on what you've found out about the Finch murder.'

'If you don't mind,' Jonah answered, with unusual consideration for his colleague's feelings. 'I wouldn't like you to think I'm trying to take over.'

The two men stood eyeing one another for a few moments. Peter, who had already been obliged to make the case to his immediate superior for his continuing as the investigating officer for the Fellowes case, was convinced that this was exactly what Jonah was hoping to do. Jonah reflected that things would be much simpler if the two murders were officially combined into a single investigation with himself in charge. As it was, he knew that Peter would be diffident over giving opinions on the murder of Arthur Finch and suspicious of any suggestions that Jonah might make in respect of the investigation into the Fellowes case.

'Sir!'

Both officers turned at the sound of Andy Lepage's voice calling excitedly to Peter as he entered the room.

'I think you ought to read this, sir,' he went on, holding out a magazine, folded back to display one of its inside pages. 'You said we ought to look for anyone else who might have a grudge against Fellowes and Finch – well, see here!'

Peter stepped forward and took the magazine from Andy's hand.

'Andy,' he said, nodding briefly towards Jonah, 'this is Detective Chief Inspector Porter. He's in charge of the Finch case. Jonah, let me introduce Trainee Detective Constable Andy Lepage.'

'Oh! I'm sorry, sir. I didn't mean to interrupt,' Andy stammered, aghast at the thought that he had burst in on a private conference between two senior officers. 'Would you like me to go?'

'No, no,' Jonah said genially. 'We were only making conversation while we waited for everyone to arrive. I'm very pleased to meet you Constable Lepage. I admire keenness. Tell us about this new evidence that you've found.'

'Well, sir,' Andy began, swelling with pride at the

commendation, 'I found this article in *Revelations* magazine. It's by Martin Fellowes. It's all about Professor George Fraser. You may have seen him: he gets interviewed on science programmes a lot.'

Peter took the magazine and started to read. He hoped that Andy was right in thinking that the article was relevant to the investigation. He did not want the young officer to feel that he had shown himself up in front of a visitor from another division.

'Popular science presenter and high-flying Oxford professor, George Fraser,' the article began, 'portrays himself as a happily-married man whose soul-mate is also a key collaborator in his work. But is that all a façade? Two sex-workers from Oxford's thriving red-light district have a very different story to tell.'

Peter continued reading to the end and then handed the journal over to Jonah.

'I take it you're suggesting that this Professor Fraser might be sore about having it trumpeted to the world that he frequents prostitutes,' he said, addressing Andy. 'But I gather *Revelations* is full of this sort of stuff; what made you pick on this one particularly? Is it just because he lives in Oxford?'

'Well, that was what made me think it was worth looking into,' Andy explained eagerly. 'So I looked him up and the thing that made me think he might be a suspect was when I found that, as well as holding a university chair, he's also a fellow at Lichfield.'

'Lichfield?' Jonah asked, looking up from his reading.

'Lichfield College, sir – the same one as Dr Riess.'

'Dr Martin Riess is the owner of the boat where Martin Fellowes was killed,' Peter explained. 'He's a tutor at Lichfield. I think Constable Lepage is suggesting that the two men would have known each other and Riess might well have mentioned to Fraser that Fellowes was staying in his boat.'

'That's smart thinking,' Jonah said approvingly. 'I'd say

this Professor Fraser is well worth checking out.'

'I've made a list of all the other people that Martin Fellowes wrote about in *Revelations* for the last nine months,' Andy added eagerly. 'There are another couple who live not all that far away. Shall I see if I can find out any more about them? Or would you like me to go back further and look at earlier editions?'

'Let's just wait for a bit,' Peter said, smiling at his young colleague's enthusiasm. 'You haven't written up what you found out from those students you were interviewing yesterday yet, and I want to hear from Philipson whether Riess's alibi holds up for Tuesday night, and there may be some results back from the lab on the clothes he was wearing. We need to be systematic about things and follow up the lines of enquiry that are most likely to get us somewhere first.'

'That's right,' Jonah agreed, making a deliberate effort to support Peter in his dealings with his subordinate. He was conscious that it would be easy, as a more senior officer coming in from outside the team, to undermine Peter's standing, and well-aware that Peter was anxious lest he take over the running of the investigation from him, 'slow and sure, that's the way to avoid making mistakes in this business. You pay attention to your boss – he taught me a lot when I was your age.'

Peter was uncertain how to react to this unexpected affirmation of his own painstaking and methodical approach, which Jonah rarely, in Peter's experience, adopted himself. He fleetingly wondered whether the Chief Inspector might be speaking ironically. He was a saved from having to formulate a response by the arrival of Anna. She immediately recognised Jonah and greeted him warmly, but at the same time glancing towards Peter, wondering whether he was being supplanted by the more senior man. Jonah recognised the hint of anxiety in her face and hastened to reassure her.

'I'm here to listen and learn,' he told her. 'It looks as if my victim may have suffered at the hands of the same killer as yours, so I want to hear everything you've found out so far – so that we don't end up covering the same ground twice.'

'I'm sure we'll all be very happy to help you,' Anna said, relieved that the smooth running of Peter's team was not to be disrupted, but, at the same time, feeling just a slight tinge of disappointment. There was something curiously attractive about Jonah's clear blue eyes and slightly lopsided smile – not to mention his contagious enthusiasm for his job.

Soon the room began to fill up, as personnel arrived and settled themselves ready for the morning briefing. Peter called them to order, banging on a table to quell the buzz of conversation as colleagues caught up with overnight news. He introduced Jonah to the group before running through a summary of the investigation so far. Then he turned to individual members of his team to report on what they had been doing the previous day.

Monica Philipson, the first up, was able to confirm that Martin Riess had arrived at his college for dinner no later than ten to seven on Tuesday evening, just as he had claimed. Not only had three of his academic colleagues, including the Master of the college, specified this as his arrival time, but also the porter had noticed him pushing his bike through the main entrance a few minutes earlier.

At this point, Rupert Andrews stepped forward, eager to share some information that he had obtained.

'We have two witnesses,' he reported, 'who saw Fellowes alive at seven o'clock that evening. It was the residents of the next boat. They were coming back from town along the towpath and they passed the *Maid of Saxony* and noticed him inside cooking a meal. He had the light on and they said he was clearly visible standing at the cooker in the galley. They'd been introduced to him when he moved in and they are sure it was him.'

'Good work,' Peter said, cutting in quickly before

Jonah could comment. 'That means that we can rule out Riess as a suspect for the Fellowes murder. Now, what about the other one? Lepage – you were checking on the tutorials that he said he was doing all day on Wednesday.'

'Yes, sir,' Andy stood up and addressed the room. 'I managed to speak to all but one of the students and they basically said the same as Riess. He had people with him from ten until twelve and then again from twelve thirty until two thirty.'

'And I checked with the staff in Hall,' Monica added, 'and they remember him coming down to lunch just after twelve.'

'Then we went round to see him at about three,' Peter mused, 'and didn't leave until half past at the earliest.'

'All of which means that he couldn't have been in Didcot doing in Arthur Finch between noon and three pm, which is what the PM report gives as the time of death,' Jonah put in. 'So I think we can rule out this Riess guy's involvement altogether. Who else do we have?'

'There's Dave Gillis,' Andrews suggested tentatively. 'His fingerprints have turned up on some of the woodwork inside the boat. So it looks as if he was there at some time, and he might well have been the man that those students saw near the scene shortly before they found the body.'

'This sounds promising,' said Jonah eagerly. 'Who is this Dave Gillis?'

'He's a rough sleeper and petty criminal,' Peter explained. 'He has no history of violence, although he wouldn't be above climbing into any boat that looked as if it was unoccupied and helping himself to anything he fancied. My guess is that he may have gone in looking for cash – or something he could easily turn into cash – and saw the body and scarpered. That would explain him looking as if he was anxious to get away when those students saw him – he wouldn't want to get himself mixed up in anything like that.'

'Well, what are we waiting for?' Jonah demanded, forgetting momentarily that he was not in charge of this end of the investigation. 'Let's pull him in and see what he has to say for himself. Even if he isn't the murderer, he could be a key witness.'

'We've got people out looking for him,' Peter said patiently, 'but he's not easy to track down at the best of times and, if the thinks he might be mixed up in a suspicious death, he'll have gone to ground somewhere that he thinks we won't be able to trace him.'

Jonah still looked dissatisfied, so Peter decided to placate him by instigating a new search for Gillis.

'OK, Andrews. Go and pick up Hughes and do another round of the homeless hideouts. He's the most likely person to have an idea where Gillis might have hidden himself, and he has the confidence of the other rough sleepers so they may possibly open up to him.'

Then Peter turned to Jonah again.

'I think the most likely suspects are the members of this Martians group,' he said. 'Two of them have been killed and the first was living on a boat that belonged to a third one of them. It's too much of a coincidence for it to have nothing to do with it. Apart from Riess, they all seem to be related by blood or marriage, and we all know that nine times out of ten the murderer is a member of the victim's family.'

'Alright,' Jonah agreed, 'Let's see who we've got there then.'

'First up there's Edwina Clarkson MEP, AKA Mrs Fellowes,' said Anna, stepping forward at a nod from Peter and writing on a large whiteboard on the wall. 'She fell out with her husband big-time about a week ago and banished him from the family home. That's why he was staying on Martin Riess's boat. She could have decided to get rid of him more permanently.'

'But, if he'd already gone,' Jonah interrupted, 'did she really need to kill him?'

'That rather depends what it was that she was so upset with him about,' Peter put in, slightly annoyed at Jonah for questioning one of his team. 'She accused him of having an *intolerable attitude*, but we don't know what about. And the other thing to consider is that she was apparently worried that divorce or separation wouldn't play well with Conservative party activists. Maybe she thought that being a widow would be more acceptable to the party faithful. Anyway, go on, Anna: could she have killed her husband?'

'Probably not,' Anna admitted. 'She was travelling back from High Wycombe to Strasbourg during Tuesday afternoon and evening. Her brother-in-law, Geoffrey Plant, says he dropped her off at the station before two.'

'And she's still in Strasbourg now,' Peter added. 'She couldn't spare the time to come back to be interviewed about her husband's death, but she's very magnanimously agreed to see me during her constituency time this weekend.'

'So, on the face of it,' she couldn't be responsible for either murder,' Jonah observed. 'Who else is there?'

'Edwina's twin sister, Martina, was at the hospital in High Wycombe all day Tuesday,' Anna said, consulting her notes. 'Then, on Wednesday she brought her daughter home and stayed in with her all day.'

'She won't admit to knowing what the row was about,' Peter added, 'but I fancy that she and her husband, Geoffrey, do both know. Assuming that they take Edwina's part, they could have conspired with her to do away with Fellowes.'

'Hmm,' Jonah murmured thoughtfully. 'So you're suggesting that Geoffrey's alibi that says Edwina was en route to Strasbourg long before Fellowes was killed could be cooked up?'

'Yes – or maybe Martina could have slipped away from the hospital for a few hours without being seen,' Peter suggested. 'I know hospitals. In the evening, there wouldn't be any more nurses on duty than they absolutely needed to look after the patients. I bet no one will be able to swear that Martina was there for the whole time.'

'And the following day,' Anna continued, 'she only has her daughter, Amber, to vouch for her having been at home all day. She could have slipped out to the Finch house in Didcot and been fairly confident that Amber either wouldn't notice or would back up her story.'

'And why would she – or Edwina, for that matter – want to kill Arthur Finch?' Jonah asked mildly.

'He and Fellowes were hand-in-glove, with this magazine that he edited,' Peter suggested. 'I think Edwina may have been including him when she talked about an intolerable attitude. It was probably something to do with the attitude that he was expressing in his articles. Maybe he was planning to run some stories that were critical of her – maybe even,' he added, a new idea occurring to him, 'writing about their marriage. Perhaps, after she chucked him out, he threatened to write about intimate details that she didn't want the general public to know, and she decided that the only way to prevent it being published in Finch's magazine was to get rid of both of them.'

'In other words,' Jonah said, 'you think that Edwina may have had a very similar motive to Professor Fraser.'

'Except that he was motivated by revenge – because the article about him had already been published, whereas I'm suggesting that Edwina – possibly in cahoots with Martina and her husband – may have been trying to *prevent* publication, which seems a much stronger motive to me,' Peter argued.

'That's a fair point,' Jonah admitted. 'So, what we really want to know is: who were the next targets for Fellowes' poison pen intended to be? And did they know that they were about to be exposed to the world?'

'We've checked the hard drive on Fellowes' laptop,' Peter told him, 'and we only found one potential victim. That was Martin Riess, and it turned out to be a load of nonsense in any case.' He briefly explained about the suggestion that Riess had killed his father and the true story behind it, carefully avoiding any mention of Bernie's involvement.

'I see,' he said at the end of Peter's story. 'Now, perhaps you'd like me to tell you what I know about your other two Martians, Coralie and Arthur Finch?'

Peter nodded agreement and Jonah stood up to address the assembly. The room immediately fell silent as he explained what his team had found out about the murder of Arthur Finch. Every eye was fixed on the handsome face of the Chief Inspector with his soulful blue eyes that shone as he became animated in his description of how his team was progressing in the investigation of Arthur Finch's death. Peter reflected on the way that his officers were hanging on every word from this charismatic man. What was it about Jonah's lopsided smile that invited adoration? What made his irrepressible enthusiasm for his job so infectious? Of course, it helped to be so good-looking. Even the greying of his hair at the temples made him appear distinguished rather than old. Peter, with once-ginger and now pepper-and-salt grey hair and the reddish skin and freckles that accompanied it, could hardly expect to compete.

'Arthur Finch spent Tuesday in his office in London,' Jonah told his eager audience. 'He left for home early that afternoon because he had agreed to look after the children while Coralie attended a parents' evening at her school. Coralie says that he got home shortly before five and she went out directly. He was at home with the children from five until nine, when Coralie returned. On the face of it, neither of them could have killed Fellowes and neither of them has a motive for wanting to. The next day, Arthur Finch is killed, apparently by the same person using the same weapon, which is another reason for ruling him out as a suspect for the Fellowes murder. Coralie was at school at the time that he was killed, so it looks as if she's out of the frame too.'

Peter listened with a feeling of annoyance – at himself for having placed too much emphasis on the link with the Martians, when on closer inspection none of them appeared to be very likely suspects after all, and at Jonah for exposing this fact to his subordinates so subtly. He had fallen into the very trap (of jumping to conclusions prematurely) that he had often criticised in Jonah, when he had been a sergeant and Jonah a mere Detective Constable. This was out of character, and Peter recognised that he had been tempted into abandoning his usual slow and cautious approach by a desire not to be outshone by Jonah, who so often appeared to solve cases by leaps of intuition rather than by painstaking collection and scrutiny of the evidence.

'It could be that someone from outside the group is trying to get rid of the Martians,' Andy Lepage suggested suddenly. 'I mean – rather than the Martians killing one another.'

'It could be,' Jonah admitted with a smile, which somehow conveyed that he remained unconvinced but admired the young man's attempt to stick up for his mentor. 'Or it could be an unhappy victim of *Revelations* magazine or something we haven't even thought of yet. So,' he went on, picking up his jacket from where he had hung it on the back of a chair by way of signalling that he was leaving. 'I'll get back to Didcot and start delving into Arthur Finch's past and *Revelations* magazine's files.'

A moment later, he was gone, striding out of the door and down the corridor with his habitual energy. Peter watched as heads turned to follow his departure. Then he rapped on the table to call the room to attention again and started distributing tasks amongst the team.

'I wouldn't mind working for that DCI Porter,' Monica Philipson confided to Anna later that morning, while they were both engaged in collating the information from the house-to-house interviews and telephone statements. 'I think he's gorgeous. Did you see how blue his eyes are and the way he smiles?'

'I think I prefer Peter,' Anna replied, loyally. 'I saw the way Porter goes on when he's in charge. He wants everything done by yesterday and expects everyone to read his mind as to what it is he *does* want. He's probably a great boss when you get things right, but I'd rather be facing old Peter if I had to own up to making a mistake.'

'Still, he must get results,' Monica argued, 'or he wouldn't be a DCI. I wonder if I could get a transfer. I might have a better chance of making inspector if I was in his team.'

'Well, if that's what you want, the best thing you can do now is to finish sorting out those interview notes,' Anna said rather shortly. 'If you do apply to transfer to DCI Porter's team, I'm sure he'll be more interested in how well you work than how much you admire his eyes!'

CHAPTER 9

The following day, which was Saturday, Peter took Andy Lepage with him to interview Professor George Fraser in his imposing detached house in Kidlington. As they walked up the drive, Peter reflected that the additional income from his radio and television appearances must have been a very welcome supplement to the academic's university salary. This was a very different property from the small terraced house in East Oxford that Bernie had occupied before her first marriage. Of course, the professor had a wife who also worked, but even two university salaries would hardly be sufficient to pay the mortgage on this impressive residence.

Andy rang the bell and they both stood back to wait for a reply. After a few minutes, the door opened and a tall, dark-featured man in his fifties looked out at them enquiringly. His wavy black hair was combed back from his face, emphasising a widow's peak above his forehead. His eyes were a deep brown. Peter explained who they were and why they had come. George Fraser's face registered concern at the mention of the murder, followed by interest at the mention of *Revelations* magazine and finally broke into a smile, which revealed a perfect set of even, white teeth, as he stepped back to welcome the police officers into his home.

He led the way into a large sitting room, furnished with a three-piece suite upholstered in leather. They all sat down and Peter began the interview by showing Fraser the article about him in *Revelations*.

'Were you angry when you saw what Martin Fellowes had written about you?' he asked bluntly.

'I suppose I was a bit annoyed at first,' Fraser admitted with a small laugh, 'but then I thought, all publicity is good publicity. I mean, it certainly increased the ratings for my latest TV series!'

'And what about your wife?' Peter asked, somewhat taken aback by this response. 'How did she react to finding out about your extramural activities?'

'Oh Sam understands that men of exceptional ability in one area are likely to have exceptional appetites in others,' Fraser laughed again. 'And, after all, it isn't like I'm having an affair, is it? I mean, it's only sex, at the end of the day. And it isn't as if I did anything illegal – or unethical, come to that. I mean – it's not as if I'd seduced one of my students!'

'I thought your wife *was* one of your students,' Andy commented quietly, 'before she married you, I mean.'

'Yes. That's true. I was supervising her DPhil. We fell in love and got married. There's nothing wrong in that.'

'I think some people would say that it created a conflict of interest,' Peter suggested.

'Not at all,' Fraser declared dismissively. 'I was her supervisor, not her examiner. She got her degree fair and square, and then she went on to join my research group, as my wife. This business in *Revelations* is just a storm in a teacup. Sam wouldn't lower herself by getting upset about it. The women were all consenting adults and I paid them a fair price for what I got – which, I might add, I needn't have done: there are plenty of women offering themselves to me for nothing after seeing me on TV!'

'Do you mean that your wife already knew – before reading about it in *Revelations* magazine?'

'Well, no,' Fraser admitted, 'but she was absolutely fine about it when she did find out. She knew when she married me that she wasn't just marrying *any* man,' he added complacently.

Peter, who had never been tempted towards infidelity in either of his two happy marriages, felt a growing distaste for this arrogant and self-satisfied man. Andy, who was aware of the struggle that his mother had gone through to raise him after being deserted by a father whom he had never known, was confirmed in his opinion that marriage, and other male-female relationships, rarely had anything in them for the women involved. For a few moments, nobody spoke. Then Peter pulled himself together and continued with the interview.

'Tell us about your movements on Tuesday evening this week.'

'Let me see,' Fraser said slowly. 'Oh yes! That's easy. I was dining on high table. The Master had a couple of important guests – potential benefactors of the college – and he wanted all of the most prestigious members of the SCR there.'

'I see,' Peter said encouragingly. 'And what time did you arrive for that?'

'I'm not sure what time I went down to the SCR – that's the Senior Common Room,' he added, for the benefit of those present who might be unaware of the jargon used by the Oxford élite, '– for sherry, but I was in college all afternoon. I dressed in my room and was in time to have a chat with the guests before we went in to dinner at seven thirty.'

'Are you quite sure about that?' Peter asked. 'Some of your colleagues have suggested that you weren't in the SCR for sherry and only arrived in hall after they had started their soup.'

Peter had prepared himself before this meeting by

reading the reports on all the interviews with Lichfield dons. Monica Philipson had noted that Fraser had arrived late and was, therefore, of no use in establishing what time Martin Riess had joined the party in the common room.

'Yes, you're right,' Fraser conceded, appearing a little flustered, but still managing to stay calm and smiling on the surface. 'I was getting confused with another occasion. I remember now – I was so intent on my work that I didn't notice the time. The Master was livid,' he went on, with a schoolboy grin. 'After all, it didn't look good having his celebrity don nowhere to be seen when his guests were expecting to be able to chat to him over drinks and nibbles. But of course, they just put it down to the normal absentmindedness of professors!'

'I see,' Peter said coldly, pausing just long enough to convey a degree of scepticism at this explanation. 'And, when you say you were in college all afternoon, were you in your room all that time?'

'Yes. I was preparing a talk that I'm giving next week at the Royal Society.'

'So, you were alone in your room from, what time?'

'Two – two thirty – something like that. Look, what *is* this? Sure you don't suspect me of doing away with that journalist fellow!'

'The editor of *Revelations* and one of his key journalists have been murdered,' Peter said calmly, enjoying the look of discomfort on Fraser's face as he started at last to take the interview seriously. 'We have to consider the possibility that the killer was one of the people who had been criticised by them in the magazine. Martin Fellowes wrote a very derogatory article about you a few weeks ago, so naturally your name was on the list of people for us to investigate.'

'Did Dr Riess tell you that Martin Fellowes was staying on his boat?' Andy asked, becoming impatient to get to the crux of the matter.

'You know, I'm really not sure,' Fraser replied

smoothly, resuming his detached smile. 'I don't have a lot to do with Martin Riess, but he may possibly have mentioned something about it in general conversation in the SCR. If he did say anything, it certainly didn't register with me – after all, it's not as if I knew this Fallows fellow.'

'Martin *Fellowes* had his name on the article that appeared about you in Revelations magazine,' Peter pointed out. 'Most people would have taken note of it.'

'Oh! I don't have time for that,' Fraser laughed. 'There are too many journalists writing about me for me to keep a record of all their names. Now, is that all? I have work to do.'

'Just a couple of things,' Peter answered, taking a certain pleasure in annoying the egotistical don. 'Firstly, is there anyone who could confirm that you were in your college room on Tuesday afternoon and early evening?'

'No, I don't suppose there is. The porters would probably be able to tell you that I called in to check for my post at about eleven in the morning; and the hall staff may remember me having lunch between twelve and one. Apart from that, I was alone, working all day.'

'Thank you. And now I need to know what you were doing the following day – that's Wednesday.

'Why do you want to know that?' Fraser asked sharply.

'That was the day that the editor of *Revelations* was killed,' Peter answered. 'So now, can you tell me where you were that day?'

'Wednesday … Wednesday?' Fraser murmured to himself. 'Oh yes! I was working on my paper for Nature. I was in my room in college all day.'

'Alone?'

'Yes.'

'No one called in?' Peter asked. 'Did you make or receive any telephone calls?'

'No, I'm afraid not. I turned my mobile off and kept the door closed to discourage visitors. I wanted to work without any interruptions.'

'And, when you say "all day" that means between what times exactly?'

'I suppose I must have got in about half past nine and left for home about five in the afternoon. I had lunch in hall at about half twelve, if that's any help to you, but I was back here by one.'

'I see.'

Peter glanced across at Andy to check that he had written all this down. Then he got up to go.

'I don't think we need trouble you any further, sir. We can see ourselves out.'

When they opened the front door to depart, Peter and Andy found a woman on the doorstep, whom they recognised from her picture on the university website as Dr Samantha Fraser, the professor's wife. She was fumbling in her handbag, searching for her keys to let herself in. At her feet lay two supermarket carrier bags bulging with shopping. They could see more bags lying in the back of her car, which was drawn up in front of the door, its boot open.

'Let me help you with those,' Andy offered, bending down and picking up the bags. 'Where would you like them?'

'The kitchen's just down the passage,' Dr Fraser answered, sounding slightly bemused, 'on the right.'

She was several years younger than her husband. According to the curriculum vitae, which she had conveniently displayed on her university web page, she was forty-five, although Peter would have judged her to be a few years older. Her dark brown hair was starting to turn grey and she had worry lines on her face. She looked tired and harassed.

Andy headed off in the direction that she had indicated, while Peter helped her to get out four more bags from the car. Soon all three of them were standing in the kitchen, looking at one another across the worktop of a peninsular unit on which they had deposited the shopping.

'Thank you very much,' Dr Fraser said breathlessly, holding out her hand towards Peter. 'I'm Sam Fraser. I suppose you've been to see my husband?'

'That's right,' Peter confirmed, shaking her hand and then taking out his warrant card. 'We're police officers. We're investigating the deaths of two people who worked for *Revelations* magazine.'

'You mean Martin Fellowes?' Samantha asked in a tone of distaste. 'The guy who wrote about George's antics with those prostitutes?'

'That's right,' Peter confirmed. 'I take it you've read the article?'

'I had to, didn't I? Everyone else seems to have done,' Samantha answered bitterly. 'You're barking up the wrong tree if you think George killed them over it, though. I think he was rather proud of it more than anything else.'

'Really?' Peter asked, unable to keep the surprise out of his voice. Fraser's behaviour was completely foreign to him and something of which he would have been deeply ashamed.

'Oh yes! He thinks it shows what a man he is. And you should see some of the tabloid headlines. Even the ones that pretend to be shocked manage to make out that it's some sort of sign of virility.' She paused for a few moments, gazing down as if contemplating the pattern on the Italian porcelain floor tiles. Then she shook herself and looked up at Peter again. 'But I mustn't keep you any longer. I'm sure you've got lots of work to do. Thank you for helping with the shopping.'

'I'll show you out,' George Fraser added from the doorway. He had evidently heard voices and come to see who was with his wife in the kitchen. He led the way back to the front door and opened it for Peter and Andy to go through.

Once it was firmly closed behind them, the two police officers looked at one another.

'I think, sir,' Andy said tentatively, as they walked

together back down the drive, 'that maybe it's Mrs Fraser who's more upset about that article. He doesn't seem bothered.'

'Yes,' Peter agreed. 'The question is: is he just putting on a show – either through bravado or in order to put us off the scent? I think you're right, though,' he added. 'It's Dr Sam Fraser who seems to have been more affected by the revelations than her husband. I suppose it's not that surprising. She must feel pretty badly betrayed, first to find out that he was visiting prostitutes in the first place and then to know that everyone else knew about it before she did.'

'There's something else I wanted to tell you about, sir,' Andy said, as they reached the end of the drive and stopped beside Peter's car. 'I've been looking into the backgrounds of those two students who found the body in the boat.'

'I see,' Peter said encouragingly, 'and did you find anything interesting?'

'Well, maybe,' Andy hesitated. 'James Pickering's father's a banker – he's something quite big in the City.'

'And?'

'Well, he was mentioned in an article in *Revelations* about six months ago.'

'An article by Martin Fellowes?'

'No – at least I don't think so. I don't think it said who had written it. The thing is, although it didn't say anything particularly bad about Edgar Pickering, it did say that there would be more revelations to come. So I was wondering whether there was any possibility that Fellowes had been nosing around Pickering, looking for stuff on his father and Pickering decided to do him in before he could write a damaging article about him.'

'Or it could even be,' Peter mused, 'that Pickering Junior had done something disreputable that would be newsworthy because of who his father was. Good work, Trainee Constable Lepage! On Monday, I'll set someone checking out both James and Edgar Pickering, in case either of them is involved. Of course, if James killed Fellowes, it looks as if the girl – Olivia, isn't it? – must have been complicit in some way, even if only by giving him an alibi.'

'But don't girls do that sort of thing all the time, when they're in love?' Andy commented. 'I mean, isn't that why so many women end up in abusive relationships? Because they're afraid of losing their boyfriend?'

Peter looked hard at his young colleague for a moment, wondering what sort of experience had prompted this observation.

'You could be right,' he admitted,' but I'm not sure many young women would want to be a party to murder, even if it was their boyfriend who was the perpetrator. Anyway, we shall see what they both say when we chase them up on Monday. Now, I know you aren't supposed to be on duty today, but if you'd like to come with me to interview Martina Clarkson MEP – for the experience – you're welcome. What do you say?'

'I would like to come,' Andy said slowly, 'but I promised my mum I'd help her in the garden. The lawn needs mowing and the hedge it getting rather out of hand.'

'In that case,' Peter said decisively,' we'd better get you back home ASAP. 'I can't have to letting your mum down – she'd only blame it on me!' he added jocularly. 'Where shall I drop you off?'

'I don't want to take you out of your way,' Andy protested. 'Just leave me in the centre of Kidlington and I can get the bus.'

'How do you know it's out of my way, if you don't tell me where you're going?' Peter demanded. 'I've seen you catching the number 8 bus from the city centre, which means you must live in the Headington direction – same as me. For all I know, we could be neighbours!'

'It's Headington Quarry,' Andy said, a little reluctantly.

'Fine,' Peter answered, realising that Andy might not

want his boss to know his address. 'My house is just the other side of the ring road, so how about I drop you at the end of Kiln Lane, where you can walk across the Ring Road to the Quarry?'

CHAPTER 10

'Wait there and I'll check whether Ms Clarkson is free to see you,' the stern-looking receptionist said when Peter explained what he was doing at her constituency headquarters later that morning. 'She has a very busy schedule today.'

Peter took a seat and waited patiently. After a few minutes, the receptionist announced that Ms Clarkson would see him now and led him through to a large office containing a desk, several filing cabinets, and some easy chairs grouped around a table. A smartly-dressed woman looked up from behind the desk and took off her reading glasses to look at Peter as he entered.

Edwina Clarkson looked like a more business-like and less glamorous version of her sister. She shared the blue eyes and perfect complexion that Peter had observed in Martina, but her hair, cropped in a pageboy style, was dark brown. Peter felt confirmed in his suspicion that the glowing red of Martina's hair was not its natural shade. The hint of grey at the roots along Edwina's parting suggested that both sisters were averse to showing their true colours in the hair department.

'Inspector!' Edwina greeted him, getting up and

offering Peter her hand. 'I'm so sorry to have kept you waiting. Please, do take a seat.'

She indicated the easy chairs with a wave of her hand and then came round the desk to join him at the low, round table.

'Bring us some coffee, please, Christabel,' she added to the receptionist, who was hovering at the door, clearly awaiting instructions.

The dour Christabel left, closing the door silently behind her. Edwina Clarkson turned to address Peter.

'Can you tell me exactly what happened?' she asked. 'I've read all the press reports, but I'd like to have the official version.'

Peter reflected that it still seemed as if she were asking for information more because it would be expected of her to know the answers to questions that might be asked of her than from any particular anxiety about – or even interest in – her husband's fate. He gathered his thoughts and gave her a brief summary of where and when her husband's body had been found. She listened attentively as if taking mental notes in readiness for possible future questioning.

'I assume that you will also have heard about the death of your husband's colleague, Arthur Finch?' Peter concluded, 'and that we think that the two deaths may be connected.'

'Yes,' Edwina admitted, in a non-committal tone, as if she were answering an awkward question about party policy from a hostile journalist. 'I did hear that. Can I ask you why you are making the connection?'

'Two reasons. Firstly, it seems too much of a coincidence that two members of your little group of friends from Cambridge should be killed in a similar fashion within twenty-four hours of one another. Secondly, and more importantly, your husband and Arthur Finch had, together, been responsible for upsetting quite a number of well-known and powerful people through that magazine of theirs. We think that may have provided the motive for the crimes.'

'I see,' Edwina said thoughtfully.

'However,' Peter went on, 'since the majority of violent crimes are committed by members of the victim's own family, I do have to ask you to tell me about your movements last Tuesday and Wednesday. Your brother-in-law told me that you flew back from Strasbourg on Monday to be with your sister, after your niece took an overdose – is that right?'

'Yes. Marty rang me that morning and I got the first flight I could. I went to the hospital and stayed with them until Amber was out of danger. Then Geoffrey gave me a lift to the station and I got a train back to London and then the Eurostar.'

'Can you give me the times of the trains that you took?'

'Yes. It was the thirteen fifteen from Didcot, and then the fifteen thirty-one from St Pancras to Paris. I had to change stations in Paris, so I only got into Strasbourg at around eleven. I went straight to my apartment and went to bed.'

'Did anyone see you arrive?'

'No. There is a concierge, but I didn't see her. I just let myself in. I didn't want to engage in conversation. It had been a hard day – and I'd had no sleep the previous night – so all I wanted was to get to bed without any fuss.'

'I see. And then the following day – Wednesday? What did you do?'

'I slept in late, and then I spent the day in the apartment, preparing for an important meeting that I had booked for Thursday. I was behind with my work – with having to rush back to be with Marty and Amber.'

'Can anyone confirm that?'

'No, I don't suppose they can.' Edwina looked a little, just a little, disconcerted by the question. 'But surely, you don't seriously believe that I might have killed Martin?'

'You weren't exactly seeing eye-to-eye with him any

more, were you?' Peter suggested, getting out a plastic wallet containing the letter that Anna had found in her dead husband's pocket. 'You *did* write this, I take it?'

'Yes – that's mine,' Edwina admitted, after glancing down at the note in Peter's hand.

'What was this *intolerable attitude* that he had adopted?' Peter asked.

'It was all to do with that wretched journal that Arthur Finch edited. Like you said, they wrote things that upset a lot of people quite gratuitously.'

'And that was enough to make you want to end your marriage of – what? – fifteen years?'

'It was more than that. What he wrote was symptomatic of his attitude more generally. When he first started out as an investigative journalist, he was concerned about exposing real hypocrisy and fraud – showing up when people in power had deceived ordinary people and taken advantage of them. Now, he doesn't seem to care about anything any more – except what will sell that horrid little magazine and make money for him and Arthur Finch. I said to him – that must have been a couple of weeks before I wrote that note – I said, "you'd accuse your own mother of multiple adulteries if you thought it would make people buy *Revelations* – even if you knew it was all lies!" I tell you: he just didn't care about anyone else any more.'

'I see. And was he, by any chance, planning to publish any personal revelations – about you and your marriage, for example?' Peter suggested. 'I mean, you are a public figure, and he was in a perfect position to make revelations – real or imaginary – about you and your personal life. And if he was as unscrupulous as you say …'

'No – nothing like that,' Edwina replied quickly. 'He knew there was nothing in my life – or in our marriage – that wouldn't bear scrutiny.'

'But you just said that he sometimes made up things,' Peter pressed her gently. 'Weren't you afraid that he might invent some sort of scandal, just to pay you back for chucking him out?'

'Oh no, it would be too dangerous to his own reputation to look as if he was carrying out a witch-hunt against his own wife. He had to keep up the pretence that he was this objective observer ferreting out the truth for the benefit of society. He couldn't risk looking like he was trashing someone's reputation just out of spite.'

'OK, let's leave that for the moment. Tell me about the Martians. You all got together while you were living in Cambridge, is that right?'

'Oh dear! Who told about all that?' Edwina gave a little laugh. 'We were all terribly young and naïve. Yes, we got together with the aim of saving the world. It all sounds rather silly now.'

'And, the original group was just you and your sister, and the two Martins: Riess and Fellowes? When did Arthur Finch come on the scene?'

'Oh, pretty much immediately. He and Martin were already great buddies. It was Arthur who came up with that silly name – all to do with Martians being little green men. It was just the sort of puerile joke that he and Martin used to enjoy.'

'Someone told me that you were engaged to Martin Riess for a time. Is that true?'

'I wouldn't go as far as to say that we were engaged, but we did go out together for a while,' Edwina said cautiously, watching Peter's face carefully as if wondering exactly what he had been told about her relationship with Martin Riess, and perhaps by whom. 'But then he went off to America.'

'You don't think he was expecting you to wait for him to come back?' Peter asked quietly. 'I mean – do you think he was surprised when he heard that you were marrying his old friend Martin Fellowes?'

'I don't know whether he was surprised. I certainly don't think he was upset at all. He sent us a wedding present.'

'But he declined to come to the wedding.'

'That was hardly surprising, seeing as he was in Massachusetts.'

'So you're confident that Martin Riess didn't hold a grudge against your husband for stealing you away from him.'

'I can't speak for Martin. You'll have to ask him.'

'Do you have any idea why your husband chose to approach Martin Riess for accommodation when you turned him out of your house?'

'No. I suppose he thought that sponging off his friends would be cheaper than a hotel.'

'Did Martin Riess ever talk to you and your husband about his past – about how he escaped from East Germany, for instance?'

'No. I knew his parents were German – because he spoke it like a native and he explained that was because they spoke German at home – but I'd always assumed he was born here. His English was perfect and I know he went to school in Oxford.'

'So you didn't know that his mother claimed political asylum in Britain and his father was killed by East German border guards when he tried to join them?'

'No. I had no idea. But what has that to do with my husband's death?'

'It looks as if he may have been planning to publish some garbled version of the story, so I wanted to know whether he would have known what really happened or not.'

'I would say that you're asking the wrong questions,' Edwina said bitterly. 'It wouldn't have made any difference to Martin whether he knew the truth or not. He'd have written whatever he thought would sell the most copies of that vile little rag of his and Arthur's.'

A buzzer sounded on the desk and the voice of the efficient receptionist came through in the intercom.

'Your taxi is here,' she announced.

'Thank you, Christabel, I'll be right there,' Edwina answered. Then she turned to Peter with a smile. 'You'll have to excuse me, I'm afraid, I have another appointment. Please keep me informed about how your investigations proceed. I'm sure I can rely on our gallant boys in blue to find my husband's killer.'

Peter accepted his dismissal graciously, recognising that he had probably learnt all that he was likely to do from this woman, who was skilled in the politician's trade of answering questions without giving away information.

CHAPTER 11

Sunday – Lucy's birthday – dawned bright and sunny, although it was a little chilly at six o'clock in the morning when Lucy demanded that they all get up, so as not to waste a minute of her special day. Bernie and Lucy went to church in the morning as usual. Peter, never a regular attender, pleaded pressure of work and stayed at home, puzzling over the notes he had made of the interviews with George Fraser and Edwina Clarkson. He was determined to make some progress with the case before the meeting that he was scheduled to have with his superior on Monday. This was a high-profile case involving an MEP and a television personality. He was all too aware that it might well be taken away from him and given to a more senior (but probably less experienced) officer – such as the charismatic Jonah Porter.

Fraser had seemed completely unconcerned about the article in *Revelations*, and Peter was inclined to believe that he was so full of himself as really to believe that it would enhance, rather than diminish, his reputation. It was his wife, Samantha, who seemed more affected by it. Could she have taken revenge by killing the author of the article? Peter made a note to interview her on her own, away from her husband.

What of Edwina Clarkson? Peter felt that he was very little better informed about exactly what she had meant in her note to Fellowes. Was it credible that she had thrown away her marriage just because his journalism was becoming less serious and more tabloid? Surely there must be something more personal involved? Apart from anything else, voters – especially Conservative voters – tended to be unsympathetic towards female politicians who failed to 'stand by their man'.

The day was marred, in Peter's eyes, by the arrival of Jonah Porter, who turned up unannounced in the middle of the afternoon. Bernie, Peter and Lucy were in the large back garden, setting up the croquet set that Bernie had given to her daughter for her birthday, when he appeared round the corner of the house, having let himself in through the side gate. He was dressed immaculately, as usual, in a beige suit, light brown shirt and chocolate-coloured tie.

Lucy saw him first, crying out in delight and running across the lawn to greet him. She flung her arms around his waist and hugged him. Then she stepped back and gazed up at his face expectantly. Jonah crouched down so that he could look her in the eye.

'Miss Paige,' he said, holding out his hand in greeting and addressing her in the formal way that he always adopted when speaking to his dead colleague's daughter, 'I do believe that you are considerably taller than when I last had the pleasure of meeting you.'

'Of course I am!' Lucy replied in a tone suggesting that Jonah must be very dense if he were surprised at that phenomenon. 'I'm seven now.'

'Indeed you are, Miss Paige, and I have brought you something to mark the occasion.'

Jonah held out a small rectangular parcel wrapped in red paper bearing the crest of Liverpool Football Club.

Lucy took it from him and soon had it unwrapped to reveal a box bearing the words, 'Junior Detective Fingerprint Kit' and a picture of a small boy using a large magnifying glass to inspect fingerprints on a wall.

Lucy read the words to herself and then hugged Jonah again, nearly knocking him over as she threw her arms around him in his crouching position.

'Thank you, Jonah. You always bring nice presents. Mam!' Lucy called out to Bernie, who had come up to welcome their guest. 'Look what Jonah's brought me. It's to take people's fingerprints – like the police do.'

'Very impressive,' Bernie acknowledged, looking at the box. 'If you take copies of everyone's prints, then I'll be able to tell who it is who keeps stealing biscuits from the tin.'

She turned to Jonah, who stood up and smiled towards her.

'It's good of you to come, Jonah. Will you be staying for Lucy's birthday tea? It's not a party – just the three of us and a couple of old friends.'

'I'd love to, but I'm afraid this has to be just a flying visit,' Jonah replied, sounding genuinely sorry to miss a treat, but also glancing in the direction of Peter, who was hanging back behind his wife, showing polite interest but lacking enthusiasm for Jonah's presence. 'My parents are visiting us this weekend and I can't leave Margaret to entertain them on her own. Dad's developing dementia and he can be quite difficult at times.'

'I'm sorry about that,' Bernie said in a tone of concern. 'You shouldn't have deserted your parents for Lucy's sake. We're always pleased to see you, but I'd hate to think you felt obliged to disrupt your own family on our account.'

'Nonsense! A couple of hours won't make any difference one way or the other to my parents – especially my dad – and I couldn't possibly miss Lucy's birthday.'

'Why didn't you come on a different day?' Bernie persisted. 'You could have waited until your parents had gone home. It wouldn't have mattered.'

'Oh yes it would – wouldn't it Lucy?' Jonah appealed to the golden-haired little girl who was now holding him firmly by one arm and gazing adoringly up at him. 'Birthdays are important, aren't they?'

'Yes,' she agreed, 'but you could come on other days too. Why don't you?'

'Once a year is plenty for you all to put up with me. If I came too often, you'd soon get fed up with seeing me.'

'No we wouldn't,' Lucy protested. 'Mam! Tell Jonah to come more often.'

'Indeed I won't!' her mother retorted with a laugh. 'You're very lucky he comes to see you at all. Just make the most of it while he *is* here.'

'I'm sorry, Lucy,' Jonah said gently, bending down and giving her a hug. 'I really do have to get back soon.'

'Well, at least you must have time for a brew,' Bernie said heartily. 'I'll go and put the kettle on.'

She headed off in the direction of the house, leaving Peter and Jonah eyeing one another, while Lucy read the instructions on the box that she had just received. Peter tried to think of something to say, but Lucy saved him the trouble of making small talk by tugging Jonah's sleeve and begging him to show her how to take fingerprints.

'Very well, Miss Paige,' he agreed, 'but we'd better take it over to the table before you open the box or some of the bits may get lost.'

They walked together to a large wooden table on a paved area at the back of the house, beneath the kitchen window and near the open French windows that led into the living room. Peter stood indecisively for a few moments while Jonah helped Lucy to tear off the protective film covering the box.

'I'll go and help Bernie with the tea,' he said at last, picking up the discarded wrapping paper and cellophane wrapper and heading into the house to join his wife.

'Why does he keep coming every year?' he asked a few

minutes later, as he stared moodily out of the window at the sight of Lucy and Jonah happily experimenting with the fingerprint kit on the table outside. 'You'd think he'd have lost interest by now.'

'He says it's for Richard's sake – taking an interest in the daughter of the man who launched his career in CID,' Bernie answered with a smile, 'but I strongly suspect that, like most of the male half of the human race, he's really a bit in love with our Lucy.'

'Or with her mother?' Peter suggested.

'Peter! The very idea!' Bernie exclaimed indignantly, pretending to be scandalised. 'He's a happily married man – and his Margaret is, by all accounts, a tough cookie and not someone to be messed with.'

'You've got a point there,' Peter admitted with a grin, his sulky mood suddenly lifting as he remembered the courtship, more than a quarter of a century ago, of the young PC Jonah Porter and his girlfriend, junior doctor Margaret Hulme. 'Getting on the wrong side of a surgeon would certainly be a risky move.'

He put his arms around his wife as she tipped biscuits on to a plate and put it on to a tray next to a teapot and four mugs. She put the biscuits down and turned to give him a quick hug to reassure him that he was the first man in both her and her daughter's hearts. Then she picked up the tray.

'Come on then,' she commanded. 'I thought you came to help. Go ahead and open the doors for me.'

'Look Mam!' Lucy called excitedly as they came out of the French windows on to the patio. 'These are my fingerprints.'

She held up a card on which were ten inky smudges, one for each of Lucy's small fingertips.

'Very good,' Peter said. 'Now we will be able to establish beyond reasonable doubt who it is who keeps leaving muddy paw prints on the wallpaper!'

'Have a look with this,' Lucy urged, ignoring his remark

and holding out a small magnifying glass. 'You can see all the different patterns.'

Peter obediently took the glass and peered through it at the prints on the card. Meanwhile, Bernie set down the tray on the table and started pouring tea. Lucy looked at the plate of biscuits and frowned.

'Why haven't you brought out my birthday cake?' she demanded. 'I want Jonah to have some.'

'I thought we'd keep that for when Stan and Sylvia come round later,' her mother explained.

'But then Jonah won't get any,' Lucy complained. 'I'm going to get it,' she added, getting up and heading towards the house. Bernie put down the teapot and followed her, calling out exhortations to her daughter as they went.

'All right, if you must have it, I'll carry it. Don't try to get it down by yourself – it's too high for you to reach. And before you touch anything else, let's get your hands washed – you're getting ink everywhere.'

Peter and Jonah were left looking at each other across the table.

'How did your interview with Mrs Fellowes go yesterday?' Jonah asked, hoping to divert Peter's attention away from the resentment that he was aware that Peter felt over his stepdaughter's undisguised pleasure in Jonah's company.

'Well, she answered all my questions,' Peter answered with a slightly rueful grin, 'but she's a politician, so I came away feeling that she hadn't really told me anything much. She doesn't seem as upset about her husband's death as you might have expected – or as interested in seeing his killer brought to justice. I rather get the impression that her main feeling about it all is annoyance that our investigation is interfering with her important work.'

'Did she tell you what it was that made her tell him to get lost?'

'Only in vague, general terms. She claims it's all to do with his journalism becoming more intrusive on people's lives and less ethical generally. I can't help thinking there'd need to be something a bit more personal to make her split with him after all these years.'

'I suppose it all depends how things had been between them up till then,' Jonah mused. 'It's difficult for the likes of you and me to imagine what would drive someone to leave their spouse after so long, but some couples never give the impression of being that close in the first place. Didn't you say something about her marriage to Fellowes being unexpected in some way?'

'Yes – sort of,' Peter admitted, a little taken aback at the way in which Jonah had bracketed the two of them together. What exactly was it that he was suggesting that they had in common? Stable marriages, he supposed. 'She admitted that she had been going out with Martin Riess – that's the guy who owned the boat where Fellowes' body was found – for most of the time that they were all in Cambridge together. And she more or less admitted that she never broke it off with him – although she denies it was a formal engagement. Riess's theory is that Edwina decided she had to get married because she couldn't let her sister get away with having something she didn't have – she *didn't want to be upstaged by Martina*, was how he put it.'

'That's interesting. If there's any truth in that, maybe, as far as Edwina is concerned, Fellowes was just a prop to help her in her career – or in some private sibling-rivalry competition – and as soon as he started to look like becoming more of a liability than an asset he had to go.'

'But, according to her, she was most likely in a train under the Channel at the time of his murder,' Peter objected, 'and that doesn't give her any motive for doing away with Finch. Moreover, Fellowes had apparently gone quietly, so there was no need to bash his head in as well as banishing him.'

'Oh I don't know. She might have thought, after he'd gone, that a disgruntled ex-husband with access to the press was too much of a risk. And that might give her a motive to get rid of Finch as well.'

'I suppose she could have got a train from High Wycombe to Oxford, instead of London, done the deed and then taken a later train to get back to Strasbourg,' Peter admitted, 'but I don't see how she could have killed Finch – unless she didn't go back until Wednesday. That might work. She admitted that she didn't speak to anyone in Strasbourg until the Thursday, because she was working alone in her flat. Well, it should be possible to find out whether she really was on the trains she said she took. I'll get someone on to that tomorrow.'

'And what about this Riess fellow? Could he have killed Fellowes in revenge for having stolen the fair Edwina away from him? Or even in the hope of winning her back?'

'No good,' Peter shook his head. 'He has cast iron alibis for both murders. Unless he's got a couple of dozen people willing to lie for him, he simply couldn't have done it. Besides,' he went on, determined to keep Martin Riess out of Jonah's sights if at all possible, 'he seems a very unlikely murderer – very quiet and unassuming, devoted to his mother, not at all your arrogant Oxford don.'

'His mother!' Jonah exclaimed, picking up on this remark. 'Could she have done it? Or does she also have a cast iron alibi?'

'As far as I know she was at home alone when Fellowes was killed,' Peter answered, rather puzzled at this unexpected suggestion. 'But what makes you think she had anything to do with it?'

'You said that Riess was devoted to his mother. I imagine she is even more devoted to him. If she blames Fellowes for destroying her son's happiness by stealing his fiancée, she might well be looking for revenge – especially if she thinks that he's now exploiting him by demanding accommodation now that the marriage has gone pear-shaped.'

'It sounds a bit tenuous to me.'

'And there's another thing,' Jonah continued, ignoring

Peter's objections. 'I remember when my sister, Sarah, turned thirty and we were both still unmarried, my mother started dropping all sorts of hints about what a pity it was that she hadn't become a grandmother yet. If she blames Fellowes for stealing the love of her son's life and thus condemning him to perpetual bachelorhood – well! I bet she'd be feeling pretty murderous towards him for depriving her of the grandchildren that she thinks are her right as a mother.'

'Well, I'll check it out,' Peter conceded, reflecting that it was not going to be easy to explain to Bernie if word got back to her that her late husband's great friend was under investigation. 'But I still think it's more likely to be something to do with *Revelations* magazine – either something that has appeared in it or something that someone wants to keep out of it.'

'George Fraser, perhaps?'

'Yes – or his wife. I've got it in mind to tackle her tomorrow.'

'Not talking shop, are you?' Bernie interrupted, arriving at that moment carrying a large birthday cake in the shape of a many-turreted castle. She put it down on the table and Lucy stepped up and put a small pile of plates next to it.

''Fraid so,' Peter answered, grinning sheepishly and trying to sound as guilty as possible in the hope of deterring Jonah from discussing the case in Bernie's presence. He did not want him discovering that she was acquainted with some of the protagonists in this drama. 'But we'll stop now that you're both back.'

'My word!' exclaimed Jonah. 'What a magnificent edifice! What is it? King Arthur's castle?'

'It's Hogwarts,' Lucy said in a tone of deepest contempt. 'Can't you see the Whomping Willow?'

'Of course! I can now. I should have recognised it,' Jonah answered, looking over the pinnacles of the chocolate-covered confection at a strangely-shaped structure on the other side. 'So, you're a Harry Potter fan, are you? You ought to meet my Nathan: he's completely obsessed.'

'How old is Nathan now?' Bernie asked. It was unusual for Jonah to speak of his family, preferring to make his annual appearance as if he were a magical Father Christmas figure with no human relations.

'Seventeen. He'll be in the upper sixth soon and off to university before we know where we are.' Jonah sounded uncharacteristically regretful, as he reflected on his younger son's all-too-short childhood, in which he had so often been too busy with his work to play a full part. 'Make the most of Lucy while she's young: you don't get a second chance with kids.'

'Light the candles, Mam!' Lucy urged, impatient with the grown-ups whose chatter seemed to her to be very much beside the point. 'You said you would.'

'Alright, alright, give me a chance, won't you?' Bernie grumbled. 'Now Jonah, I hope you're in good voice. Lucy is expecting you to sing Happy Birthday to her.'

She struck a match and lit the seven candles perched on the towers of the school of witchcraft and wizardry. Then she stepped back and gestured in an exaggerated imitation of a musical conductor to indicate when they should start singing. Jonah joined in with a will as Bernie and Peter sang. As soon as the verse was over, Lucy stepped forward and blew out the candles, carefully directing her breath at each one to ensure that they were all extinguished in a single exhalation.

'Well done!' Jonah commented. 'Did you make a wish?'

'Don't be silly!' Lucy retorted, in a tone that suggested that she was disappointed in him for asking such a foolish question. 'Wishing doesn't work. There's no such thing as magic really – only in books.'

'That's telling you, Jonah,' Bernie said, smiling. 'You can't fool our Lucy: she knows the difference between stories and real-life!'

'And there's no such thing as the tooth fairy or Father

Christmas, either,' Lucy added, just to make her belief-system crystal clear. 'They're just made up by grown-ups to make children behave themselves.'

'And of course, you are always so perfectly well-behaved that your Mum doesn't need to resort to such subterfuge,' Jonah suggested, amused at Lucy's precocity.

'If only!' Bernie laughed. 'I'm just not much good at telling lies, that's all.'

'Where's the knife?' Lucy asked suddenly. 'Oh Mam! You've forgotten to bring one. I'll go and get it.'

She turned to go, but Jonah called her back.

'Hang on there! I think you really ought to keep this cake for your friends to see. It would be a pity to spoil it just for me.'

'But I want you to have a piece,' Lucy said sulkily. 'And it's *my* cake,' she added, frowning and giving her mother a hard stare, as if daring her to disagree.

'Tell you what,' Bernie suggested. 'How's about I get the spare bits that I cut off and we all have some of those?'

'Will it have the chocolate on it?' Lucy asked, still frowning.

'I've got a bowlful of the chocolate icing left over,' her mother assured her, 'so we can all dip into that. Will that satisfy you?'

'OK,' Lucy conceded, still sounding somewhat aggrieved.

Bernie went off to the kitchen to find the cake trimmings and soon all four present were engaged in dipping pieces of chocolate cake into a gooey mixture of chocolate, butter and sugar. Jonah ate sparingly but with evident relish and congratulated the cook on what he termed a culinary triumph. Then, wiping sticky fingers on a paper serviette, he got up to go.

'I'm sorry, Lucy,' he apologised. 'I really must make a move now.'

'Oh Jonah!' Lucy pleaded. 'Can't you just have one game of croquet? It won't take long. Please!'

'No, Lucy. Jonah explained why he has to go,' her mother reminded her. 'We're very lucky that he could come at all, under the circumstances.'

'Goodbye, Miss Paige,' Jonah said solemnly, resuming his habitual formality. 'I hope to see you again when you reach the advanced age of eight!'

At this, Lucy launched herself at Jonah, hugging him round the waist with sticky fingers and pressing a chocolate-smeared face against his chest. He returned the hug then gently but firmly removed her arms from around him and turned to say his farewells to Bernie and Peter.

'Oh Jonah!' Bernie exclaimed, looking in dismay at the chocolatey smears on his smart jacket and shirt. 'Another suit bites the dust at the hands of our Lucy! Oh Lucy! What are you like? Look at the mess you've made with your sticky paws!'

'Not to worry,' Jonah assured them, cheerfully, winking at Lucy. 'It's all washable. I'll sneak them into the machine when Margaret isn't looking. She's always telling me I don't take enough care over my clothes.'

He made his escape, leaving Bernie attempting to clean chocolate icing off her daughter's hands and face while Peter collected the crockery together and carried it into the house. As soon as Jonah was out of sight, Lucy turned her attention to Peter.

'Daddy!' she called after him, as he stepped through the French window on his way to the kitchen, 'will you play croquet with me now? You said you would.'

CHAPTER 12

The following day was the May Day public holiday, but, with a double murder on their hands, neither Peter nor Jonah could take time off. Lucy was indignant when Peter told her that he would be going off to work as usual, leaving her with just her mother for company.

'Why can't you stay at home like everyone else's daddy?' she demanded, as he put on his jacket and prepared to leave. 'I wanted to take your fingerprints. I've only got mine and Mam's so far.'

'It'll have to wait until I get back, sunshine,' Peter said apologetically, giving his stepdaughter a quick peck on the cheek as he headed for the door. 'I must go now – I'm late enough already.'

'But why?' persisted Lucy. 'It's a holiday!'

'Lucy, love, just let Peter go, there's a good girl,' Bernie intervened. 'Policemen often have to work when other people are on holiday. You know that.'

'And right now,' Peter added over his shoulder, in an attempt to persuade Lucy of the importance of his job,' I'm on the trail of someone who's killed two people, so it's important to try to catch them before they do it again.'

'Do you think they will?' Lucy asked, wide-eyed as she

took this statement in. 'Will they try to kill *you*?' she added, running after Peter and pulling at his sleeve. 'If you try to catch them, I mean?'

'Whatever put that idea into your head?' Peter asked, turning to look at Lucy, who was gazing up at him with a worried expression.

'Like what happened to my real dad,' Lucy explained, still looking anxious. 'He was trying to catch someone, wasn't he? When he died.'

Lucy's father had been one of Peter's police colleagues. He had fallen to his death following a scuffle while pursuing a suspect across the rooftop of one of the Oxford colleges, several months before Lucy was born.

'Oh dear, Lucy!' Peter bent down, picked up the little girl and hugged her close. 'Don't you worry about me. Nobody's going to kill me. I'll be back home before you know it, and you can take my fingerprints all you like. OK?'

'Are you sure?'

'As sure as I can be.' Peter answered, conscious that his wife, who did not believe in hiding hard realities from children, would not permit him to give assurances that went beyond the demonstrable truth.

'Lucy, love,' Bernie added, 'policemen do sometimes get killed. It's part of the job, but it only happens very rarely. It's not something to get worried about.'

'But my dad …' Lucy persisted.

'Richard – your dad – was much braver than me,' Peter intervened. 'He took all sorts of risks that I'd never dare to take. You don't need to worry that anything will happen to me – really.'

Lucy still looked dissatisfied, so Peter reached into Bernie's back pocket and took out her mobile phone. He handed it to Lucy.

'Tell you what,' he said. 'If you really can't stop thinking about it, just send me a text whenever you want and I'll text you back to say I'm alright. How's that?'

Lucy took the phone in her hand and bestowed a beaming smile on Peter, nodding her acquiescence to this arrangement.

'Mind you,' he went on, 'I may not be able to reply right away – if I'm in a meeting with one of the bigwigs for example. So don't start panicking if you have to wait a few minutes, will you?'

'And I'll have that phone back, if you don't mind,' her mother added, taking the device out of her daughter's hands and replacing it in her pocket. 'I can't have you answering all my private calls or ringing Australia. You can have it back if you feel the need to check up on our Peter, but I'll look after it in the meantime.'

This little drama made Peter late for work, something that he rarely allowed to happen and about which he felt irrationally angry with himself. Anna greeted him as he entered the incident room.

'The Chief Super wants to see you, sir,' she informed him. 'He said to go straight through to his office.'

Chief Superintendent Adrian Fuller was four years younger than Peter. He was a plump man with brown eyes and a receding hairline. He looked up from his desk as Peter entered the room and gestured to him to take a seat.

'Ah Peter!' he said. 'Thank you for coming in. How's the Fellowes murder investigation going?'

'We're following up a number of leads,' Peter answered, unsure where this conversation was going and playing safe by supplying minimal information until he knew what his superior was getting at.

'But an arrest is not imminent?' Fuller enquired, smiling acknowledgement that they were both speaking formulaically.

'That's right, sir,' Peter grinned back. He and Fuller were old friends and understood one another well.

'I gather it's almost certain that the same killer was responsible for the other murder, over at Didcot,' Fuller went on. 'The Deputy Chief Constable has decided that the two investigations should be run as one.'

He paused and looked at Peter, who looked back with an interrogative expression on his face, waiting for the inevitable announcement.

'That being the case,' Fuller went on, 'he's putting DCI Porter, from South Oxfordshire, in overall charge. You'll carry on looking after the Oxford end of things, but you'll be reporting to him. Of course, I'll want you to keep me fully informed as well.'

'Yes, sir.'

Peter wondered briefly how long Jonah had known about these new arrangements. Was he, too, being briefed by his superiors at this moment or had he already been aware that he was to be put in authority over Peter when they met socially yesterday? If the latter, he had at least been good enough not to risk spoiling Lucy's day by mentioning it.

'The DCC is taking a personal interest in this, Fuller went on. 'His wife's a conservative councillor and she knows both the Clarkson twins socially. So it's important we don't have any slip-ups.'

'I'll do my best.'

'And you'll see to it that there's no argy-bargy between your team and this Jonah Porter's men? We've got to be joined-up about this.'

'Yes, sir,' Peter replied, trying to keep out of his voice the resentment that he felt, firstly about being made answerable to Jonah and, more importantly, at Fuller having felt the need to spell out what was expected of him, as if the professionalism of his team could not be taken for granted.

'I gather you know the man?' Fuller continued. 'You've worked with him before?'

'He and I both cut our teeth in CID under Richard Paige,' Peter answered, referring to Lucy's father, who, as Detective Inspector Paige had been Peter's mentor in his early years as a detective and had been instrumental in having Police Constable Jonah Porter transferred to his plain-clothes unit.

'Good. Then you shouldn't have any difficulty with this operation. Very well then – you'd better get on. You can expect Porter over here later this morning to agree how you're going to manage things. I told him not before ten, to give you time to brief your lot.'

Peter went back to the incident room and called his team to attention. He briefly explained the new working arrangements, emphasising the need to co-operate fully with the South Oxfordshire CID and not to allow any petty rivalries to get in the way of the investigation. When he mentioned Jonah's name, a low ripple of conversation went round the room, especially amongst the female officers present, and Peter noticed Monica Philipson exchanging a meaningful look with Anna. Some, at least, of his team appeared to welcome this development.

Then he summarised what he had found out himself from George Fraser and Edwina Clarkson during the weekend and invited suggestions from the floor for additional lines of enquiry. No new ideas being forthcoming, he then set to work distributing tasks amongst his officers.

He paired Andy Lepage with Monica Philipson and commissioned them to look into Andy's hypothesis that the student, James Pickering, could have killed Fellowes to protect his father. This was something that he had not yet mentioned to Jonah. Peter made a mental note to include that in his first report to DCI Porter. It would not do young Andy Lepage's career any harm to have his good idea brought to the attention of an up-and-coming man like Porter – and Jonah appreciated the sort of enthusiasm Andy was exhibiting over this investigation.

He set Anna Davenport sifting through the transcripts of telephone calls received from the public over the weekend, in the hope of finding something that might give them a new lead. She could come with him later to see

Samantha Fraser, but he had better stay in his office until after Jonah's promised visit that morning.

The thought of Jonah's imminent arrival reminded him that he had done nothing about checking on the whereabouts of Eva Riess at the times of the murders. Perhaps he ought to speak to her himself. It needed careful handling to avoid upsetting a potentially vulnerable woman – or giving her son cause to complain that the police were ignoring his request to act sensitively towards her. On the other hand, she might be made more anxious by having the officer in charge of the case – well, a senior officer leading the Oxford end of the enquiry, he corrected himself – interviewing her.

In the end, he called Sergeant Andrews over and told him to ring Eva to make an appointment. Martin's clothes had come back from forensics with a clean bill of health, so he could arrange to return them to her and then quiz her tactfully about her movements on Tuesday and Wednesday.

When he got back to his office, intent on making the arrangements to meet with Samantha, Peter found Jonah Porter sitting at his desk waiting for him. Seeing Peter come in, he looked up from the laptop computer that he had brought with him and smiled apologetically.

'I assume you've been told that Sir Rodney has put his oar in and decided that there has to be one person heading up this investigation?' he said, closing the lid of the computer and getting up to allow Peter to take his chair. He walked round the room and sat down again, facing Peter across the desk.

'Did you want to speak to everyone?' Peter asked. 'I'm afraid I've just sent most of them off on errands.'

'No, no,' Jonah shook his head emphatically. 'I'm not here to take over. I just thought I ought to see you face-to-face to make sure there's no misunderstanding and so we're agreed on how we're going to work this. You're still in charge of the Oxford end of things. The only change is that you need to keep me up to speed on what you're up to. There's concern at the top that this is going to be very high profile, what with MEPs and TV personalities being involved and, probably more importantly, the press seeing it as an attack on two of their own. Whatever they may have thought about Fellowes and Finch, every journalist in Fleet Street is going to be watching us like a hawk hoping to be able to denounce police incompetence or even to accuse us of bias against the press.'

'Put like that, I suppose I ought to be grateful that you'll be the one taking the flack,' Peter observed drily.

'Oh yes – that's the other thing. My instructions are that nobody else is to speak to the media. Any press conferences will be headed up by me – or by Sir Rodney himself if he thinks more weight is needed – and any approaches from the press are to be strictly directed through the proper channels. No chattering to journalists – not even the local papers.'

'Don't worry. My team all know the score,' Peter assured him. 'And as far as press conferences are concerned, you're welcome.'

'You never did like being in the limelight, did you Peter?' Jonah smiled. 'Never mind, I'll do my best to keep the spotlight off you and give you a chance to get on with solving the case while all the journalists are watching to see me making a balls-up of it!'

At that moment Peter's mobile phone played an alert to notify him of an incoming text. Taking this as an opportunity of avoiding the need to formulate a suitable reply to Jonah's unexpected remark, Peter fished the phone out of his jacket pocket and put it down on the desk in front of him.

'From Bernie?' Jonah asked, seeing the name displayed. 'You'd better read it.'

'From Bernie's phone,' Peter confirmed, 'but it'll be from Lucy.'

He opened the text and they both read the message: *I*

love you Daddy. Peter hastily typed a reply: *I love you too, precious.* Then he pocketed the phone and looked up at Jonah, who was watching impassively.

'Sorry about that,' Peter apologised. 'I made some stupid remark to Lucy about needing to catch our killer as quickly as possible, before he had a chance to strike again, and she's got it into her head that I might be in some sort of danger. Bernie told her all about how Richard died, you see, and she's been putting two and two together and making out that all policemen are under constant threat. Now, on the subject of keeping you up to speed, you ought to know that we've identified another potential suspect.'

Peter told Jonah about the motive that they had postulated for James Pickering to have killed Fellowes and Finch, giving Andy Lepage full credit for the discovery and detailing their plans for testing out the hypothesis. Then, thinking that perhaps he had been unfair in singling out Lepage for praise, he went on to detail Monica Philipson's work with the dons and staff of Lichfield College that had enabled them to establish that Martin Riess had an alibi for Fellowes' murder while George Fraser did not.

'She passed her sergeant's exam a couple of years back,' he went on, 'but she keeps getting pipped at the post when I put her forward for shortlisting. It wouldn't do her any harm to get some experience in another division. If you have any vacancies you could do a lot worse than to give her a trial.'

Jonah smiled but said nothing, so Peter continued, describing their plans for the day, emphasising his confidence in the ability of Rupert Andrews to obtain the necessary information from Eva without alarming her and praising Anna for her competence and attention to detail.

'She's ripe for promotion,' he ended. 'She'd have been an inspector before now if she didn't keep having babies.'

'And what about you?' Jonah asked, smiling broadly now, 'You've told me about everything your team have been doing and why they ought to be given more recognition for it, but what about your contribution?'

'Oh, you know me,' Peter said, giving a shrug of his shoulders and a nervous laugh. 'I don't have brilliant ideas that change the course of an investigation; I just plod along doing the routine stuff and pulling things together in the hope of making sense of it all in the end.'

This description of Peter's approach to police work was so precisely Jonah's own opinion that for a moment he was unable to think of a reply. Peter took advantage of the pause to press home his advocacy of the young trainee detective.

'Young Andy Lepage, on the other hand,' he went on, 'has a real flair for the job.'

'Well, I'll certainly keep a close eye on him, if he gets a placement in my division,' Jonah promised, still smiling with amusement at the way that Peter refused to be deflected away from his determination to support his team members and towards consideration for his own promotion prospects. 'But now we'd better decide on our next move. I agree that this Edgar Pickering needs to be looked into. There's someone I know in the Met who specialises in financial stuff. I'll get him on to checking out whether there could be anything dodgy going on that might be grist for the *Revelations* mill. And, if you don't mind, I'll also talk to someone who can do some digging around the neighbours of the Fellowes' flat in London and see if we can find out any more about how their relationship was going before they split up, and what really caused the rift.'

Peter remembered that, a few years previously, Jonah had spent eighteen months on secondment to the Metropolitan Police. Presumably he had connections with all sorts of useful people as a result. Peter had not been able to understand why someone would voluntarily work in London when he had a perfectly good job in rural Oxfordshire, but now he realised what an astute career move it had been.

'And I'll be going through all the files in the *Revelations* offices as a matter of routine for the Finch murder,' Jonah continued, becoming animated as he thought about his plans for taking the investigation forward, 'so I'll let you know if anything turns up that's relevant to the Oxford end of things. Now, what else is there? Oh yes! Did you ever manage to track down that rough sleeper you were telling me about who may be a witness?'

'Yes,' Peter answered, glad that a call had come through that morning to say that Dave Gillis had been found at last. 'Constable Hughes has tracked him down and is going to bring him in later this morning. I doubt if he'll be able to tell us much, but at least if he admits to having been the man on the towpath who bumped into Olivia Best and James Pickering, we can stop looking for anyone else.'

'Hughes? D'you mean Gavin Hughes?' Jonah asked in tones of surprise. 'Is he still around – and still a PC?'

'That's right. I'm surprised you remember him. He can only just have joined the force when you moved to South Oxfordshire.'

'I was on the panel that interviewed him. To be honest, I was against taking him. He seemed so slow. I thought he'd never make the grade.'

'He's not what you'd call *dynamic*,' Peter agreed, 'and he won't contemplate taking his sergeant's exams. But he seems to have found his niche working with the homeless community. He's done more to reduce crime there – both crime done to them and done by them – than all our clever initiatives put together. They trust him, you see, which doesn't often happen where the police are concerned.'

'OK,' Jonah said, drawing the conversation to a close and getting up, eager to get on with his own work. 'I'll leave you to it. Just be sure to keep me informed. I don't want to look stupid if the DCC calls me in wanting chapter and verse on what we've been doing.'

'Don't worry. I'll get Andy Lepage to email you a daily

summary. He's good at reports – must be something he learned at university – and it will be good for him to get a view of how the whole team works together.'

'Good. I know I can rely on you. Now I'd better get off.' Jonah opened the door and then turned back for a moment. 'Take care of yourself. Lucy needs you.' Then he was gone.

Peter sat for a moment, staring into space. Suddenly the resentful and discontented mood that had been upon him, ever since he had found Jonah at Finch's house and realised that he was likely to be made subordinate to him, evaporated. It was as if he had been looking at the world through a misty lens and now everything had clicked back into focus. Jonah was not trying to displace him at home – it was absurd paranoia to imagine that he could have done even if he had wanted to – and, as for work, if Jonah cared to climb the greasy pole in the direction of Chief Constable and a knighthood, good luck to him! Detective Inspector suited Peter very well, and he was starting to look towards his retirement in a few years' time. He would have the opportunity then to spend more time with his family: Lucy, of course, but also his daughter Hannah in Leeds, and perhaps he could even make a trip to Jamaica to visit his son, Eddie, who had settled there after his mother died.

Then he pulled himself firmly together and, smiling at his own foolishness and in anticipation of a good day ahead, he strode back to the incident room.

He found Anna in conversation with Rupert Andrews over a report that had come in over the weekend of a mysterious stranger seen crossing the grounds of Worcester College on Tuesday night. The students reported the sighting admitted to having been the worse for drink at the time and Anna was inclined to think that their call to the police hotline on Saturday evening was likely to be the result of bravado brought on by a similar indulgence. Peter listened to both sides and agreed with

Anna that it was unlikely to lead anywhere, and with Andrews that nevertheless it had to be followed up.

'I thought you'd be on your way to see Eva Riess,' he went on, addressing Andrews. 'I told DCI Porter that you would be on to her this morning.'

'I haven't forgotten,' Andrews defended himself. 'But she's not in. I rang and there was no reply.'

'All right,' Peter conceded, 'keep trying, and meanwhile, check out this mysterious stranger in the quad story.'

'I've been on to Samantha Fraser,' Anna said, eager to show that she was also doing her bit to keep up the good name of Peter's team. She says we can go to see her at her lab any time today. Apparently the university doesn't take much notice of bank holidays and she's working as usual. I told her we'd try to come this morning – I wasn't sure how soon you'd be free.'

'Good. We'll go right away. I have a feeling in my bones that she may have something important to tell us.'

CHAPTER 13

Meanwhile, back at *Llanwrda*, the large detached villa that Bernie's late husband had inherited from his father and grandfather, Bernie was doing her best to keep Lucy entertained and to distract her from thinking about imaginary dangers that her beloved stepfather might be facing. They were busy cleaning the working surface in the kitchen, after cutting out gingerbread men, when the doorbell rang. Bernie quickly rinsed her hands under the tap and went out into the hall, drying them on her trousers as she went.

When she opened the door, she was surprised to see the diminutive figure of Eva Riess standing on the step and looking up at her with an apologetic expression on her face. She seemed to be having difficulty deciding what to say, so Bernie opened the conversation.

'Eva!' she said cheerily. 'How nice to see you after so long. Are you coming in or what?'

'So you do remember me,' Eva stammered. As usual, she was rather unsure of herself in the presence of Bernie's hearty Scouse accent and turn of phrase. 'I was afraid you would have forgotten after so many years.'

'I could never forget you,' Bernie assured her, 'after all

those evenings of listening to you and Richard playing duets, and hearing all about your incredible escape from the Stasi. How's your son?' she went on innocently. 'It was his boat where that journalist was found dead, wasn't it? I saw the TV reports.'

'Yes. That's what I came to see you about. I was wondering – do you still have contacts with the police?'

'Yes,' Bernie smiled, realising that Eva did not know about her marriage to Peter. 'You'd better come in.'

Eva hesitated, so Bernie repeated her invitation.

'Come in – please! You must come and meet our daughter, Lucy. She'll be so pleased to see you. She always likes talking to people who knew Richard.'

'Your daughter?' Eva repeated in a puzzled tone. 'I don't think I understand.'

'She was born in the May after Richard died,' Bernie explained, stepping back to allow Eva to enter, and nearly tripping over Lucy who had crept up behind her to see who was at the door.

'It was my birthday yesterday,' Lucy added helpfully. 'I'm seven years old now.'

'My goodness!' Eva said, in a suitably impressed tone of voice. 'And you are Richard's little girl? I had no idea!'

'I hadn't got round to telling him when he died,' Bernie went on, 'so it's not surprising that the news didn't reach you before you went to America. I really ought to have made contact before now – as soon as I knew you were back. I'm sure that's what Richard would have wanted. Now, Lucy,' she added, turning to her daughter, 'this is Eva Riess. She was friends with your father for years – long before he met me.'

She led the way into the large living room and they all sat down. Eva looked intently at Lucy, and Lucy gazed back in return.

'Yes,' Eva said at length, 'I can see the resemblance. There's certainly something of Richard there, in your face.'

'Where? What?' Lucy asked eagerly, getting up and

standing in front of Eva and looking her in the eye.'

'I am not sure,' Eva said slowly, 'something about the eyes, I think. Yes – the eyes … and the set of the jaw. You have a very determined look about you – just like your father.'

Lucy smiled broadly.

'Would you like to see my book?' she asked eagerly. 'My mam made me a book all about my dad. It's got pictures and stories in it. Shall I get it for you?'

'I'd like that very much,' Eva replied seriously, 'but just now there's something I need to talk to your mother about.'

'Another time, love,' Bernie said, seeing her daughter's face fall. 'I'm sure we'll be seeing a lot more of Eva now we've met up again after all these years. Now, Eva, what was it you wanted to see me about?'

'It's Martin. As you said, it was one of his friends who was killed last week and he was staying on Martin's boat when it happened. I'm worried that Martin is not being quite as … co-operative, as he might be, with the police. He does not talk about it with me – he just tells me not to worry – but that make me worry more. I know that he had nothing to do with the man's death, but I know he is under suspicion and I think his attitude is making them suspect him more.'

'How do you mean – his attitude?' Bernie asked, puzzled. From what Peter had told her, Riess appeared to have been very open and helpful towards him.

'Principally the way he tells them not to bother me – as if I could be intimidated by a British policeman after having been interrogated by the Stasi! They sent a man round to borrow his clothes for tests while he was out. He was very angry about it and it was all I could do to stop him making an official complaint. And the other thing is that I'm sure he has not been completely open about the way Martin Fellowes stole his girlfriend from him. They are bound to find out about it and then it will look bad that he did not tell them himself.'

'But, even if he has a motive for killing Martin Fellowes,' Bernie argued, 'he can't have had any reason to attack the other man – Arthur Finch.'

'There you are wrong. Arthur Finch telephoned the house the day after Martin Fellowes died, wanting to speak to Martin. I told him that Martin was in college and he said that he would ring him there. I do not think that Martin has told the police about that.'

'And what do you think Finch wanted to talk to him about?' Bernie asked, becoming interested in this new development.

'I do not know,' Eva shrugged. 'Arthur was a bad egg. He would sell his grandmother for a good story for his nasty little paper. But I worry that the police will think that Martin killed Fellowes and that Arthur knew and was threatening to expose him.'

'So, what were you hoping I could do?'

'I am not sure,' Eva said, hesitatingly. 'I suppose that I just thought: if Richard was still here, I would go to him and he would know what to do. And then I thought of you, and I thought that perhaps you still knew people in the police force who might be able to help in some way.'

'Well,' Bernie said slowly. 'I do still know people in the police-'

'My Daddy's a policeman,' Lucy interrupted.

'She means her stepdad,' Bernie explained, seeing Eva's puzzled expression. 'DI Peter Johns.'

'Peter was my godfather,' Lucy declared forcefully, determined to be part of the conversation, 'and now he's my daddy.'

'Richard must have talked to you about Peter,' Bernie said, turning towards Eva and, at the same time, signalling with her hand to Lucy to keep quiet. 'He was his right-hand man for years.'

'Peter Johns,' Eva repeated to herself. 'Yes the name is certainly familiar. I think Richard told me about a Sergeant

Peter Johns, but he was married to a West Indian, I thought.'

'Yes, that's right, but Angie Johns died nearly four years ago, and Peter and I married last year.'

There was a long pause while Eva took all this in.

'I can see you don't approve,' Bernie said, smiling, but half-serious. 'I suppose you think that no one could replace Richard – and you're quite right – but I think he'd approve of me and Peter, I really do. He had tremendous respect for him.'

'Yes. I know he did,' Eva agreed. 'And I'm sure it's better for your little girl to have two parents. I hope your second marriage lasts longer than your first,' she added, recalling that Richard had died only two years after marrying Bernie.'

'Gosh yes!' Bernie said with feeling, but in a jokey tone. 'I can do without being widowed a second time!'

'You said Peter wasn't in danger!' Lucy cried out indignantly, unexpectedly picking up on this reference to her stepfather's potential demise. 'You promised!'

She threw herself at her mother and demanded to be given the use of her phone. Bernie handed it over without speaking, realising that any protest would only confirm Lucy in her belief that something sinister was being kept from her. Lucy carefully selected Peter's name from the list of contacts and started composing her text. Bernie hastily explained to Eva the circumstances that had led to her daughter's anxiety. Lucy pressed the send button and they all waited anxiously for a reply.

Bernie was just about to start explaining to Lucy that Peter might not be able to answer immediately, when the response came through. Bernie breathed a sigh of relief as she read Peter's text over her daughter's shoulder.

'There you are,' she said. 'Peter isn't in any danger. We were only talking hypothetically – that means we were imagining what it would be like if something really unlikely happened. Now, let's go and see how those gingerbread men are coming on, shall we?'

Eva waited in the living room while Bernie and Lucy returned to the kitchen to get the biscuits out of the oven. She looked around at the pictures on the wall, nodding approvingly at a portrait of Richard and sadly at the photograph of his wedding to Bernie. She turned as Bernie and Lucy returned a few minutes later with a pot of tea, three bone-china mugs and a plate containing three warm gingerbread men fresh from the oven.

'You made Richard very happy,' she said to Bernie. 'He told me many times that you were the best thing that ever happened to him.'

'Really? I always thought I was more trouble than I was worth most of the time,' joked Bernie, who was always uncomfortable at receiving praise. She busied herself with pouring tea, whispering to Lucy to hand round the biscuits.

'Did you make these?' Eva asked as Lucy held out the plate towards her. 'I can remember making gingerbread with my mother when I was a little girl.'

They all sat down again and Bernie turned to Eva.

'I'm not sure that I understand what you're asking me to do,' she said. 'I'm afraid I can't talk to Peter about the case, because he has to be impartial. If it looks as if he's got a conflict of interest, he'll just be taken off it. But I can assure you he will be absolutely fair and he won't accuse anyone without proper evidence.'

'I am not sure,' Eva admitted. 'I did not think it through – I just decided I needed to speak to someone who knew the police, and you were the only one I could think of. Perhaps you could speak to Martin yourself – tell him to be honest about the way he felt when Edwina told him she was marrying Martin Fellowes. They are bound to find out about it and then it will look bad for Martin. If you can convince him that he can trust this Peter, perhaps he will stop keeping things back.'

'Are you sure that he is?' Bernie asked. 'I mean, he can't

have felt that badly towards Martin Fellowes to have allowed him to sleep in his boat. Maybe he's put it all behind him and forgotten about it. And then it wouldn't be relevant to the enquiry, would it?'

'No. I know Martin. He does not put things behind him. He broods on them and they get bigger in his own mind. I do not know why he allowed the man to stay on his boat – I can only imagine that he just could not think of a way of making him go away. But I do know that he did not tell me about it, which means that he knew I would not have approved. You do not understand how bad it was. Martin went away to America to get experience that would help him to make a career and support himself and his wife. He was planning to come back after two years to marry Edwina. The first that he knew that she had changed her mind was when he got an invitation to her wedding to Martin Fellowes!'

'That must have been a shock,' Bernie agreed.

'It was a dreadful blow. It was almost like losing his father over again. He abandoned his plans to come back to England and got another job in America. It was another ten years before he could face coming home to Oxford.'

'Did he blame himself?' Bernie asked suddenly. 'Did he think that it was his own fault that Edwina left him?'

'Why do you ask that? He had nothing to reproach himself for.'

'No. I didn't mean that. I meant,' Bernie paused to think. 'Apparently he told Martin Fellowes that he felt responsible for his father's death – which I know is nonsense – so I wondered whether he could have imagined in his own mind that it was also his fault that Edwina gave up on him. That would explain why he didn't hold it against Martin Fellowes, wouldn't it? And maybe he didn't tell you that Fellowes was staying with him because he knew that you blamed Fellowes for taking Edwina away from him.'

'I do not know,' Eva said, shaking her head. 'There may

be something in what you say. I do not know. I thought I knew my son so well and now what you say has made me think that perhaps I do not know him well at all. Would you come and talk to him? Tell him that he can trust the police and tell him that he does not need to try to protect me from anything.'

'If that's what you'd like,' Bernie replied. 'I don't know what good I can do, but if it will help to put your mind at rest …'

'Good! Are you free this morning? We can go at once. He is on his boat, tidying it up and cleaning it after the police went through everything. The car is outside. I can take you right away.'

'If that's what you'd like,' Bernie agreed, smiling at Eva's sudden enthusiasm and energy. 'Lucy, love, get ready to go out: Eva's going to take us down to see a man in a boat.'

'Do you mean a house boat?' Lucy asked. 'Does he live there?'

'Sort of. It's a canal boat – with bunks and somewhere to cook and everything, so you can live in it, but he doesn't live there all the time – just for going off on holidays.'

'Is it one of those boats with the big rudder and the writing on the side? Will we go far in it?' Lucy's eyes lit up with excitement.

'I'm afraid we won't be going anywhere,' her mother answered with a smile. 'It's moored down behind Worcester. We're just going to visit the man who owns it. But you will get to see what it's like inside. How's that?'

CHAPTER 14

'Come in here,' Samantha Fraser greeted Peter and Anna when they arrived at the laboratory in the university science area, where she worked. She led them into a cramped room adjacent to one of the labs and moved piles of papers off the chairs to make room for them to sit down. 'Would you like a drink?'

Peter followed her gaze towards two brown-stained mugs, which stood on the crowded desk, looking as if they had not been washed up for several days.

'No thank you,' he answered for both of them. 'We'll just ask a few questions and then get out of your hair.'

Dr Fraser sat down and looked at him attentively.

'How did you feel when you read that article about your husband?' Peter asked. 'It must have been quite a shock.'

'Yes,' Samantha answered with a tinge of bitterness. 'I was stupid enough to be surprised – and of course it was galling that I hadn't known. But it was what came afterwards that was far worse.'

'And what did come afterwards?' Anna asked, intrigued.

'People's reactions. Most people – most of my friends

anyway – were sympathetic, but even then, their sympathy tended to include offering me advice on how to improve our sex life. And there were some people who were openly critical and told me to my face that I had only myself to blame.'

'How did they make that out?' Peter asked, shocked at this suggestion.

'The basic problem is that everyone assumes that George and I must not have an active sex life. It doesn't occur to anybody that he could be going off to use prostitutes despite everything being perfectly fine in that department. So, there are those who berate me for not giving him his conjugal rights and those who offer suggestions for places that I can get help for my frigidity and those who slip advertisements for sex-aids into my pigeonhole. They just don't get it that George has been doing this in addition to having regular sex with me!'

'Were you angry with him?' Anna asked.

'I was bloody furious,' Samantha admitted, 'but there wasn't anything I could do about it – except getting myself off to the STD clinical for an AIDS test.'

'And what did you think of the man who wrote the article?' Peter asked.

'I suppose he has his job to do,' Samantha sighed. 'And George was asking for it, the way he seeks out publicity all the time. I suppose he told you that he sees it as a recognition of his virility?'

'Something like that. And you think that's genuinely what he thinks? He's not just putting on a brave face to hide his embarrassment?'

'Embarrassment!' Samantha snorted. 'He doesn't know the meaning of the word. It's all just good publicity for his next TV series as far as he's concerned.'

'He's not afraid of the effect that it might have on his academic career?' Peter asked. 'I mean, the university might not look too favourably on one of their professors being well-known for frequenting prostitutes.'

'He just keeps saying that he's done nothing illegal,' Samantha insisted. 'And he's right: they were all consenting adults and however he found them it wasn't through kerb-crawling his way round the red light district.'

'What will you do now?' Anna asked. 'Will you stay with him?'

'I don't know,' Samantha sighed. 'When you've been married for twenty years, it's difficult to imagine how it would be to be single again. And at the moment I really don't think I could cope with all the publicity that a divorce would bring with it. And then there's our work. It would be very awkward still working together if we'd split up, and my work is so much associated with his that I doubt I'd get a job anywhere outside his research group. So I suppose we'll just carry on the way we are and I'll manage somehow.'

The door opened and the tousled head of a young woman appeared round it.

'I'm sorry,' she apologised when she saw Peter and Anna. 'I didn't realise you had visitors.'

'This is my post-doctoral research assistant, Hannah Frinton,' Samantha explained. 'She's working with me on our latest project. It's alright, Hannah, I'll be with you in a few minutes.'

The head disappeared and Samantha turned back to face Peter.

'I really don't think there's anything more I can tell you.'

'For the record, I need to ask you where you and your husband were on Tuesday and Wednesday last week,' Peter told her. 'Let's start with your husband. He says that he worked in his college room on both of those days and dined on High Table on the Tuesday evening, dressing in his room and going straight down to the dining hall.'

'If that's what he says, then I suppose that's what happened,' Samantha answered, not sounding particularly interested.

'Is that what he told you he was doing on those days?' Peter persisted.

'Well, he wasn't at the lab and he wasn't at home when the postman called to deliver a parcel, so I suppose in his college room is as likely a place as anywhere.'

'I see. And now, what about you? Where were you on Tuesday from, say, five p.m.?'

'I was working here all day. I went out for a sandwich at about one-thirty and came straight back. Then I stayed here until … let me see … it was gone ten before I left. I'd got a bit of a build-up of work to be done and George was going to be late because of dining on High Table, so I stayed here and tried to get the project back on track.'

'Was anyone else there? Is there anyone who can confirm that you were here all evening?'

'Hannah stayed until about half past six, but after that I was working alone.'

'I see. And on Wednesday?'

'I was here all day, working on the project.'

'With Hannah?' Anna asked.

'Yes.'

'OK,' Anna said quietly. 'Now, can you tell me how well you know Dr Martin Riess?'

'Who?'

'The man who owned the boat where Martin Fellowes was killed,' Anna explained. 'He was a tutor at Lichfield, so I thought you might have met him.'

'But I'm not at Lichfield. My post is attached to different college. I suppose George probably knows him, but he's never mentioned it.'

'Well, thank you,' Peter concluded the interview. 'I think that's all for now. We'll find our own way out.'

As they walked down the corridor towards the stairs, they saw Hannah Frinton coming towards them. She disappeared through a door on the left marked Female Toilets.

'Excuse me, sir.'

Anna followed the research assistant through the door and Peter stood outside, waiting. A few minutes later, Anna emerged with a look of satisfaction on her face.

'Well?' Peter asked, as they resumed their walk toward the exit.

'She confirms Dr Fraser's movements on Tuesday and Wednesday – up to a point. However, as well as not being able to vouch for her after half past six on Tuesday, she says that Samantha was working on her own in her office with the door closed for most of the afternoon on Wednesday. The other interesting thing that I learnt is that Professor George Fraser is not as universally popular – at least among the female members of his own department – as he would have us believe.'

'And what exactly do you mean by that?' Peter asked with interest.

'Well, according to Hannah, they all think that it's his wife who does all the work and has all the bright ideas and it's George who gets all the credit. There's quite a groundswell of opinion among the women that the department would be a pleasanter and more productive place – and better for their career prospects – without him.'

CHAPTER 15

After his meeting with Peter, DCI Jonah Porter headed south towards Didcot, with the aim of interviewing Coralie Finch. He judged that by now she should be in a better frame of mind to answer questions. He wondered to himself, as he drove down the A34 past Abingdon, how Arthur Finch's wife really felt about his death. She had appeared distraught the previous week, but how much had that been due to her having just discovered his body and how much was grief at his loss?

Jonah knew that he would have been devastated if his own wife, Margaret, had suffered a violent death, but he would not have given way as Coralie had done. He would have wanted to be actively doing something to bring her attacker to justice. Peter Johns had lost his first wife in some sort of violent incident. Jonah did not know the details and had never liked to ask. How had *he* felt when he heard the news?

He parked outside Coralie's parents' unassuming semi-detached house and strode up the short drive with his usual energy. He rang the bell and stood on the step, waiting. He was just about to ring again when the door opened and a grey-haired man looked cautiously out.

Jonah held up his warrant card and explained why he had come, with what he hoped was a reassuring smile on his face.

'Coralie's not in,' the man said shortly, attempting to close the door.

'Then perhaps I can have a word or two with you and your wife?' Jonah suggested. 'You *are* Mr Fergus Thornton, I assume. Mrs Finch's father?'

'Yes, that's right. I suppose you'd better come in.'

He opened the door wider and stepped back a little to allow Jonah to enter. Then he closed the door firmly behind them both.

'Come through to the back room,' he invited, grudgingly. 'Carol's in there with the kids.'

Jonah followed him into a small living room crowded with furniture and toys. A small girl was sitting on the floor playing with a dolls' tea set. A woman, whom Jonah deduced must be Mrs Carol Thornton, was sitting in an armchair with a younger child – Jonah judged that she must be less than eighteen months – sitting on her lap with a picture book. They all turned their heads to look at Jonah as he entered.

'This is Detective Chief Inspector Porter,' Mr Thornton explained. 'He wants to ask us some questions.'

Mrs Thornton got up to shake hands with Jonah, holding the toddler in one arm as she did so. Then she looked round as if thinking and finally addressed the little girl on the floor.

'Louise, sweetheart,' she said, 'be a darling and read to Agnes for a little while. This policeman wants to talk to me and grandad.'

Agnes looked up from her tea party with a pensive expression. Then, after sizing up the situation, she nodded and permitted her grandmother to settle her down on the chair with her sister next to her and the book across their combined laps. Mrs Thornton signalled to the men to follow her into the kitchen.

They sat down around an oval table in the centre of the room. Mrs Thornton offered coffee, which Jonah waved away.

'What is it you want to know?' Mr Thornton asked bluntly.

'First of all,' Jonah said, glad to be getting down to business. 'Can you tell me how I can find your daughter? I need to ask her some more questions about her husband. You said that she was out. How long will she be? Or can you tell me where she is?'

'I'm afraid we can't help you,' Fergus Thornton answered for both of them. 'She just asked us to look after the girls so that she could have some time by herself. She wanted to think things through.'

'And where did she go, to do this thinking?' Jonah pressed him.

'She didn't say where she was going. She just took the car and went off.'

'She told us not to expect her back for lunch,' his wife added. 'We always look after the kids during the day when Coralie's at work, so it's no bother for us and she needed some peace and quiet.'

'Don't you have any idea where she may have gone?' Jonah persisted, starting to become slightly concerned that all might not be well with Coralie Finch.

'She probably went walking on the Ridgeway,' Carol Thornton suggested. 'She always used to go there to think during the time when she was going through the fertility tests and everything. She said the fresh air helped her to think straight.'

'Any particular part?' Jonah asked. 'Where would she have been likely to park, for instance?'

'Probably the Step's Hill car park near Ivinghoe Beacon. She likes the beacon. There's a magnificent view. She says it puts everything into perspective.'

Jonah reflected that it also provided possibilities for throwing oneself down from a great height and he had to suppress his immediate instinct to set off for Ivinghoe himself in search of Coralie. If she was genuinely overwhelmed with grief at losing her husband, who knew what she might be intending to do? Perhaps life no longer seemed to her to be worth living.

'What sort of frame of mind was she in when she went out?' he asked. 'I mean, did she seem depressed or anxious at all?'

'She's just lost her husband in very distressing circumstances,' Carol said, rather coldly. 'So naturally she was upset.'

'But she wasn't suicidal, if that's what you're getting at,' Fergus added quickly. 'She would never do that, for the sake of the children, if nothing else.'

'She just needed some space to think through how she was going to organise her life now that Arthur is gone,' Carol explained. 'That's why she went out. It's difficult to think when you have two under-fives running around.'

'If you ask me,' Fergus went on darkly, 'she'll be a lot better off without him. He's always been a bloody waste of space. About the only good thing he ever did for Coralie was to give her two lovely children.'

'He even took his time about that,' commented Carol grimly. 'Poor Coralie went through all sorts of tests and procedures and they all came out saying there was nothing wrong with her and there was no reason why she should have any difficulty getting pregnant, but would he agree to having a sperm count? No he would not!'

'Things seem to have progressed quite quickly once they got started,' Jonah observed. 'I mean, there isn't a very large age gap between your two granddaughters.'

'No,' growled Fergus. '*I* reckon he didn't really *want* children. He's certainly never taken any interest in them after they were born.'

'He prefers being the centre of attention himself,' Carol put in. 'He's just an overgrown kid who wants his wife's undivided attention with no distractions. He was quite rude to me when I said I thought it was time I became a grandmother.'

'Are you suggesting that he was doing something to prevent his wife falling pregnant?' Jonah asked.

'I don't know about that,' Fergus admitted. 'I'm just saying that he never wanted kids and wouldn't co-operate with poor Coralie when she was making the rounds of fertility clinics and all that.'

'OK. Now, I really do want to speak to Coralie. Could you give me her mobile number?' Jonah asked.

'You can have it,' Fergus replied, 'but it won't help you this morning. She left it at home. She said she didn't want to be pestered by any more journalists and nosey so-called well-wishers.'

'Has there been a lot of that?' Jonah asked.

'Too right there has!' Fergus answered vehemently. 'Ringing her mobile and calling at the house, at all times of day and night too! People claiming to be offering sympathy, but really, they just want to be able to boast that they know someone who's in the news.'

'And every journalist in the country claims to have been Arthur's bosom friend,' Carol added. 'But, of course, they're just hoping to get a story out of it.'

'We can arrange to have a police officer outside the house to keep people away,' Jonah suggested. 'Would you like me to do that for you?'

'No, no,' Fergus said hastily. 'We don't want the kids to think we're under siege.'

'Well, let me know if you change your mind – or if Mrs Finch would find it helpful. Now, I have a few questions for *you*. First, can you tell me a bit more about your daughter's relationship with her husband? You say they didn't see eye-to-eye about having children. Was that the only area on which they disagreed?'

'I don't know,' Carol sighed. 'I really don't know why she married him. I never liked that whole bunch that she started going round with in Cambridge – especially those

Clarkson girls. They were typical Oxbridge types, with a rich daddy and thinking they owned the world. I always thought Coralie was keen on one of the other men – Martin, his name was. She joined the group because of him, but he wasn't interested in her.'

'Which Martin was that?' Jonah asked, with interest. 'Was it Martin Fellowes or Martin Riess?'

'It was Fellowes,' Fergus answered for his wife. 'The same guy that was killed in Oxford the other day. Poor Coralie never had a chance with him. He was on the lookout for a wife who could help to give his career a leg-up. Little Coralie, with her teaching certificate and two primary teachers as parents, had nothing to offer. She was a bridesmaid at his wedding, when he married one of the Clarkson twins.'

'And then Arthur Finch proposed to her and I suppose she was afraid of being left on the shelf and she agreed to marry him.' Carol concluded.

'Are you suggesting that she never loved him?' Jonah asked.

'I wouldn't go as far as that,' Fergus said hastily, 'but I don't think it was exactly a marriage made in heaven, if you see what I mean.'

'And things definitely got worse when there was still no sign of any babies on the way after seven or eight years,' Carol put in.

''Well, you must admit, you can't have made it any easier for them with all your hints about wanting to be a grandma.' Fergus muttered. Jonah looked at him. This was the first time that the Thorntons had seemed less than totally united in their views. So Mrs Thornton had been disappointed not to have become a grandmother sooner, had she? But, of course, unlike Mrs Riess, she no longer had any reason to feel resentment against the man whom she blamed for that situation, since he appeared eventually to have fulfilled his obligations in this respect. Still, it looked as if there was no love lost between her and her son-in-law.

'I was only backing Coralie up,' Carol protested. 'Trying to get Arthur to agree to taking the tests to find out what the problem was. Anyway, it's all water under the bridge now.'

'Did Arthur Finch have any enemies that you know of?' Jonah asked, steering the conversation away from a topic that appeared to divide husband and wife.

'I would have said he could have had a good number,' Fergus replied. 'He didn't pull any punches when he wrote about people in that nasty little rag of his.'

'But we couldn't name anyone specifically,' his wife added hastily. 'Not anyone who might have done that to him.'

'No threatening letters or phone calls?'

'Not that we know of,' Fergus said firmly.

'All right,' Jonah said, taking out a business card from his pocket and holding it out. 'That's all for now. Please ask your daughter to ring this number when she gets in. I really do need to speak to her.'

Jonah sat for several minutes in his car outside the Thorntons' house, debating what to do next. He wanted to speak to both of the Clarkson sisters about their relationships with the two dead men, and in the hope of getting a clearer idea of what exactly had caused Edwina to make the final break with her husband; but he had a nagging doubt about Coralie Finch. Whatever her parents might say, he could not get rid of the feeling that, in her distress, she might do something rash and harm either herself or someone else. In the end, he decided to follow his instinct and look for Coralie Finch at Ivinghoe Beacon first. He could easily make his way to the Fellowes' Beaconsfield house from there, taking in Martina and Geoffrey in High Wycombe on the way.

There were several cars in the car park at Ivinghoe when Jonah pulled in, but there was no sign of the blue estate car that he had noticed outside the Finch's house when he had been called there to investigate Arthur's death. He got out, wondering what to do next and momentarily doubting that he had done the right thing in coming on what might well be a wild goose chase. After all, he had only Mrs Thornton's hunch to suggest that Coralie had come here at all.

He saw a woman with a dog coming back into the car park from the footpath and accosted her. He showed her a picture of Coralie Finch, which had appeared in one of the newspapers, and asked whether the woman had seen her. The woman shook her head.

'No. I've only seen the usual morning dog-walkers,' she replied brightly. 'This is the woman whose husband was battered to death isn't it? Has *she* gone missing now?'

'No. It's just that I was hoping to talk to her and we thought she might have come here. It's one of her favourite places apparently. Never mind. I'll catch up with her later.'

'Come to think of it,' the woman added, peering carefully at the picture in Jonah's hand. 'I think I *have* seen her here before – not for a good while though. I remember now. It must have been two or three years ago at least, because she commented on what a lovely coat my previous dog had. He was an Afghan and he was rather beautiful.'

'Well, thank you anyway.'

Jonah returned to the car and set off for High Wycombe to visit Geoffrey and Martina, hoping vehemently that the woman would not spread any stories to the effect that the wife of the dead magazine editor was missing and being sought by police. It looked as if following his instinct to try to find Coralie had been a bad move, but if she had been here – and in particular if she had been here and about to do something silly – it could have saved her life.

What would Peter have done? Most likely, what Jonah did now, which was to pull up in a layby and to contact a senior member of his team and ask them to organise for officers across the region to be on the lookout for Coralie Finch. Jonah was not given to self-doubt but, on this occasion, he had to admit that his passion for action and personal involvement had led him to working less effectively than had he delegated the job of finding Coralie immediately.

Geoffrey Plant answered the door and led Jonah into the large sitting room at the back of the house, where Peter and Anna had interviewed them the previous week. Martina was there, looking as glamorous as usual, reading a newspaper. She got up as Jonah entered and he waved her to stay seated.

'I won't keep you long,' he promised. 'I'm just trying to get my head around who everyone is and how they fit together. I gather that, when you were at Cambridge together, there were seven of you in a group called the Martians, is that right?'

'Yes,' Geoffrey admitted, sounding a little annoyed. 'Who told you about that?'

'Several people told my colleague,' Jonah said vaguely. 'Some of them seemed to think that it was significant that two of the group have been killed, so now I'm interested to hear more about it and more specifically about how far the relationships formed then continued after you went your separate ways.'

'Well, we all exchange Christmas cards,' Martina volunteered, 'but that's about all – except for me and Edwina, of course.'

'Of course. And on the subject of your sister. I'd really like to know what it really was that made her split with her husband.'

'We told your colleague,' Martina said coldly, 'that he would have to ask Edwina about that.'

'He did. And she said that it was to do with the things he was writing in *Revelations*.'

'There you are then!'

'And,' Jonah went on, 'she denied that it was that she

was afraid of anything he might write about her.'

He paused to let this sink in.

'But I'm convinced that there must be something more personal in all this. I don't buy the idea that she would tear up her marriage vows and ditch her husband – particularly when it might well alienate the constituency party members that she's hoping will choose her as their next parliamentary candidate – unless there was something more to it than a principled objection to his methods. And if she's not afraid of what he might write about her, maybe he's concerned about someone close to her – someone else in the public eye, whose reputation might be damaged. Am I getting warm?'

'Oh all right,' Martina said sulkily, darting a look towards her husband. 'I can see you're not going to give up until you get the whole story. And it'll be better if you hear it from us. The truth is, he was planning to write an article about Amber's mental health issues.'

'We could hardly believe it when Eddie told us, but she'd actually seen the notes he'd been making.'

'Amber has been having problems for a long time,' Geoffrey explained. 'she started self-harming when she was only ten – although she managed to keep it secret from us for over two years – and she has periods of depression that sometimes mean that she can't even get herself out of bed in the morning.'

'We thought she was coming through it all,' Martina continued, 'but then last year she got bullied at school and it all started up again. I think that must have been what made Martin think of writing about it.'

'Eddie told us that he seemed to be planning to put a spin of "career mother's neglect causes daughter's depression" on it – which is so completely unfair on Marty,' Geoffrey added.

'Thank you. I can see how that would make your sister feel that she couldn't live with her husband any more. Now, before I go, can you think of anyone who might want to kill Martin Fellowes and Arthur Finch? Someone else who was in their firing line, for example?'

Martina and Geoffrey both shook their heads.

'In that case, I'll bid to goodbye. I can see myself out.'

Jonah found Edwina Clarkson busy clearing out items of her husband's clothing from their shared wardrobe in the Beaconsfield house where they had lived together – when Edwina was not needed in Brussels or Strasbourg and Martin could get away from the London flat. Once she knew that her sister had told him about the proposed article detailing her niece's mental health, she confirmed that this had been what had prompted her to sever her links with her husband. On being asked to suggest possible enemies who might have wanted to kill the two journalists, she shrugged her shoulders.

'I'm sure there must have been lots of people – practically everyone that they ever wrote about in that sordid little magazine of theirs – but the only specific people I could name are me and Martina, and, I'm sure you will have checked us out and discovered that we both have alibis for both murders.'

She spoke with a calm confidence that made Jonah realise that, despite her apparent lack of interest in the investigation of her husband's killing, she had taken some trouble to keep abreast of the case. There was nothing to be gained from prolonging the interview, so he made his excuses and left.

CHAPTER 16

Eva Riess parked her small car in the Worcester Street car park and got out. Bernie climbed out of the back and they all made their way to the path, which led between the Castle Mill Stream and the beginning of the Oxford Canal. They soon came in sight of the first of the canal boats moored a few feet to the right of the path.

'Which one are we going on?' Lucy demanded eagerly.

'She's called the *Maid of Saxony*,' Eva answered. 'It's just round the corner – there you are!' she added as Martin's boat came into view. See the gangplank on the side? That's so he can get a new gas cylinder on board, for the cooker. He told me it needed replacing.'

Lucy ran on ahead and was soon climbing the ramp. Bernie hurried after her, wondering what Martin Riess would make of having a small girl descending on him unannounced, and hoping to intercept her daughter before she had an opportunity to find out.

Lucy stepped down into the stern of the boat and found that she was looking into a narrow room with a bench seat at one side and a table in the middle. At the far end, she could see a door leading to another room. To her surprise, there was someone standing by the door, apparently intent on peeping in through a small crack to watch something in the room beyond. Lucy was not sure whether it was a man or a woman. The figure was taller than Bernie, but not as tall as Peter, and was dressed in trousers and a light waterproof coat. The strange thing was that, although it was not raining and in any case it was indoors, the hood was up, so that Lucy could not see the person's hair or face.

Lucy stood staring as this person raised its right hand, which Lucy now saw was gripping a large hammer, and sprang through the door, pushing it wide to reveal a small kitchen and a man crouched down near the cooker, intent on making adjustments to some controls beneath it. The hammer came crashing down on his head and Lucy saw blood appearing as it broke the skin on the back of his skull.

'Stop!' Lucy shouted at the top of her voice, leaping forward instinctively towards the hooded figure. 'Don't do that! Stop hitting him!'

The figure leapt up in surprise at the sound of Lucy's voice and glanced round to see who had entered. Lucy caught a glimpse of a woman's face, framed by a few strands of brownish hair, before the would-be murderer made her escape through a door at the other end of the kitchen. Lucy stepped forward and put her arms around the man who was now sitting hunched up on the floor with his head bowed.

'Don't worry,' she told him. 'My mam will be here soon and she'll know what to do.'

'And who might you be?' Martin asked, trying to focus his eyes on this unexpected apparition, while fighting off the feeling of light-headedness that threatened to render him unconscious.

'I'm Lucy Paige,' Lucy said in a matter-of-fact voice. 'We were coming to see you.'

Bernie entered the boat just in time to see Martin's assailant disappearing towards the front of the boat. She quickly took in the situation and decided to try to capture the runaway. Climbing nimbly up on to the roof of the boat, she ran along it hoping to reach the prow before her quarry. The woman was too quick for her, however, and Bernie reached the other end of the roof at the same moment that she climbed out of the prow of the boat on to the bank, hurling the hammer away into the canal as she did so. Bernie leapt from the roof in an attempt to bring her down, but the bank was slippery and her feet slid from under her, bringing her down in a muddy heap. She watched impotently as the hooded figure made off along the towpath at a trot.

'Are you all right?' Eva's voice reminded her that there was unfinished business to deal with aboard the boat.

Bernie looked up to see the German woman gazing anxiously down at her. She quickly got to her feet and led the way to the galley of the *Maid of Saxony* where she found Lucy helping Martin into a seat in the dining area.

'This is Martin,' Lucy told her. 'His head's bleeding.'

'So I see,' Bernie acknowledged, handing Lucy a handkerchief. 'Hold this on the wound and press down as hard as you can to stop the bleeding,' she ordered. 'I'm going to ring for the police and an ambulance.'

While Bernie made phone calls, Lucy settled herself next to Martin and pressed the folded handkerchief firmly down on his head.

'I told you my mam would know what to do,' she said complacently. 'Now this may hurt a bit, but I've got to press hard to stop the bleeding.'

Martin sat there feeling bemused. His head ached where something had hit him hard. Right after that, this strange little girl had appeared and had announced, as if it ought to tell him something, that her name was Lucy Paige. Her solicitude for his welfare included helping him on to the seat where he was now and examining the head wound meticulously, all the time murmuring reassuring words in his ear. Then another unexpected guest had arrived in the person of his colleague, Bernie Fazakerley, who appeared to be the little girl's mother. That, he realised, explained the name. This must be Richard Paige's posthumous daughter – and a very mature and capable young lady she appeared to be, considering that she must be only seven or eight years old. But then, Martin could not imagine Bernie being fazed by anything, however bizarre and unexpected, so presumably Lucy took after her in this respect.

'Well now, Lucy! It looks as if you ought to be a nurse when you grow up.'

Martin turned his head at the sound of his mother's voice. So she was here too – and apparently had come in the company of Bernie and her daughter. Why had she never mentioned that she had renewed her acquaintanceship with Richard's widow?'

'No. I don't want to be a nurse,' Lucy said seriously. 'I'm going to be a forensic pathologist.'

'There's no answer to that,' Martin observed, smiling to see his mother's surprise at this statement. 'So, Lucy Paige, what made you decide on pathology as a career?'

'I want to cut up dead people to find out what killed them.'

'Lucky for us,' Bernie joined in, putting away her mobile phone, 'you survived that attack or we'd have had Our Lucy wanting to assist with the post mortem, and I'm sure there are all sorts of rules and regulations that prevent seven-year-olds from dissecting human corpses.'

CHAPTER 17

Peter was about to start questioning Dave Gillis, the homeless man who had been seen on the towpath on the day of Fellowes' murder, when the call came through from Bernie to tell him about the attack on Martin Riess.

'I've phoned for police and ambulance,' she said, 'but I thought you'd want to be in on it too, with it being another attack like the ones you're looking into.'

'You're right, he agreed. 'I'll come straight over.'

He was about to end the call when a thought occurred to him.

'What about Lucy?' he asked. 'Where is she? Did you leave her with Stan and Sylvia?'

'No, she's here with us,' Bernie admitted. She had deliberately omitted to mention Lucy's involvement in the incident, knowing that Peter would worry at the idea that his precious stepdaughter had been exposed to the sight of a violent assault. 'She's enjoying herself hugely, playing nursemaid to poor Martin.'

'I'll be right over.' Peter ended the call and stood outside the interview room for a few moments, thinking. He would have liked to interview Gillis himself, but the business with Martin Riess might take some time and he could not justify holding him until the following day. He considered his options and decided to delegate the task to Rupert Andrews. It would be good experience, he decided, for Andrews to take the lead, instead of acting as Peter's assistant. Anna would probably have been a safer pair of hands, but Peter wanted her with him in case he needed someone he trusted to look after Lucy. He turned to Andy Lepage, who was waiting with him.

'Go on in and wait with them,' he instructed. 'Tell them someone will be along to interview Gillis in a few minutes.'

Then he headed for the incident room, instructed Andrews to take over the interrogation of Gillis and called to Anna to come with him.

'There's been another attack on the little green men,' he told her. 'This time it's Martin Riess who's the victim, but luckily they were interrupted and he's got away with a nasty bang on the head, so with any luck we'll get a description – or he may even be able to identify the perpetrator.'

Andy entered the interview room and saw a rather dishevelled man with grey hair wearing a long, rather dirty, gabardine raincoat of indeterminate dark colour. That must be Dave Gillis. Sitting next to him was a smartly-dressed man, whom Andy vaguely recognised. It must be the duty solicitor, who had been called in to advise the suspect. He was staring straight ahead and looked extremely bored. Andy introduced himself, trying to remember all the things that PC Hughes had told him about dealing with members of the homeless community in general and with Dave Gillis in particular.

'I'm sorry to keep you waiting,' he said to Gillis. 'DI Johns has been called away, but someone else will be here soon to talk to you.'

Gillis continued to stare down at the table in front of him and did not acknowledge that he had heard. Andy tried again.

'Would you like a cup of tea while you're waiting?' he ventured.

Gillis still did not respond. Andy sat down opposite him, trying to think of something else to say to engage his attention. He was relieved when Sergeant Andrews entered a few minutes later to start the interview.

Rupert Andrews was delighted to have been chosen to conduct this interview and was determined that it would produce results. He introduced himself and shook hands with the solicitor, who grudgingly confided the information that he was John Rudge of *Semple and Rudge*. Then he indicated to Andy that he should move into the seat opposite Rudge so that he could sit directly opposite Gillis.

Once both policemen were seated, Andrews began the interview by reminding Gillis that he was suspected of involvement in the murder of Mr Martin Fellowes and the theft of his wallet. Andy, who knew that Peter was convinced that Gillis had nothing to do with the murder, wondered at this aggressive approach, but said nothing. Although Gillis had already been cautioned, Andrews repeated the formula, so that there could be no doubt that his suspect had been made fully aware of his rights, before launching into a volley of questions.

'We know that you entered the narrowboat *Maid of Saxony* last Tuesday evening – why was that?'

'No comment,' Gillis muttered without looking up.

'Your fingerprints were found in the boat. What were you doing there?'

'No comment.'

'We have witnesses who saw you hurrying away from the scene shortly after Fellowes was killed. What were you doing there? Did you kill him when he found you rifling through his things?'

'They must've been wrong,' Gillis asserted, looking up briefly and then resuming his contemplation of the table. 'I weren't there.'

'You're lying. How do you account for your fingerprints being all over the inside of the boat?'

Gillis did not reply. After the effort of his previous response he seemed to have slipped back into a truculent trance. Andrews leant forward and spoke directly into his face.

'You went on board to steal, didn't you? You thought the boat was empty and, when you found it wasn't, you hit the man who tried to stop you. That's what happened isn't it? Isn't it?' he repeated, raising his voice.

'My client is entitled to remain silent,' the solicitor said coldly, appearing to take an interest in the proceedings for the first time.

Andrews paused to collect his thoughts and Andy took advantage of the lull to try a different approach. He knew that Peter was convinced that the rough sleeper had nothing to do with the murder. Hughes had advised him not to intimidate Gillis, who mistrusted the police and was unlikely to co-operate if he felt threatened. Andy tried to reassure him.

'Mr Gillis,' he began, 'DI Johns told me that he knows you didn't kill anyone.'

Andrews gave Andy an angry look and opened his mouth to intervene, but changed his mind and allowed him to continue.

'He thinks that you found Mr Fellowes after he was already dead and ran away because you were afraid that people would think it was your fault.'

Gillis said nothing, but raised his head a little and gave a furtive look towards Andy, as if trying to decide whether this was some sort of trick.

'Maybe you saw him lying there and thought he'd had an accident and went to see if you could do anything to help him.' Andy suggested. 'Is that how your fingerprints got on the table where he was lying?'

'Yes.' Gillis nodded, looking up properly for the first time. 'I touched him and he was dead. I knew if you found me there you'd say I done it, so I got out.'

'What time was that?' Andrews asked quickly.

'Dunno,' Gillis shrugged, visibly tensing at his voice.

'You must know about what time it was,' Andrews insisted. 'Was it early evening or later? Had you had dinner?'

'Dinner?' Gillis laughed very briefly at the word. Andy wondered whether this was because he associated it with a midday meal or because he rarely got the opportunity to eat anything sufficiently substantial as to be given this grand name. Seizing another lull in Andrews' interrogation, he asked another question in what he hoped was a sympathetic tone.

'Can you remember whether it was dark?'

'It wasn't dark outside,' Gillis answered, looking Andy in the eye. Andy smiled back and nodded encouragement. 'But it was dark in the boat. I never saw him until I put the light on.'

'So you did go in, thinking the boat was empty!' Andrews exclaimed triumphantly. 'What was it you were after? Anything you could lay your hands on, I suppose?'

Andy managed, with difficulty, to keep his temper and maintain an impassive expression on his face, as he saw Gillis slump down in his seat and return to staring at the table. He was convinced that this was not the way in which Peter would have conducted the interview and equally convinced that Peter's less confrontational approach would have been more productive. He looked towards Rudge hoping that he might intervene, but the solicitor, having made one contribution on behalf of his client, appeared now to consider his job done and to have fallen asleep once more.

'I didn't take nothing,' Gillis mumbled without looking up.

'His wallet and credit cards were missing,' Andrews pointed out remorselessly. 'You're not trying to tell me that's just a coincidence, are you? You thought the boat was empty and went in to take whatever you could find, and then you either killed Fellowes and took his wallet or-'

'Mr Gillis,' Andy interrupted rashly, knowing that it was out of order for a trainee to interrupt a sergeant in the course of interviewing a suspect, but unable to contain his rising frustration. 'We aren't interested in who took the wallet.'

Andrews was so taken aback by this intervention that for a moment he was unable to speak, giving Andy the opportunity to continue.

'We'll probably never know what happened to it; but we really do need to find out who killed the man that you saw on the boat, and you are a key witness. It would help us a lot if you could tell us exactly what you saw. Can you remember anything – anything at all?'

For a moment there was silence. Andrews was still struggling to think of a way of reprimanding his junior colleague without showing him up in front of the solicitor. Andy could feel his heart beating against his chest as he waited, hoping that Gillis would respond and realising that he had overstepped the mark and would probably be disciplined once the interview was over. Gillis slowly raised his head and looked at him.

'There was this bird,' he said slowly. 'Come off of the boat.'

Everyone waited without speaking, as he seemed to be gathering his thoughts before continuing.

'The light went off on the boat and then I saw her get out on the bank. Then I got in and I couldn't see nothing 'cos it was dark. But there was a light switch by the door, so I put it on and then I saw him.'

'And you went over to see what was wrong,' Andy prompted.

'That's right,' Gillis agreed gratefully. 'But I could tell he was dead – when I got up to him, like.'

He looked round at Andy and Andrews and then at the solicitor, as if sizing them up. Then he took a breath and went on.

'He was dead, so he didn't need money any more, did he?' he said defensively. 'I felt in his pockets and found the wallet. I admit I took that, but I never laid a hand on him. He was dead when I found him, like I said before.'

'We believe you, Dave,' Andy assured him.

'Tell us about the woman,' Andrews urged, trying to follow Andy's lead in avoiding accusations, now that he could see that they only antagonised the witness. 'What did she look like?'

'Dunno. I wasn't looking.'

'It might help us a lot if you could remember,' Andy suggested. 'Did you see which way she went?'

'Back towards the road.'

'You mean Worcester Street?'

'Yeah. I suppose.'

'And which way were *you* going?'

'I come from there. I was going home.'

'Home?' queried Andrews.

'Under the canal bridge at Aristotle Lane,' Andy explained, remembering that Gavin Hughes had told him that this was Gillis' preferred sleeping place.

'So you must have passed one another,' Andrews said, with a small note of triumph in his voice. 'Surely you can remember something about the woman. Was she tall or short? How old was she? What colour was her hair? What was she wearing?'

'I told you, I don't remember,' Gillis answered sulkily.

'Don't worry,' Andy said reassuringly. 'I know it's hard, but if you can think of anything at all, it might help us to catch someone who's killed two people – maybe three,' he added, remembering Bernie's recent telephone call, from which he had not been able to be sure how serious the injuries to Martin Riess had been.

'She had red hair,' Gillis muttered eventually. 'But that's all I can remember,' he added defiantly.

'Go and get that photo of Mrs Plant,' Andrews said

excitedly to Andy, who obediently went and fetched a picture of Martina, looking even more glamorous than she had done in real life. Andrews took it and put it on the table in front of Gillis.

'Was it this woman?' he asked.

'Dunno. The hair's right.'

'So it could have been her that you saw?'

'Yeah. I suppose.'

Andrews decided that the interview had achieved as much as they could have hoped for and decided to bring it to an end. He told Gillis that they had no further questions at that stage, but that DI Johns might want to talk to him when he got back. At that point, Rudge roused himself from his stupor sufficiently to demand that his client be permitted to leave, but when Andrews declined the request he made no further protestations as Gillis was led away to the cells.

When they were alone together, Andrews and Lepage looked at one another. Andy wondered whether he ought to apologise for having interrupted Andrews' interview. He was still searching for the right words when Andrews spoke.

'Well done!' he said, as heartily as he could manage. He was smarting from the mortification of discovering that a trainee detective had been more adept at questioning a key witness than he had been himself, but he recognised that, without Andy's help he might well have had nothing to show for his efforts and might even have been responsible for preventing this important evidence from coming to light. He was also well aware that DI Johns had a soft spot for this particular trainee and it would not do his own reputation with his boss any harm to show magnanimity towards him. 'How did you know how to get Gillis to talk?'

'I've had Gavin Hughes taking me round the homeless hostels,' Andy explained. 'He told me that if they think you're accusing them of something they just clam up. He said you've got to try to stop them seeing you as a threat. I hope I did the right thing,' he added, apologetically, 'giving him the impression that we won't prosecute him for stealing the wallet.'

'I wouldn't worry about that. Old Peter won't want to pursue that, so unless Fellowes' wife kicks up a fuss, I reckon he'll drop it. The main thing is: we probably know who the murderer is now.'

CHAPTER 18

Peter and Anna hurried along the path towards the *Maid of Saxony*. Anna had to run to keep up with her colleague who was striding out with his long legs in an uncharacteristic burst of energy. When they arrived at the boat, she saw Bernie waiting for them and realised what had prompted his haste. He would want to reassure himself that his wife was safe and to pack her off home out of harm's way as soon as possible.

Two uniformed officers were engaged in cordoning off the crime scene with tape. Peter nodded a greeting and instructed them to carry on. Then he climbed into the boat and peered into the small room at the back where Martin Riess was sitting. Lucy was still kneeling on the bench pressing the handkerchief against his head, while Eva Riess was sitting opposite them on small seat that flapped down from the wall.

'Daddy!' Lucy exclaimed as Peter's head appeared round the door. 'Mam said you were coming. This is Martin. Someone hit him with a hammer, so I'm looking after him.'

'So I see,' Peter agreed, smiling at her and feeling thankful that she did not appear traumatised by what she had witnessed. 'You're doing a great job there, but now it's time for you to go home.'

'But I'm looking after Martin,' Lucy protested. 'Mam told me to hold this on his head to stop the blood.'

'That's all right,' Peter said gently. 'I'll take over now, and the ambulance will be along any minute.'

'But *I* want to do it,' Lucy insisted. 'Why do I have to go?'

'Come on Lucy, love,' Bernie intervened. 'It's time for us to go now. We'll only be in the way when the SOCOs arrive. It's a nuisance to the police to have a load of civilians milling around when they're trying to work. And don't worry about Martin. Peter will see he's OK.'

Lucy pulled a face, but reluctantly consented to hand over the handkerchief to her stepfather, emphasising as she did so the importance of pressing hard on the wound to staunch the blood. Peter nodded and promised to do his best.

'I'll drive you back,' Eva offered, remembering that Bernie and Lucy had no transport.

'Thank you, Mrs Riess,' Peter said. 'And then, please could you stay at our place? I'll need to speak to you all later.'

They set off along the path, leaving Peter and Martin eyeing one another. Anna stood on the bank, watching for the arrival of the ambulance and wondering to herself how her own daughter, Jessica, who was just one year younger than Lucy, would have coped if faced with this situation. She could not imagine her taking it all in her stride in the way that the self-assured Lucy appeared to have done.

'Daddy!' Martin exclaimed eventually, giving Peter a look of exaggerated disgust. 'And you told me that you *believed* that Richard Paige's widow had married again!'

'Yes, I do,' Peter answered, smiling broadly.' And as you can see, I had very good grounds for that belief.'

'But you let me go on and on,' Martin groaned. 'And then I suppose you told Bernie everything that I said about

180

her?'

'Maybe I did,' Peter said with a shrug. 'Would you like me to tell you what she said about you?'

'If it won't be too damaging to my self-esteem,' Martin answered guardedly.

'Well, to begin with she was reluctant to give much away,' Peter began, enjoying this opportunity of teasing the little don. 'But she revealed that you always choose coffee in preference to tea and you drink it black with a ridiculous amount of sugar.'

He caught Martin's eye and they exchanged grins.

'Pretty damning stuff,' Martin observed, deadpan.

'That's what I thought,' Peter agreed. 'She went on to tell me that, when you're getting bored with some of the old fogeys on that committee that you both go to, you keep your head down and pretend to be very busy reading the meeting papers so no one will know what you're really thinking. She said you're a valuable ally in her quest to bring the university kicking and screaming into the twentieth century.'

'That's very generous of her.'

'When I pressed her, she wouldn't commit herself as to whether or not you were capable of murder, but she begged me, if it turned out that you were guilty, to put off arresting you until after the next meeting of your precious committee because she's banking on you to get some motion or other passed.'

'A kind thought.'

'Finally, she told me that she wished she could find a way of telling you who she was and getting to know you properly, but she could never find the right time to introduce the subject and she was afraid to talk about you and Richard and your escape from East Germany in case it opened up old wounds that you were trying to forget about. In fact,' Peter concluded, looking Martin full in the face, 'if you could both stop pussy-footing around worrying about treading on each other's sensitivities and start talking to one another you'd get on like a house on fire.'

For a moment, there was silence as Martin took in this long speech. Then a smile flashed briefly across his face and disappeared as quickly as it had come.

'It's all very well you saying that,' he muttered in a grumbling voice, 'when it's too late for me because you've already stepped in and snatched her away from under my very nose!'

'If it makes you feel any better,' Peter said kindly, 'you'd never have had a chance even if you had managed to screw up courage to speak to her earlier.'

'Is that so?' Martin demanded, putting on a mock aggressive tone. 'Who says so?'

'I do. I know for a fact that there's only one person in the whole world that Bernie would ever have considered marrying after Richard died.'

'And that's you? How do you make that out?'

'Because I'm the only person who satisfies two essential criteria.'

'And they are?'

'First off, my late wife was Bernie's best friend, and Bernie considers that she owes it to Angie to look after me and see that I don't take to drink or stop eating properly or go off the rails in any other way, now that I haven't got her to keep me in order. And secondly, I'm Lucy's godfather and her very favourite person and hence the only acceptable daddy for Richard's daughter.'

'I reckon I'm not doing too badly as far as ingratiating myself with Lucy is concerned,' observed Martin.

'Maybe, but in the helpless-widower stakes you are absolutely nowhere.'

'I could make myself into a helpless bachelor,' Martin suggested optimistically.

'It's not the same thing at all,' Peter said scathingly. 'If a bachelor can't look after himself then he's just a useless tosser; if a widower can't look after himself it's because he's been used to relying on the more intelligent, competent and all-round more capable half of a partnership in which he naturally played a very secondary role, and so he is deserving of every woman's pity.'

'So you're saying all those hours I spent trying to pluck up courage to ask Bernie out were wasted?'

'I'm saying that you never had a hope in hell of getting her to marry you, if that's what you were after,' Peter agreed. Then he paused for a moment before adding, 'so you'll just have to make do with an extra-marital affair, won't you?'

Martin stared at Peter in disbelief. Then a smile slowly crept across his face and he laughed out loud.

'Inspector Johns!' he said at last. 'You must be one of the luckiest men alive!'

'Why's that?'

'To be so sure of your wife's fidelity that you can make an outrageous suggestion like that.'

They sat looking at each other for a minute, enjoying the joke.

'Mind you,' Martin said mischievously, 'now that you've thrown down the gauntlet like that, you do realise that I feel honour-bound to take up the challenge.'

'Do your worst,' Peter said, continuing to smile broadly. 'I will watch your progress with interest. And now,' he added, turning towards the green-suited paramedic who had just climbed aboard the boat, 'I think this is your escort to take you to the hospital.'

'Are you sure that's necessary?' Martin protested. 'It's only a bang on the head and the bleeding's stopped now. I'll be alright without hospital treatment.'

'Now listen here,' Peter said in a low voice, taking Martin's arm and helping the paramedic to assist him out on to the bank. 'When I get home, I'm going to have to face three women, all of whom will want to know, before anything else, how you are. If I can't assure them that you have received the best possible medical treatment and are following the doctor's orders to the letter, my life won't be worth living. So you are going in this ambulance to the hospital, where you will submit to all the scans and tests and what-have-you and generally behave like a model patient. Do you understand?'

'Yes, officer,' Martin said meekly, allowing himself to be led away between two of the ambulance crew.

Peter went with Martin to the hospital, leaving Anna to supervise the forensic examination of the crime scene and the search beneath the water of the canal for the discarded hammer. Pathologist Mike Carson greeted them on arrival, having been summoned by Peter to view Martin's head wound before the emergency staff stitched it up. He gave the opinion that it could well have been caused by a hammer of the same design as the one used in the other attacks.

Peter put off informing Jonah about the third hammer attack for as long as he dared, which was that evening, after Lucy had reluctantly gone to bed. He squared this delay with his conscience by telling himself that there was no point in alerting Jonah to the development until he had completed the initial local investigation of the incident and could give him a full account of what had taken place. In reality, his motive was to reduce the likelihood of Jonah descending on them in his usual energetic manner and insisting on interviewing the witnesses in person. In particular, Peter was determined to shield Lucy from being subjected to the kind of questioning that he remembered his colleague using when he was an overenthusiastic Detective Sergeant carried away by the thrill of the chase.

Most of the afternoon was taken up at the hospital with Martin Riess, who had his head stitched and his brain scanned, coming away at last with instructions to take it easy and to come straight back if he experienced blackouts, double-vision or any one of a number of other symptoms that might indicate brain injury. Peter escorted him home, reiterating the doctor's instructions before turning to leave.

Martin called him back.

'I just wanted to ask,' he said diffidently. 'I'd like to thank Lucy for saving my life – and for looking after me,' he added seeing Peter's raised eyebrows at the suggestion that Lucy's intervention had prevented Martin's assailant from completing her murderous intentions. 'I was wondering … would it be OK for me to call round to your house one evening, to thank her in person?'

'I'd say that you should consider that duty compulsory,' Peter answered. 'I hope you realise that the only thing that is going to convince her that you are really safe and sound is for her to examine you for herself? Moreover, if she harbours any suspicions that you may not be in the robustest of health following this little incident, I am the one who will get the blame. So I will expect you at six-thirty prompt tomorrow, to pay your respects.'

Peter's next call was at his own home. He told himself that he needed to speak to the eye-witnesses at the earliest opportunity, but in reality his main concern was to assure himself that Lucy had not been adversely affected by her experience. He need not have worried. She was still excited at having been part of such a dramatic event and eager to hear how her patient was doing. Peter assured her that Martin Riess had come to no serious harm and then shooed her into the kitchen with Bernie while he questioned Eva. He was conscious that he must find out whether she could have been the killer of Fellowes and Finch. Even though it now looked as if the murderer had designs on her son as well, it was premature to assume that the same person had carried out all three attacks.

It did not take long to establish that Eva had no alibi for either murder. She had spent Tuesday evening at home alone, after Martin had left for his dinner engagement. On Wednesday, she had also been at home. She could provide Peter with the names of her piano pupils whose lessons covered two hours in the morning and three in the evening, but there was nobody to vouch for her during the crucial period from noon until four in the afternoon. She took his questioning calmly, with no hint of resentment at having her movements investigated. Her only anxiety appeared to be for the well-being of her son. Peter reflected that Martin's concern to protect his mother from any involvement in the case was unnecessary and his assertion that she might be nervous of speaking to the police was unfounded. She was clearly a strong character – stronger, perhaps, than her son.

It was not difficult for Peter to prolong the conclusion of the initial investigation until the end of the working day. By the time Eva had been safely despatched home and he had been back to the incident room to bring the rest of the team up to speed on this third attack and listened to Andrews' account of the interview with Gillis, it was already later than his usual departure time. He decided go home and have tea with Bernie and Lucy and then ring Jonah after Lucy was safely in bed and unable to insist on contributing to the conversation.

As Peter knew he would be, Jonah was excited to hear about this latest attack and keen to get involved.

'It's certainly beginning to look as if someone has got it in for our extra-terrestrial friends,' he observed eagerly. 'And that's one up to you,' he added generously, remembering that Peter had said from the start that the Martian link was significant. 'And this time the victim survived. Was he able to identify his attacker?'

'Unfortunately, no,' Peter said ruefully. 'He didn't see anything. The first he knew was a blow on the head, which knocked him off balance. By the time he was in any position to notice anything, the attacker had made a run for it.'

'Didn't he even get a feel for whether it was a man or a woman?' Jonah sounded disappointed.

'No, but we do have a witness who got a glimpse of her face,' Peter admitted reluctantly.

'Excellent! So it was a woman, was it?' Jonah burst in,

excitedly. 'What did they say about her? Did they recognise her?'

'Yes, it was a woman. And, no, they didn't recognise her.'

'And who was this witness?' Jonah asked, detecting Peter's reluctance to tell him the whole story.

'It was Lucy.'

There was silence for a moment. Then Jonah spoke.

'Lucy? You mean your Lucy – Lucy Paige?'

'That's right. Eva Riess asked Bernie to speak to Martin about being more co-operative with the police – it turns out they used to be friends, way back in the mists of time – and she and Lucy came to visit him on his boat.'

'And Lucy saw this woman, whoever she was, attacking Martin Riess?' Jonah exclaimed, a tone of alarm entering his voice. 'What happened? Is Lucy all right?'

'At the moment she's just very excited at having frightened the woman away and very pleased with herself for taking care of Martin afterwards. I don't know how it will pan out later, though, when she realises what it was that she saw and how serious it could have been.'

'You say Bernie was there too,' Jonah resumed, getting back to the business of the police case. 'Did she see the woman's face? Have you tried showing her any of our suspects?'

'No. Bernie says she only saw her from behind. She agrees with Lucy that it was a woman, but she can't tell us anything about what she looked like. Eva Riess says the same. She was the last on the scene and she saw even less than Bernie.'

'So Lucy is our only real witness?'

'More or less.'

'And what has she been able to tell you? Did she describe the woman? Does it sound like anyone we've got in the frame?'

'I haven't interviewed her yet,' Peter said, trying to quell the rising irritation that he was feeling at Jonah's eagerness to press forward with what he saw as a considerable ordeal for his beloved stepdaughter. 'I don't want to push her too hard.'

'It might be better if … someone else were to interview her,' Jonah suggested, realising in time that his colleague might well resent any proposal that Jonah himself might perform this duty, 'to avoid any suggestion of a conflict of interest.'

'I've already arranged that,' Peter told him. 'Sergeant Davenport is going to conduct the interview and Bernie is going to be there as the appropriate adult.'

'Good idea,' Jonah said warmly, knowing how much it must have cost Peter to give up the opportunity to be the one putting potentially difficult questions to the little girl of whom he was so fond.'

'I'll just be an observer,' Peter added. 'So I can stop the interview if it's too much for Lucy.'

'I rather fancy Our Bernie would have no difficulty doing that,' Jonah observed drily.

'You're probably right, but I'll feel more comfortable if I'm there.'

'Just so long as it doesn't look as if anything Lucy says is just to please you,' Jonah cautioned. 'If she does manage to identify our killer, we want her evidence to stand up in-'

'There's no way I'm letting Lucy into the witness box,' Peter interrupted. 'You know as well as I do that, however compelling her evidence is, any decent defence counsel will run rings around the jury and convince them that she's too young for what she says to be trusted. I'm not having her put through cross-examination by some clever dick lawyer who doesn't care about anything apart from winning his case.'

'OK, OK. Keep your hair on. Who said anything about putting Lucy in the witness box?'

'You just said … Well, anyway, as you well know, if Lucy does manage to identify the woman she saw, we'll still have it all to do to prove that she's really picked out the perpetrator. Unless we can find some other convincing evidence, there won't be any point charging anyone – and then, if we've got the evidence, there won't be any need for Lucy to be called as a witness.'

'Right,' Jonah agreed, wishing privately that Peter would relax and stop worrying about Lucy for long enough to make the most of whatever evidence she could give them. 'So the main thing is to find out how much she saw and then take it from there. Will you be recording the interview?'

'Yes. It will be exactly by the book,' Peter assured him. 'I suggested to Bernie that we might do it at home, but she thinks Lucy will be disappointed not to come down to the station to be questioned in a proper interview room. She's probably right, so that's what I've arranged.'

'Right you are. Let me know how it goes. Now I have some news for you,' Jonah said, ending the discussion. He went on to tell Peter about Fellowes' plan to write an article exposing Amber Plant's mental health problems and the clear resentment felt by Geoffrey Plant and both the Clarkson sisters. 'Any of them have a clear motive for wanting to do away with Finch and Fellowes,' he concluded.

'But not Riess,' Peter commented.

'Unless they held him responsible in some way,' Jonah suggested. 'Because he put Fellowes up, for example. Or maybe they were afraid that Fellowes had confided in him and he might decide to publish the article posthumously on his behalf. Or even,' Jonah paused to think for a moment. 'Riess could even have tried to blackmail them by threatening to publish.'

'That doesn't fit in with what I've seen of Riess,' Peter objected. 'But I suppose they may not have known that he wouldn't publish, and decided to make sure that he couldn't. Are you suggesting that it may have been a conspiracy between the three of them? If so, it's going to be difficult to prove anything because they all have alibis for at least one of the attacks.'

'Yes, well let's just wait and see what young Lucy can tell us tomorrow, shall we?'

CHAPTER 19

Lucy was excited to be going to the police station for her interview. This was far more fun than school! She had been to Peter's place of work before, but only to wait in reception, chatting to the desk sergeant. Now she would be going behind the scenes to see what a real police interview room looked like. And she was going to be interviewed by a real police sergeant, just like on the television detective shows. Lucy had never met Anna, but Peter had assured her that she was one of his best officers and Lucy was prepared to be impressed.

She was disappointed to hear that her mother would be there as well. That was not how it happened on the TV, but she grudgingly accepted Peter's explanation that he would be in serious trouble if he allowed a minor to be interviewed without a parent present.

'You'll be there,' she pointed out,' so why does Mam have to come too?'

'But I'm the police officer in charge of the case,' Peter explained patiently. 'So I might be tempted to put the interests of the investigation ahead of what's best for you. Your mam will only be thinking about your welfare.'

'What if you were both in the police?' Lucy wanted to

know.

'Then I suppose we'd have to get a social worker to sit in to safeguard your interests,' Peter answered, wishing, not for the first time, that Lucy had a less enquiring and logical mind. 'Now, come and meet Anna.'

'You mean, Detective Sergeant Davenport?'

'Yes, that's right. She's going to ask the questions. I'll just be watching.'

Anna led Lucy into the interview room and helped her on to a seat. Then she sat down on the other side of the table and Peter took his place beside her. Bernie sat down next to Lucy.

'Now, Lucy,' Anna began, 'I'm going to ask you some questions and I want you to answer as well as you can. If there's anything you don't remember, just say so. Do you understand?'

'Yes,' Lucy nodded, 'but aren't you going to start the tape? I thought you were supposed to record everything.'

'It's OK to wait until after I've explained about what's going to happen,' Anna told her. 'But if it makes you feel happier, let's start it now.'

She pressed the record button and recorded the standard message detailing who was present. Lucy watched intently, taking it all in and checking it in her mind against scenes from television dramas that she had watched.

'Now, Lucy,' Anna began, speaking softly in what she hoped was kindly manner. She was well-aware that her boss would not forgive her if she were to upset this particular witness. 'Can you tell me what you saw yesterday, starting from when you went on board Dr Riess's boat?'

Lucy, who had been rehearsing what she was going to say, in her own mind, ever since bedtime the night before, took a deep breath and began.

'I got down into the room at the back and I saw someone standing there, looking through a little gap in the door into the next room. She didn't see me because she was looking the other way. I thought it was funny because she had her hood up even though it wasn't raining.'

'Hang on a minute,' Anna interrupted gently. 'You said she. Does that mean it was a lady you saw?'

'I wasn't sure *then*,' Lucy said emphatically, 'but afterwards, when she looked round and I saw her face, I knew it was a *woman*.' She pronounced the word *woman* in a tone that somehow suggested that *lady* was not a term that she permitted in her own vocabulary.

'I see. I'm sorry. Please go on with your story. What happened next?'

'She was holding a hammer in her hand,' Lucy resumed, 'but I didn't notice that at first. Then she suddenly pushed open the door and I saw Martin crouching down on the floor. The woman hit him on his head with the hammer and he fell down. I shouted at her to stop and she looked round. That's when I saw her face. Then she ran away and I went to look after Martin.'

'Thank you, Lucy, that's all very nice and clear. Now, can you tell me what the la- woman's face looked like?'

'Not very well,' Lucy admitted. 'She still had her hood up and she ran away as soon as she saw me.'

'That's all right,' Anna said, try to sound reassuring. 'Just tell me as much as you can.'

'She had red lipstick on,' Lucy said, after a long pause, 'and her hair was a sort of brown colour. I … I don't really remember any more than that.'

'That's OK. You're doing fine. Now, I'm going to show you some pictures and I want you to tell me if any of them look like the person you saw. Is that all right?'

'Yes,' Lucy nodded eagerly.

Anna got out a collection of a dozen photographs, among which were the Clarkson twins, Samantha Fraser, Coralie Finch and Olivia Best. The others were photographs of some of her female colleagues, which Peter had insisted that she include, in order that any positive identification by Lucy of one of the suspects would be more convincing. She spread them out on the table. Lucy looked at each one intently.

'It definitely wasn't this one,' she said at last, pointing at Olivia's picture. 'She was much older. And these two have got the wrong colour hair,' she added, removing two of the pictures of police officers from the array and continuing to study the remaining photographs.

'This one has the wrong hair too,' Lucy declared a few moments later, handing Martina Clarkson's picture to Anna. 'It's too long and the wrong colour. The woman I saw had a fringe – like these,' she added selecting Samantha Fraser, Coralie Finch and one of the policewomen, and pushing all the other pictures away.

Anna hesitated, wondering whether to say anything. It was interesting that Lucy had managed to choose two of their suspects from among the photographs, but it might just be chance that they were closest to what she remembered of the woman in the boat. She did not want to precipitate a false identification by encouraging Lucy to select one of the three.

'I don't think it was this one,' Lucy went on, continuing to study the remaining photographs intently. 'Her nose is too big. But it might be one of these.'

Anna and Peter looked down at the last two photographs lying in front of Lucy. She had selected Samantha and Coralie.

'Thank you Lucy,' Anna said warmly.' You've been a big help.'

'But I'm not sure,' Lucy added anxiously, remembering that Bernie had given her clear instructions to own up if she could not remember anything that she was asked about. 'I didn't see her very well.'

'That's all right,' Peter assured her, speaking for the first time. 'You've still been very useful. Look at all the people that we've been able to rule out, thanks to you,' he added, pointing to the pile of discarded photographs.

Lucy smiled broadly at these words of praise.

'And now,' Peter went on, 'I think that will do. Sergeant Davenport, stop the tape and we'll all go and get a cup of tea.'

It took some time to extricate Lucy from the police station and send her on her way to join her classmates in school. Word had got around amongst the officers and civilian staff that DI Johns' little stepdaughter had foiled a murder attempt and was now a key witness in the case. Everyone was keen to make a fuss of her and do something to make her visit there a treat to remember. Peter's idea of a quiet cup of tea for the four of them in his office quickly had to be abandoned.

Eileen Brookes, the Chief Superintendent's secretary, had been out and bought a cake, and one of the police constables provided Coca Cola as being more likely to appeal to a seven-year-old than tea or coffee. (Lucy, who had been drinking tea almost from birth, seemed about to insist on having the same as the grownups, but a meaningful glance from her mother prompted her to accept the offer without fuss.) Then the custody sergeant took her on a tour of the cells, which she seemed to find very interesting. She was less impressed by the records clerk's attempt at showing off a room full of filing cabinets and document storage boxes, asking in a scornful voice why they did not store everything on a computer.

'It looks as if Lucy is well on the way to following in her father's footsteps,' Eileen observed to Peter, as she watched Lucy frowning in concentration as she studied images of fingerprints on a computer screen, assisted by Sergeant Andrews and watched closely by her mother.

'Yes,' Monica Philipson agreed. 'She looks just like you. She's got the same expression you have when you're thinking hard about a case.'

There was a moment's silence while Peter and Eileen tried to think of a way of pointing out that any physical resemblance between Peter and his stepdaughter was purely coincidental and that the father, to whom Eileen had been referring was a different man altogether.

'Lucy's dad was my boss for a long time,' Peter said at last. 'It's not surprising if I've picked up some of his habits.'

It was strange, he reflected, how often people seemed to see a family likeness between himself and Lucy when they saw them together. This was in contrast to the reaction that people usually had as far as his own two children were concerned. Peter could not remember anyone ever having suggested that either of them took after their father. Everyone subconsciously compared the frizzy afro hair and dark skin with Peter's thick red thatch and pale complexion and became oblivious to any of the less obvious facial characteristics.

'I'm sorry,' Monica said in some confusion. 'I thought ... I mean ... I hadn't realised ...'

'Lucy's father was Detective Superintendent Richard Paige,' Eileen explained. 'He was accidentally killed while he was on duty seven and a half years ago.'

'Before your time,' Peter added, waving aside Monica's apology. 'So it's no wonder you didn't know about it.'

'She looks as pretty as a picture, anyway,' said Sergeant Underhill, a middle-aged uniformed officer with two granddaughters who aspired to be Disney Princesses, 'wherever she gets it from.'

Peter ignored the observation and hoped that Bernie had not heard it or else would resist the temptation to speak her mind on the subject. Such a remark would be sure to win Underhill her lasting disapprobation. He wondered how much of Lucy's ability to win the heart of practically every adult that she met was down to her gently curling golden hair and cornflower blue eyes. He had never brought his daughter, Hannah, to work with him, but he could not picture her attracting as much attention and admiration. True, on the rare occasions when she consented to allow her mother to plait her hair in intricate patterns across her head, people had often commented on how attractive it looked, but he could not imagine anyone being much impressed by her more normal unrestrained mop of black curls.

'Of course, you have mathematicians to thank for these fingerprint pictures,' Bernie said to Lucy, raising her voice enough for it to attract the attention of a wider audience and so distract Monica from her embarrassment and to draw attention away from Underhill's poorly-judged comment. 'They invented the wavelet transformations that are used to compress the images so that they can be stored on a computer.'

'How?' demanded Lucy, in her usual direct way.

'Digital images – like those you're looking at now – are stored as an array of numbers that tell you what colour each bit of the picture has to be. That takes up a lot of space in the computer, so if you've got a lot of pictures to store you need a lot of storage space. Mathematicians have invented a way of reducing the amount of storage space by taking advantage of the fact that most real-life images have areas where the colours don't change much.'

'Is that what you do?' Lucy asked, as if wondering for the first time whether her mother's work might be almost as interesting as her stepfather's.

'I've done some work in image processing, but not with fingerprints,' Bernie admitted. 'And it was a woman in America, called Ingrid Daubechies, who invented the wavelet transforms that are used to compress these sorts of pictures. The thing about maths is that we just work out the theory behind things and then leave someone else to use it in practical situations. I was just making the point that, behind almost every scientific advance, there's some mathematics that it all depends on.'

'I think being a policeman is more interesting,' Lucy said, turning back to Rupert Andrews. 'Now will you show me the hammer that the woman hit Martin with?'

'I'm not sure if I ought to have promised to do that,' Andrews answered, conscious that he was being observed by his commanding officer and the Chief Superintendent's secretary.

'It's all right,' Peter told him. 'We'll stretch a point, just this once.'

Eventually, Bernie insisted that Lucy had lost enough school time for one day and that they must go away and leave the police to do their jobs. Lucy shook hands solemnly with her new friends. Then she suddenly seemed to remember her fears for her stepfather's safety and gave Peter a long hug before finally allowing her mother to lead her away. Peter turned to Anna.

'We'd better have another word with Dr Fraser,' he said. 'See if you can find out where she is and make an appointment for us to call on her, while I give DCI Porter an update. I imagine he'll want to be the one who tackles Mrs Finch.'

Anna turned to go, but Peter called her back.

'One more thing,' he said. 'Can you remember whether Samantha Fraser was wearing red lipstick when we interviewed her yesterday?'

'She wasn't,' Anna answered promptly. 'She had peach lip-gloss on.'

'And there's a difference between lipstick and lip-gloss?'

'Yes. Lipstick stays on better, but lip-gloss gives a nicer sheen. It's more liquid you see, so you have to keep applying it during the day.'

'And what about on Saturday?'

'Peach lip-gloss again.'

Jonah appeared to be very pleased with the way the interview with Lucy had gone and expressed satisfaction both with the way that Anna had conducted it and with the final result.

'It looks as if we may be narrowing down our suspects very nicely,' he observed. 'After all, it must be more than coincidence that Lucy managed to pick two of our five suspects out of a line-up of twelve.'

'That's what I said to Bernie,' Peter told him,' and she says there's a fifteen percent chance that it could have happened by chance.'

'That's well below evens,' Jonah pointed out. 'And, in fact, she's done better than that, because she's picked the two most likely out of the five. Olivia was always an outsider and the Clarkson twins were both speaking to me in locations well away from the crime scene only a short time before Riess was attacked. In fact, I may well have actually been speaking to Edwina when it happened.'

'According to Bernie, there's a one in sixty-six chance that Lucy could have picked Coralie and Samantha completely at random.'

'That sounds pretty good odds to me – certainly good enough to give us an excuse to ask them to explain their whereabouts yesterday morning.'

'Dr Fraser was in the labs with me until about ten forty-five. I suppose something that we said to her might have precipitated the attack – if she suddenly started thinking that Martin Riess was partly responsible for the article about her husband.'

'Right,' Jonah said decisively. 'You speak to her and I'll deal with Coralie Finch. She never got back to me yesterday, so she shouldn't be surprised to find me chasing her. She's the one my money's on at the moment.'

'What motive does she have for killing Fellowes and Finch?' asked Peter. 'I agree that she's the one with the best opportunity for attacking Riess, but why would she want to harm either of the others?'

'You're the one who said it was likely to be all about this Martian business. Maybe she's been harbouring some deep resentment dating right back to their Cambridge days – something to do with wanting Fellowes and only managing to get Finch. Anyway, she can tell me all about it – if I can manage to track her down this time!'

All right. You tackle Coralie and we'll take care of Samantha. Anna's checking out where she is right now.

Oh! And Andy Lepage has found out that James Pickering was in a seminar when Finch was killed, so he's out of the frame for that one at least.'

'Has he checked properly?' Jonah asked a little sceptically. 'Just because a student is *supposed* to be in a seminar, it doesn't necessarily mean that he *was* there.'

'He was one of the ones giving a presentation,' Peter assured him. 'So there isn't any doubt that he was there – and we've got confirmation from the lecturer in charge and written evidence in the form of copies of the critiques that the other students had to write about each of the presentations.'

'It sounds as if your trainee constable has done a very thorough job,' Jonah commented,' slightly amused at Peter's robust defence of his young colleague.

'I told you he was good.'

Peter put the phone down and turned to discover Anna waiting to speak to him.

'Samantha Fraser will see us at home,' she reported. 'Her husband is out all day filming one of his TV documentaries. She sounded a bit rattled when I told her we wanted to speak to her again, but she didn't make any fuss about us going round there.'

'Right. Now I want you to take the lead,' Peter told Anna, as they made their way to Kidlington. 'You interviewed the witness who identified Dr Fraser as possibly the woman who attacked Martin Riess. Don't let on who the witness was or that we have someone else who also fits the description.'

'OK, Sir. I understand.'

They pulled up outside the Fraser's spacious residence and walked up the drive to the front door, which opened as they reached it to reveal Samantha Fraser's slim body encased in denim dungarees and a checked shirt. She ushered them in and took them through to the kitchen, where there was a jug of fresh coffee and three Portmeirion mugs on the working surface. They sat down round the table.

'What can I do for you?' Samantha asked, apparently calm, but Peter noticed that her face was slightly flushed and her hand shook almost imperceptibly as she poured the coffee.

'Dr Martin Riess was attacked yesterday,' Anna told her.

'That's the man who owns the boat where that journalist was killed?' Samantha asked, as if playing for time.

'That's right. He was in the boat at the time. Someone came up behind him and hit him over the head with a hammer.'

'Like the others?' Samantha asked, opening her eyes wider. 'Was he killed too?'

'No. Fortunately the attacker was interrupted and ran away before she could finish the job.'

'She?' Samantha said weakly, looking from Anna to Peter and back again.

'That's right. We have a witness who says that it was a woman answering your description,' Anna replied, pressing her advantage in the hope of startling Samantha into revealing more than she intended. 'Can you tell us where you were yesterday morning – after we left your office?'

'I was working in the lab.'

'And there are other people around who can vouch for that?'

'Hannah was there until about eleven, but then she had to go home. She has a young child and the child-minder would only do half a day because it was a bank holiday. She can confirm that I was still there when she left.'

'And after that?'

'I was on my own. In fact, I only stayed until – oh, I don't know – about twelve thirty, I suppose. I had been meaning to put in the whole day, because we're getting behind on the project, but after Hannah left I suddenly thought, what does it all matter anyway? I'm thinking of jacking it all in and trying something completely different.'

'Such as?' Peter asked, with interest.

'I don't know! I used to do a bit of singing – for parties and in pubs and clubs, that sort of thing – maybe, with the notoriety that this business has brought, I could break into show business with that. Or I might just apply for a job as a biochemist in a hospital lab. Anything, really, to get away from Oxford and George and his women!'

There was a long pause after this outburst.

'I'm sorry,' Samantha said at last. 'You were asking about what I was doing yesterday. As I said, I left the lab at about twelve-thirty and came home. George will be able to confirm that. We had lunch together and then he spent the afternoon in the lounge reading the papers – looking for more coverage of his sexual exploits, I expect – and I hoovered the floor and did the washing. We had coffee in the middle of the afternoon and then he said he was going out for a walk.'

'But you think otherwise?' Anna asked, picking up on the sceptical tone in Samantha's voice.

'He was going to see his mistress,' she answered. 'The same as he did on Wednesday afternoon, when he claimed to have been working in his room at college. I knew that was a lie, because I tried to see him there. I rang him first and then, when he didn't answer the landline and the mobile was switched off, I went round. I knocked on the door and called to him, but he wasn't there. Then, after you'd come to the lab asking questions and I could see that we were both under suspicion, I confronted him and in the end he admitted that he was in a hotel on the Abingdon Road having it off with one of the lab technicians.'

'So much for *it isn't like my having an affair* and *I paid them a fair price for what I got*,' Peter muttered under his breath, remembering Fraser's words to him regarding his use of prostitutes.

'That's very interesting,' he said aloud. 'Can you give me the name of the hotel and of the woman involved?'

Samantha tore a page off a pad of paper that hung above the fridge, wrote down the information and handed it to him.

'I suppose that takes him out of the frame for murdering Finch,' she said, as if she wished that it did not, 'and probably puts me into it, seeing as I lied to you about being in the lab all day on Wednesday.'

'We'll be the judge of that,' Peter said, folding the paper and putting it away in his jacket pocket. 'Now, is there anything else that you told us before that you'd like to modify on reflection?'

'No, I don't think so.'

'Well, if you do think of anything – or anything else that could help us at all – give us a ring on this number,' Peter said, handing her one of his business cards and getting up to leave.

Samantha showed them to the door.

'I really didn't do in those journalists,' she said as they left. 'If I was going to kill anyone it would be George. I feel such a fool!'

CHAPTER 20

Jonah found Coralie Finch at her parents' home, playing with her children. She seemed happier and more at ease than Jonah had seen her before, as she sat on the floor narrating a story about the adventures of various toy animals, putting on different voices for each character.

"'Ho, ho ho," laughed Barnaby Bear,' she said in a deep, throaty voice, bouncing the teddy bear on the floor to indicate that he was shaking with mirth, "'You do look funny!" "Oh no I don't!" Molly Mouse squealed,' she went on, in a high-pitched squeak, picking up a floppy toy mouse in a pink dress and making it wave its arms around wildly. "'I don't! I don't!" and Molly Mouse ran -'

Coralie broke off suddenly as she realised that her audience had increased. Looking up at Jonah, smiling down on her, she turned bright red and dropped the toys. Then she scrambled hastily to her feet and extended her hand towards him. Jonah noted that her lips were painted a deep red, contrasting starkly with her pale face.

'I'm sorry,' she apologised. 'I was meaning to ring you, but it was quite late when I got home last night and then, this morning I wanted to spend some time with the girls.'

'Not to worry,' Jonah said equably. 'But now that I've

found you, I do need to ask you some questions.'

Coralie's parents took the children out to the park, leaving Jonah and Coralie to speak undisturbed. They sat eying one another across the untidy floor, which was still littered with soft toys. Jonah paused, debating the best starting point for his inquisition.

'Where were you yesterday?' he asked at last. 'It wasn't very sensible going off without letting anyone know where you were.'

'I know,' Coralie admitted, looking slightly relieved, as if she had accepted the implication that his main concern was for her own welfare. 'I just wanted to get away from everyone. I needed to be alone, to think things through.'

'I see. And did you come to any conclusions?'

'I suppose only the obvious one.'

'Which is?'

'That, from now on, it's just me and the kids, and what I've got to do is to make things as good for them as I can.'

'But that's going to be quite difficult all the while we're still looking for their father's killer, isn't it?' Jonah commented. 'So we need you to help us find them.'

'Yes, of course. What is it you need me to tell you?'

'Let's start by you answering my question. Where were you when I called round yesterday?'

'I went for a walk.'

'Where?'

'The Ridgeway.'

'Whereabouts?'

'I don't remember. I wasn't thinking about it. I just went and parked and then walked about.'

'Where did you park?'

'The usual place.'

'Steps Hill?'

'Yes – no – I don't remember. I was on autopilot. I just got in the car and drove around and then I found myself by the Ridgeway and I thought that would be a good place to blow the cobwebs away.'

'I don't think you went to the Ridgeway at all,' Jonah said quietly. 'I think you went to Oxford. I think you probably parked in the Worcester Street car park. It's got CCTV cameras – we can easily find out. And then I think you walked along the path to Martin Riess's boat.'

'No. I went for a walk on the Ridgeway,' Coralie insisted. 'You ask my mum. She'll tell you that's where I always go to think.'

'She already did,' Jonah told her, 'but I think you'd already done your thinking. I think you'd decided that Martin Riess needed to be punished. I think you took a hammer with you and crept up behind him while he was bending down to adjust the connection between the gas bottle and the cooker and then you hit him over the head.'

'No. I didn't go near him or his boat.'

'We have a witness who saw someone just like you, standing in wait for him and then hitting him with a claw hammer.'

'It may have been someone like me,' Coralie said, flushing red and looking rather flustered, 'but it wasn't me.'

'So you'd have no objection to taking part in an identity parade?' Jonah asked, becoming convinced that Coralie was lying.

'None at all,' she answered defiantly. 'At least – no, I don't have any objection, but I don't see why I should.'

'If you weren't there it will help us to eliminate you from our enquiries, and if it *was* you …'

Coralie sat looking down at the floor. Jonah waited for her to speak again. When she remained silent for several minutes, he continued.

'Of course, the forensic evidence will probably clinch it anyway. It's very difficult not to leave some sort of trace – a little piece of your DNA that shows you were here.'

'All right,' Coralie sighed, continuing to stare at the floor. 'I admit that I did hit Martin Riess over the head – but I didn't kill my husband or Martin Fellowes.'

'Thank you. Now we're getting somewhere. Do you mind explaining why you did it?'

'Because he killed Martin, of course!'

'Did he?'

'He must have done. Who else could it have been? He must have hated Martin for stealing Edwina from him and bottled it all up and then, when he got the chance – wham!'

'But she'd already left him, so why did he need to kill him?'

'I told you. He must have hated him. He pretended he didn't mind, but underneath, he must have really hated poor Martin. He was like that – always. He never forgot and he brooded on things and made them bigger and bigger. And then, this was his golden opportunity. Poor Martin came and put himself right there in his hands!'

'OK. So let's suppose Martin Riess did kill Fellowes in revenge for stealing his girlfriend. What about your husband? Did he kill him too?'

'Yes, he must have.'

'Why would he do that?'

'Because it was Arthur who was behind Edwina marrying Martin.'

'Really? How was that then?'

'When Martina fell pregnant, she was really upset that it might mean the end of her TV career, but Arthur worked it all out that it could all become good publicity and make her even bigger in the end. He dreamt up the idea of a double wedding – and Edwina leapt on it, because she couldn't bear to have Martina stealing the limelight. Geoffrey – boring old Geoffrey – was delighted, because all he wanted was a nice quiet family life with Martina and she'd been a bit reluctant to tie the knot with someone as ordinary as an accountant. I think at first Arthur thought that he might be able to bag Edwina, but she plumped for Martin, who was better looking and generally a lot nicer than Arthur.'

'Which rather begs the question,' Jonah interjected, 'why did you marry Arthur when you apparently have such a low opinion of him?'

'You know,' Coralie said, giving Jonah the briefest of smiles, 'that was the key question that I was trying to think out the answer to yesterday, and I still can't work it out!'

'But I'm still confused,' Jonah confessed. 'If Martin Riess was so keen to marry Edwina, and if she didn't really care who she married so long as it happened at the same time as her sister's wedding, how come Edwina didn't marry Martin Riess?'

'He was in America.'

'He could have come back.'

'But he would have expected his wife to go back with him until his contract ended, and that would have got in the way of her career.'

Jonah sat for a few moments, ruminating on what he had just heard. It still made no sense to him.

'I suppose you'll have to arrest me for assaulting Martin Riess,' Coralie said. 'How is he? I was watching the papers for news, but it wasn't reported.'

'We're trying to keep it out of the papers to dampen down speculation. Lucky for you, Riess has a hard skull and you only managed to inflict superficially injuries. It'll be up to him to decide whether to press charges.'

'What happens next?'

'Well, I have to decide whether or not I believe you when you say that you weren't responsible for either of the deaths. And at the moment I'm really struggling to understand some of the things you've just been telling me.'

'Such as?'

'Well, for a start, when I asked you why you tried to kill Martin Riess, you said it was because he killed Fellowes. And then, afterwards, you said that you though he'd killed your husband too. What I don't understand is why it was Fellowes that you thought of first. What is he to you?'

'He's the only man I ever really loved,' Coralie said

simply. 'And,' she added, after a short pause, 'he's the father of my children.'

'So there you have it,' Jonah said to Peter on the phone later that afternoon. 'It turns out that both Fellowes and Coralie were fed up with their respective marriages and had found true love at last – on Coralie's side anyway. But, according to her, both Arthur and Edwina were too self-absorbed to notice.'

'And do you believe her when she says she didn't kill either of the others?' Peter asked. 'By her own admission, she had no time for her husband any more and she *was* the one who found the body.'

'Yes, but what possible motive could she have for killing Fellowes? She seemed to be genuinely concerned for him and upset about his death. I could see why she might kill her husband in order to marry Fellowes – especially after he left Edwina – but why would she want to kill *him*?'

'To stop him telling Finch that he was the father of the kids he'd been supporting, maybe.'

'Yes,' Jonah said slowly. 'That might work. How about this? When she hears that Fellowes has left his wife, Coralie expects that he'll marry *her* and it'll all be happy families the way she had hoped for, way back in their Cambridge days. She goes to see him aboard the boat, but he laughs at her and says he's not getting himself into another marriage when he's still suffering from the first. She gets angry and threatens to tell everyone that he's the father and he says *do your worst* and threatens to set Finch against her over it. She can see herself ending up with no husband at all and no financial security, so, after she leaves, she turns round and creeps back and hits him over the head.'

'With a large hammer that she just happens to have in her pocket at the time,' Peer finished for him. 'No. These murders have to be pre-planned. Anyway, wasn't Coralie at a Parents' Evening the night Fellowes was killed? I can just about buy the idea that she could have slipped away unnoticed for, say half an hour, which might just have given her time to drive to Oxford, hit Fellowes over the head and drive back, but definitely doesn't allow for this heart-to-heart conversation that you're imagining.'

'It doesn't have to have been on the same occasion,' Jonah pointed out.

'She's still got a pretty good alibi. And if she killed Fellowes to stop him telling Finch about the kids, why would she go on to kill Finch as well?'

'By all accounts, Finch was no loss to anyone,' Jonah muttered. 'However, I'm inclined to agree with you. Coralie has alibis for both murders and no clear motive for either. She's probably telling the truth when she says that she attacked Riess because she blamed him for killing Fellowes – which brings us on to the question of whether she's right to blame him.'

'I'd say, definitely not,' Peter answered promptly and with more decisiveness than Jonah expected of him. 'Unless he's managed to persuade an inordinate number of people to lie for him, he can't have committed either crime. The whole of the Lichfield College SCR – with the notable exception of George Fraser – can vouch for it that he was with them when Fellowes was killed, and on Wednesday he had tutorials all day with students who have no reason at all not to tell the truth. Besides, I've met the man, he's not the type.'

'You used to tell me that there was no *type*. You said anyone could commit a murder. And didn't you say that his own mother described him as brooding on things from the past?'

'Yes, but not like that,' Peter answered, wishing that he had not mentioned to Jonah the words that Bernie had used to explain Martin's guilt feelings about his father's death. 'She said that he broods on things and it makes him blame *himself.* I expect he thinks he wasn't good enough for Edwina and that's why she chose Fellowes. You shouldn't take everything Coralie says at face value. Remember, she's got to paint Martin Riess as black as she can, in order to justify what she did.'

'OK,' Jonah conceded. 'If it wasn't Coralie and it wasn't Riess, who have we got left?'

'There are the Frasers – neither of them have got what I'd call watertight alibis. Which reminds me: according to Samantha, George has a mistress with whom he spent a good part of Wednesday afternoon. I don't know whether that makes either of them more or less likely to have done away with the journalists that exposed his other sexual misdemeanours. What about Edgar Pickering? Has your man at the Met come up with anything on him yet?'

'Not yet.'

Peter felt an unreasonable tinge of satisfaction that Jonah's connections at Scotland Yard had not produced any instant results to help their enquiries. For a moment or two, neither spoke as they tried to think what the next move ought to be.

'It's just occurred to me,' Peter said, eventually, 'that, if Arthur Finch had found out about his wife's liaison with Fellowes, that gives him the best motive so far for wanting to do away with him.'

'Maybe, but if Coralie attacked Riess, and Finch attacked Fellowes, we have to assume that the three attacks were all carried out by different people,' Jonah objected.

'Yes,' Peter agreed with a sigh. 'You're right. We've got to assume that we're looking for someone who wanted to get rid of both Fellowes and Finch.'

'Which brings us back to people who had either appeared in *Revelations* or thought that they were about to appear and didn't want to.'

'Or else, to one of the Martians for whatever bizarre reason their contorted mind managed to find,' Peter commented in a despairing voice. 'I reckon they were right describing themselves as aliens from outer space. The way they behave is certainly completely alien to anything I can understand!'

'I don't know,' Jonah replied in an amused tone, 'ambition, greed and marital infidelity aren't that uncommon.'

'Huh!' snorted Peter, whose personal views on love and marriage were of a very conservative kind. 'There's Coralie, who marries a man she can't stand just in order to have children …'

'Something that he turns out to be singularly ineffectual at,' Jonah commented wryly.

'And Fellowes, who's supposed to be such a good friend of Riess's, but doesn't hesitate to steal his fiancée while he's out of the country; and Edwina throwing over the man she loves and marrying someone else, just so that her sister doesn't get to have a wedding before her …'

'That's only Coralie's take on it,' Jonah pointed out.

'No it isn't. Martin Riess said the same. Everyone seems to agree that the Clarkson girls were fiercely competitive and neither wanted the other to appear to have achieved something they hadn't.'

'So, I wonder how Edwina felt about Martina's children,' Jonah murmured. 'Suppose she had wanted some, but Fellowes wouldn't agree? She'd have a right to feel miffed if she found out about Coralie's kids, wouldn't she?'

'Yes, but we already have a perfectly good motive for either of the Clarkson sisters to want to do away with Fellowes,' Peter objected. 'That's the other thing that I can't understand. They're all supposed to be such good friends, but then Fellowes and Finch come up with the idea of exposing Amber Plant's mental health problems to the world, just to sell a few copies of their paper. If Martina took the law into her own hands and silenced them both with a hammer, I can't honestly say I'd blame her!'

'You always used to say,' Jonah said, breaking the pause that had followed this outburst, 'that there was never any justification for taking the law into your own hands.'

'I know,' Peter admitted, feeling a bit ashamed at having displayed his feelings so openly. 'And I still say it, but I've been thinking about what it must have been like for the Plants after Edwina told them about the article Fellowes was writing. Think of the damage that it could have done to Amber – knowing that everyone was reading about her and talking about her. And what could Martina do, legally, to stop it? Attempting to take out an injunction could have produced the very publicity that they wanted to avoid – or it could have prompted Finch to publish the article sooner. In Martina's place, I know I'd have been desperate to prevent Fellowes and Finch from printing anything that might make my daughter's mental state worse; and if they wouldn't listen to reason … well, I don't know what I might have done.'

'You're right,' Jonah agreed. 'Martina has by far the best motive for killing them both. At least, I'd say Martina and Edwina together. I know they were competitive over some things, but they were twins, after all, and pretty close in many ways. And it was Edwina who alerted Martina to Fellowes' plans for the article about Amber.'

'Which reminds me,' Peter added. 'We've discovered that Edwina lied about which train she got back to Strasbourg last Tuesday. Constable Philipson finally managed to get the information: she's been like a terrier with a bone over that, these last few days, and all her hard work finally paid off.'

Jonah smiled to himself at Peter's determination to give credit to the younger officer for something that he had almost certainly initiated himself. It was no wonder Peter had never climbed above inspector rank! Jonah imagined the scene at the promotion interview with Peter in the hot seat.

Now Johns, what would you say was your greatest

achievement? – I'm not sure I can answer that, sir. I have such a good team that I never seem to need to do much myself. – Tell us why you should have this DCI post. – It's time I moved on out of the way of junior officers coming along behind. There are two or three detective sergeants I could recommend, who deserve to be promoted.

'Martina told us that she got the fifteen thirty-one Eurostar from St Pancras,' Peter went on, breaking into Jonah's reverie, 'but we couldn't find any trace of her on that one. It turns out she missed it and actually left London at half past eight in the evening.'

'Still too early to have killed Fellowes,' Jonah observed. 'Or do you think it could have been done? With a fast car from Oxford to London, perhaps?'

'It would be incredibly tight, but I suppose if we assume that the time of death was as early as it possibly could be – which is shortly after seven – then it might just be possible. Edwina definitely couldn't have killed Finch, because we have confirmation that she was in Strasbourg on Wednesday, but if the sisters were working together …'

'Yes, Jonah agreed. 'The only witness to say that Martina wasn't out making murderous attacks on magazine editors on Wednesday afternoon is Amber Plant, who most probably shut herself up in her room all day and wouldn't know – or care – whether her mother was there or not.'

CHAPTER 21

Bernie had a church meeting that evening, so Peter and Lucy were at home alone enjoying a game of draughts when Martin Riess called to thank Lucy. Peter answered the door and ushered him into the large living room. Lucy immediately ran forward and asked how his head was. He bent down obligingly and allowed her to inspect the stitches, before reaching inside his jacket and bringing out an envelope. He handed it to Lucy.

'This is to say thank you for looking after me,' he said solemnly. 'I don't know what I'd have done without you.'

He watched as Lucy opened the envelope and took out a card. It had a cartoon of a nurse and the caption *Thank You for Looking After Me*. She smiled broadly and held the card out for Peter to see.

'I'll make a brew,' she said, remembering that tea was a necessary part of receiving guests and seeing herself as hostess in the absence of her mother. She turned to go, but Martin called her back.

'Just a minute! I've got something else for you – from my mother.'

Lucy stopped in her tracks and looked up at him expectantly. He reached into his jacket pocket again and produced a small photograph album, which he held out towards her. She took it, a puzzled frown on her face.

'Open it,' he urged. 'Have a look inside.'

Lucy did as she was told. The first page had a portrait of a man in his late thirties with blue eyes and an unruly mop of fair hair. Lucy looked at it carefully. Then she looked up and went over to the fireplace and compared it with a portrait of an older man that stood on the mantelpiece. Gradually her face lit up in a smile.

'It's my dad, isn't it?' she said at last.

'That's right,' Martin confirmed. 'My mum took that picture when I was only a couple of years older than you are now. He was a very, very good friend of ours. He helped us a lot.'

'Did he?' Lucy asked, wide-eyed. 'Tell me about it.'

'I will, if you like, but have a look at the other pictures first.'

'I'll put the kettle on,' Peter said, getting up and heading for the kitchen. 'It's black coffee with three sugars, isn't it?'

'That will do nicely,' Martin agreed, returning Peter's grin. 'Now Lucy, this is your dad helping me to learn English.'

'Why?' Lucy asked, looking down at a photograph of a man and a boy poring over a book together.

'When I first came over here, I could only speak German,' Martin explained. 'I had English lessons at school and my mum taught me, but Uncle Richard – that's your dad – used to read stories with me and help me say the words right. If it hadn't been for him, I vood probably shtill be shpeakink viz a shtronk German aksent, like zis!'

Lucy giggled as Martin put on an exaggerated accent, reminiscent of a comedy German from television shows. Then she turned the pages of the album again and he told her what each picture depicted. When they reached the end, she looked up at him, eyes shining.

'Is it really mine – to keep?'

'Yes. My mother wants you to have it – to go with your book. She told me you have a book about your dad.'

'That's right. Would you like to see it?' Lucy asked eagerly, 'I'll get it.'

Peter returned to find Lucy and Martin sitting together on the sofa, engrossed in studying hand-written stories, which various friends and acquaintances had composed, at Bernie's request, to provide the little girl with a vision of the father that she would never meet. He put down the mugs that he was carrying and sat down quietly on a chair, trying not to disturb them.

When Bernie returned two hours later, Lucy ran into the hall to greet her, brandishing her new album and talking excitedly.

'Martin's asked me to go out in his boat on Saturday,' she said, pulling at her mother's hand to lead her into the living room. 'I can go, can't I? Daddy says I can.'

'Well, if Peter has already given you permission, who am I to disagree?' Bernie said with a smile.

'You're welcome to come as well,' Martin assured her, hurriedly, 'if you think she needs someone with her – and your husband too, of course.'

'I'm quite sure that Lucy will enjoy herself far more,' Bernie answered, seeing her daughter's face fall at the suggestion that her mother might accompany her in the trip, 'if she can command your undivided attention. So, if you're prepared to take her on without any assistance, that's fine by me.'

'Lucy frowned briefly at the suggestion that anyone might need help in order to cope with looking after her and then decided that her mother was teasing her and smiled again at the thought of the boat trip. Her face fell again, however, shortly afterwards when Bernie declared that it was bedtime and escorted her out of the room and upstairs to the bathroom, leaving Peter and Martin looking at one another rather awkwardly.

'I'd better go,' Martin said, at last. 'But before I do,

there was one thing I wanted to tell you.'

'Oh?' Peter said encouragingly, when he did not continue.

'My mother says I ought to be more open with the police – about Martin's death and everything.'

He stopped again and Peter looked at him silently, wondering what it was that he was finding so difficult to say.

'The thing is,' he went on, after another long pause, 'I don't like getting other people into trouble. I mean, I wouldn't want something I said to be what put someone in the dock.'

'Even if they were guilty?'

'I suppose not. Well, I don't know.'

'Whatever you tell me won't lead to a prosecution unless it fits with other evidence to prove that the person is guilty,' Peter told him. 'And if you don't tell me and the murderer goes on to kill again, then you might be partly responsible.'

'Yes. I know. Well, here goes then.' Martin paused again and then continued. 'The thing is, Martina and Geoffrey Plant were absolutely furious with Martin just before he died.'

'Because of the story he was writing about their daughter?'

'You know about that?' Martin asked in surprise.

'Yes. It took us a long time before we found out, but we know that he was planning to write about Amber's mental health problems and we know that it was that plan that made Edwina finish with him and turn him out of the house.'

'And did you know that Geoffrey threatened to kill him?' Martin asked quietly.

'No! When was that?' Peter demanded sharply.

'The Sunday before he died. I went round to see Martin that afternoon. I wanted to apologise for my behaviour the previous night. Well, actually it was mainly that I wanted to try to find out what sort of nonsense I might have been talking. I couldn't remember much about Saturday night, if I'm honest, and I had a feeling that I'd probably made a fool of myself. Anyway, while I was there, Geoffrey turns up and starts pleading with Martin to leave his wife and daughter alone and not to write about their private family problems. Martin just laughed and told him that he'd better grow a thicker skin if he was going to be married to a TV celebrity. Geoffrey got angry and started shouting and calling Martin all sorts of things that I won't repeat. He said that Amber was in a bad place at the moment and the last thing she needed was to have her privacy invaded by the likes of him and Arthur.'

'And wouldn't Fellowes accept that?' Peter asked.

'Not at all. He just kept laughing and calling Amber an attention-seeker. He was unbelievably obnoxious – which is why I really can't blame Geoffrey for storming out with a threat to kill him if he went ahead with publishing the story.'

Peter could not think of anything to say. He imagined how he would have felt if one of his own children had been self-harming or suicidal and someone had been threatening to expose them in the press. What would he have been prepared to do to protect them? He remembered the sounds from Amber's bedroom when he and Anna had visited the Plants at home – and the anxious looks on her parents' faces. He wondered how he and Bernie would have coped if it had been Lucy pacing the floor and crying out in frustration and fear.

'Do you think he did it?' Martin asked, breaking into Peter's thoughts.

'I don't know – do you?'

'I can't really believe so. He was such a placid, laid-back sort of guy. He used to annoy me because he never seemed to get passionate about anything,' Martin said with a short nervous laugh. 'I never understood why he joined us when he didn't seem to feel that strongly about the environment, but I suppose in fact it was just that he was less idealistic and silly than the rest of us – being an accountant.'

'What about Martina? Did she get passionate about things?'

'Oh yes! She was very good at being passionate.'

'You make it sound as if she wasn't sincere.'

'Well, I always suspected that a lot of it was put on. I used to think that Edwina was the one who really cared about things and her sister just jumped on the bandwagon because she didn't want to be left behind, but after Eddie joined the Conservative Party, I came to the conclusion that they were both rather flexible in their ideals. No, maybe that's unfair. Eddie's probably right that she's got a better chance of making a difference by being a *successful* Conservative candidate than an *unsuccessful* Green Party one. I suppose it's her pragmatism that means that she's on her way into parliament while I'm likely to spend the whole of my life tutoring students and writing articles that nobody reads.'

'Depending on who your students are,' Peter observed, 'you might be the one making the difference in the long run.'

'What will happen to him?' Martin asked, abruptly returning to the subject of Geoffrey Plant. 'If he's found guilty?'

'We haven't decided to charge him yet,' Peter pointed out, playing for time.

'Yes, but if you do and the jury decides that he killed Martin and Arthur?'

'There's a mandatory life sentence for murder.'

'But in these circumstances,' Martin persisted. 'Wouldn't the mitigating factors bring it down to manslaughter? Doesn't provocation come into it?'

'I don't know. It would be very unusual for a serial killer to get away with manslaughter on the grounds of provocation. But I suppose, it would all depend on whether the jury accepts that Plant's threat to publish his story amounts to a trigger that caused loss of control.'

'And you don't think it does?'

'I think it all depends on what you think about that sort of article. Some people would say that Martina made herself into a public figure and so ought to expect that sort of thing. On the other hand, if Geoffrey gets himself a good lawyer, he may well be able to convince them that he was just doing what any father would have done to protect his daughter.'

'And what about his daughter?' Martin asked sharply. 'How do you think she's going to feel while the court case drags on and her whole history is played out in front of everyone? Who's going to explain to her that none of this is her fault?'

CHAPTER 22

And then,' Peter concluded, when he rang Jonah the following morning to report what Martin had told him, 'the next day, his daughter tries to commit suicide and Geoffrey spends the next twenty-four hours in the hospital wondering whether she's going to pull through. If he did grab a claw hammer from his toolbox and go off to Oxford to have it out with Fellowes, you can't help feeling it was understandable.'

'Why on earth didn't this Martin Riess fellow tell us about Plant's threat in the first place?' Jonah wondered. 'Surely it must have been obvious to him that it was important evidence?'

'He didn't want to accuse his friend of murder,' Peter began.

'But what about his other friends?' Jonah interrupted. 'Didn't he care about bringing their murderer to justice?'

'And there's the girl, too,' Peter added quickly. 'Amber Plant. The last thing she needs is to see her father dragged through the courts for killing someone to protect her. And Martin Riess knows all about being a child who feels responsible for their parents doing things for them that turn out badly. Think about it, Jonah! Whatever happens now, the whole business is going to be a big mess. Even if, by some sort of miracle, neither Geoffrey Plant nor his wife and sister-in-law, get charged with murder, we're going to have to go crawling all over their homes and families looking for the evidence. How do you think that's going to affect Amber – or the other Plant kids, come to that? And all for the sake of two ruthless journalists who didn't care about anything except selling their sordid little paper! Sometimes, I don't like our job one little bit,' he concluded with a sigh.

'Come on, Peter,' Jonah urged, taken aback by this outburst. 'Aren't you forgetting the victims in all this? I don't mean Fellowes and Finch, who I agree are no great loss to the world, but what about Coralie and her kids? They've just lost both the father they knew and the real father they didn't know about. And Finch has a doting mother who's desperate to know why he died.'

'Better for her if she never finds out,' Peter muttered. 'It's hardly likely to give her something to feel proud of her son for.'

'And, now that we've got to this stage,' Jonah went on, ignoring this interjection, 'whatever we do won't make much difference to Amber and her siblings, because there'll still be speculation in the press and reporters knocking on their door and fingers pointing in the street. Much better to get it over with as soon as possible so they can start to rebuild their lives.'

'With one or both of their parents in jail,' Peter observed bitterly. 'I know you're right, but that doesn't make it any easier to be part of. And I was only trying to explain why Riess didn't tell us that Geoffrey Plant had threatened Fellowes,' he added defensively.

'OK then,' Jonah said briskly. 'Where do we go from here? We can't charge Plant on the evidence we've got so far, but we can use it to justify a search warrant for his house-'

'Better get warrants to search Edwina's house and flat

too,' Peter interposed, becoming the efficient policeman again. 'Just because Geoffrey was the one who made the threats doesn't mean we can rule out anyone else being involved. It could easily have been a conspiracy between him and the two Clarkson sisters. Remember – Edwina lied about which train she got on Tuesday, and Martina only has Amber to vouch for her whereabouts on the Wednesday. Oh! And I haven't told you – we've got a witness who saw a woman answering Martina's description getting out of Riess's boat on Tuesday night.'

'Who? When? Why didn't you tell me before?' Jonah cried out excitedly.

'You remember the rough sleeper that those students say they bumped into just before finding the body?'

'Yes. Didn't you say you were bringing him in on Monday?'

'That's right. While I was ministering to Martin Riess, DS Andrews and young Lepage managed to get him to admit that he went on board and took Fellowes's wallet – and he told them that he saw a woman getting out. He didn't exactly give a positive ID, but he was definite that it was a woman with long red hair, like Martina's.'

'Is he a reliable witness?'

'I shouldn't think so. At least, I reckon he's probably telling the truth, but getting him into the witness box is going to be tricky – he's likely to abscond at the mere suggestion – and even if we do, any decent defence counsel would have no difficulty convincing the jury that he's making up a story to get out of being charged with theft.'

'So we've got another witness that we can't afford to have giving evidence,' Jonah observed drily. 'That means we need to do everything we can to find some independent proof. I'll apply right away for warrants to search all three premises and we'll go over them all simultaneously to make sure there's no opportunity for anything to be removed after they get wind of what we're up to. We also need fingerprints and DNA from all three of them.'

'Of course, we'd expect Geoffrey Plant's fingerprints to be on the boat, from when he visited Fellowes that Sunday,' Peter pointed out, 'but we've no reason to believe that either Martina or Edwina ever went there to see him and left him alive.'

'Yes. If Geoffrey Plant did it, we're going to have our work cut out proving it,' Jonah agreed. 'If he keeps his nerve and continues to deny everything we may end up with it being clear that one or other of them – or a combination of two or more – did it, but without the evidence to pin it on anyone in particular. Now, we've got to do this right – both for the sake of the kids and because we could end up being accused of police harassment. Neither Edwina nor Martina is the sort of person to put up with being arrested and fingerprinted and having their house searched, without kicking up a fuss. And, whatever they may think of the press, it'll be fair and square on their side against the police right up to the moment that we find definitive proof that they did it.'

'I'll organise a team to search the Plants' house,' Peter suggested. 'Wycombe is nearer to me than you.'

'OK. I'll arrange squads for Edwina's flat and her Beaconsfield house. Let me know when you're ready and we'll launch a co-ordinated operation.'

'I'll need time to organise care for the kids,' Peter warned. 'I'm not having anyone turning up at the door with a search warrant until we've got something set up to take care of Amber – and the younger ones too, for that matter. They went to stay with their grandparents when Amber was ill, so that might be a good place for them to be while we go over the house and interview Geoffrey and Martina.'

'OK, but don't let on to the grandparents in advance what we're doing or they'll warn Geoffrey.'

'Of course not. I was thinking that we can start the

search while they're all at school – apart from Amber and the youngest one, I suppose – and Social Services can go round to Geoffrey's parents at the same time to try to organise for them to pick the kids up at the end of the afternoon. Amber's the big problem. She needs to be in the hands of professionals who know about her mental health needs, but we know she's frightened of being taken into a psychiatric hospital. I wonder if I could get someone who knows her from the community mental health team to come with us,' Peter mused. 'And would she be able to go to Geoffrey's parents too? Or what about her other grandparents? I wish we knew more about the family, so we could work out what was going to be best. I'm almost tempted to take her home with me and put her in Bernie's hands, but I don't know how Amber would react to being with strangers.'

'Peter,' Jonah said gently, breaking into his thoughts. 'This isn't your problem. Get on to Social Services and leave them to make the arrangements for looking after the kids. Your job is getting the house searched and taking Geoffrey and Martina back to the station, so that they can be questioned under caution. Once they realise that they are under serious suspicion, they may start talking.'

'Sorry,' Peter apologised. 'You're right. I just keep remembering how distressed Amber was, just knowing that the police were in the house. Goodness knows how she'll react when we turn up demanding to search the place.'

'OK. Put whatever arrangements you need in place and then let me know.'

It took the rest of the day to make all the preparations in readiness for the operation. Jonah paced the floor of his office, full of pent-up energy and frustrated at his forced inaction. He had the search warrants there in front of him and teams in London and Beaconsfield primed and ready to go, but Peter was still not satisfied that they were ready for the assault on the Plant family home.

At last, the call came through. They agreed that they would wait until the Plant children were safely at school the following morning. Then teams would call simultaneously at their home in High Wycombe, at Edwina's house in Beaconsfield and at her London flat. Fortunately, Amber was staying with her maternal grandparents in Suffolk, to allow her parents to get back to work and Aaron was still in the care of Geoffrey's parents. Jonah breathed a sigh of relief when Peter reported that none of the children would be present when the police arrived at their home. Now they could concentrate on the murder investigation and leave the welfare of Martina's offspring to someone else.

CHAPTER 23

Everything went surprisingly smoothly. By ten o'clock the following morning, there were teams in High Wycombe, Beaconsfield and London, busily taking apart the homes of Geoffrey and Martina Plant and Edwina Clarkson, while those three individuals were sitting in separate interview rooms in Oxford waiting to be questioned about the murders of Martin Fellowes and Arthur Finch.

'You take Geoffrey,' Jonah said to Peter. 'You were the one that Riess confided in about his threats towards Fellowes. He'll find it harder to dismiss them, coming from you. I'll tackle Edwina first and then we'll compare notes before seeing what Martina has to say.'

Peter and Anna went into the interview room and sat down opposite Geoffrey, who was sitting at the table, staring belligerently at a cup of tea that someone had brought for him. His solicitor, a middle-aged woman with dark-framed glasses and black hair cut in a neat bob, sat next to him. In the next room, Monica Philipson closed the door and sat down next to Jonah, her heart beating unusually fast at the thought that this was her opportunity to impress this officer whom she so admired. Across the table sat Edwina Fellowes and her solicitor, both dressed in smart business suits.

'Now, Mr Plant,' Peter began, after allowing Anna to go through the routine of starting the tape and reminding the suspect that he was under caution. 'I wonder if we could go through again what you did after you left the hospital last Tuesday afternoon.'

'I told you. I took Edwina to the station.'

'Arriving at what time?'

'I don't know exactly. One fifteen, one thirty, something like that. What does it matter? The papers said that Fellowes wasn't killed until the evening.'

'Did you see your sister-in-law on to the train? Or did you just drop her at the station and go straight off?'

'I pulled up outside and let her get out and then drove away. There's nowhere to park if I'd wanted to see her off – and it's not as if she'd got lots of luggage that she needed help with.'

'So, for all you know, she may not have got on a train for some time? And she could have got a train to Oxford, rather than to London? Or she could even have left the station in a taxi without catching any train at all?'

'I suppose she could,' Geoffrey answered, visibly relaxing as he realised that these questions related to suspicion of Edwina rather than himself. 'But why would she? She told me that she was in a hurry to get back to Strasbourg'

'Yes. She intended to get the fifteen thirty-one Eurostar, but we know that she didn't in fact make it, and she had to get a much later train. Did she tell you about that – afterwards, I mean?'

'No. But then we've had rather a lot of more important things to talk about, haven't we?'

'Now, Mrs Fellowes,' Jonah said, smiling pleasantly at Edwina across the table. 'We've discovered that you haven't been completely frank with us about your movements last Tuesday afternoon.'

'What do you mean?' she asked sharply.

'I mean that you gave us the impression that you went straight to London after your brother-in-law dropped you off at High Wycombe station and caught the fifteen thirty-one Eurostar to Paris, but in fact, you didn't leave St Pancras until half past eight that evening. Where did you go during that time?'

'I – I …' Edwina was, for once, lost for words.

'Did you get a train to Oxford and go and see your husband?'

'No! Well … yes. At least … I actually got a taxi. The trains aren't good from Wycombe to Oxford. I went to plead with him not to run that dreadful story about Amber and Martina. I thought that, if he knew how bad Amber was, he might realise that he just couldn't expose her to that sort of publicity.'

'And did he listen to you?'

'Yes. He did, as a matter of fact. He said that he couldn't guarantee that Arthur wouldn't try to run a story based on what he'd already told him, but he promised that he wouldn't write anything himself and that he'd talk to Arthur. I think he was a bit shocked that Amber had nearly died. Up until then, I think he was treating it all as some sort of game.'

'Thank you. That's better. So you went to see your husband in Oxford. Was that on board the *Maid of Saxony*?'

'You mean that boat? Yes. He'd told me that was where he was staying. I got the taxi to drop me off in Worcester Street and called unannounced. He was very civil, in fact he actually told me that he missed me. I think he wanted to come home and he may even have already decided to shelve the article. It certainly didn't take much to persuade him.'

'And you left at what time?'

'I'm not sure. I was in time to catch the fifteen forty-three from Oxford to Paddington, so I must have left

Martin in time to walk to the station and buy a ticket, but I can't remember the exact time. Before half past three.'

'Alright,' Peter said to Geoffrey Plant, 'let's forget Mrs Fellowes for the time being. Tell me about what you did after you left her at the station – bearing in mind that we've found your fingerprints inside the boat where Fellowes was killed.'

'I told you: I went home and fed the cat and then I rang Martina and she told me Amber was sleeping, and then I rang my parents to sort out getting the kids back. You've got it all in my statement.'

'I was wondering whether you might want to change your statement – in the light of the fingerprints. I thought they might have jogged your memory into recalling a visit to Martin Fellowes that afternoon – after you'd fed the cat and before the children arrived home.'

'No. I've already told you what I did.'

'In that case, perhaps you visited Fellowes later that day – after the children were in bed. Did you leave them sleeping and drive over to Oxford to make sure that he wasn't in any position to traumatise your daughter by writing about her?'

'No! I stayed with the kids. I couldn't leave them alone – they're only ten and eight.'

'And the fingerprints? How do you account for them?'

Plant looked towards his solicitor, who looked back and raised her eyebrows. Peter surmised that this was a development that Plant had not been expecting and had not, therefore, briefed his solicitor about.

'I'd like a few minutes alone with my solicitor,' he said at last.

'Very well.'

'Thank you, Mrs Fellowes,' Jonah said, leaning back in his chair and considering what she had just told him. 'So, you left your husband – fit and well, presumably – under the impression that he was going to drop the story about your sister's family. Did you tell her about that?'

'I tried to ring her, but her phone wasn't working. I expect she was still in the hospital – reception always seems to be bad there.'

'So, as far as you're aware, she still believed that he was going to run the story, right up to when he died?'

'She still does. After he was dead, I didn't see the point in telling her.'

'And your brother-in-law? Does he still think that your husband was planning to write about his daughter's illness?'

'Geoffrey? Oh yes – I never thought of ringing him.'

When Peter and Anna returned to the interview room, Geoffrey was sitting very upright in his chair, as if bracing himself for what was to come. He hardly gave them time to sit down before launching into his story.

'I can explain why my fingerprints are in Martin's boat. That was from the Sunday before. I went round to try to persuade Martin to see sense and leave Amber alone. We talked for a few minutes and then I left.'

'That's better,' Peter said encouragingly. 'You talked with him about his appalling plan to expose your daughter in the press in a way that you thought would make her psychological problems worse. You must have been very angry with him.'

'Yes, I was.'

'Angry enough to kill him?'

'Angry enough, maybe, but I didn't do it.'

'Perhaps you didn't, but you did threaten him, didn't you?

'I may have done – in the way you do, not intending to actually do anything.'

'According to your other friend, Martin Riess, you stormed off when Fellowes wouldn't listen to you and the last thing you said to Fellowes was that you were going to kill him.'

'Like I said – everyone says that sort of thing without meaning it.'

Did your sister or brother-in-law ever talk to you about doing anything to stop Fellowes and Finch from writing about their daughter's problems?' Jonah asked Edwina.

'Taking out an injunction, you mean?'

'Yes – or maybe something more ... permanent?'

'They didn't kill them, if that's what you're getting at. We were all just as surprised as everyone else when it happened.'

'Did your sister tell you that she left the hospital on that Tuesday night, while Amber was asleep, and drove to Oxford to visit your husband?'

'No. Did she tell you that she did?'

'We have a witness who saw her – or someone very like her – getting out of the *Maid of Saxony* just as it was starting to get dark. Are you sure she didn't mention anything about it to you? I thought that twins always told one another everything.'

'I know nothing about any such visit – probably because it never took place.'

'Alright, Mr Plant,' Peter said calmly, watching his interviewee carefully for signs that he was getting rattled. 'Let's assume that you're telling the truth and you never intended Mr Fellowes any harm. I guess you were still very angry with him, weren't you?'

'Yes. I told you I was.'

'And your wife must have been angry too.'

'Yes, of course,' Plant said irritably. 'We were both angry, but that doesn't mean that we went off on a killing spree as a result. We aren't maniacs!'

'It would have been understandable if you – or your wife – decided that he only way to save your daughter was to get rid of the two men who were threatening her mental stability. I know how I'd have felt if it had been my daughter.'

'Yes. We've established that, haven't we? I was angry. So was Martina. But that was all. We didn't do anything about it – there was nothing we could do.'

'Did your wife tell you that she left the hospital after you'd gone and went to see Martin Fellowes?'

'No!' Plant gasped in astonishment. This was clearly something new to him. 'And I don't believe that she did,' he added hurriedly, regaining his calm with evident difficulty.

'We have a witness who saw a woman answering her description climbing out of the boat shortly before Fellowes' body was found.'

'It couldn't have been her. She would never have left Amber. And she definitely couldn't have killed Martin.'

'You sound very sure about that?'

'Yes. I am,' Plant said firmly. Then he looked briefly towards his solicitor, who shook her head as if advising him not to say any more, and then at Peter and Anna in turn. He hesitated, as if wanting to speak but uncertain what to say. Peter and Anna remained silent, waiting.

'I'm quite, quite sure that my wife did not kill Martin Fellowes,' he said at last, 'because *I* did.'

'Do you think Plant is telling the truth?' Jonah asked Peter, putting down the copy of the statement that Geoffrey had signed. 'As far as I can see, it looks consistent with the facts. He says he left the children in bed and slipped out, drove to Oxford, parking in a side street to the north of the moorings to avoid the CCTV cameras in the Worcester Street Car Park-'

'That's something that none of the others thought of,' Peter observed, 'which makes his story more plausible.'

'I'm not sure, sir,' Anna said hesitantly, uncertain whether she ought to intervene in this discussion between more senior officers but feeling that she ought to point out a possible flaw in the case. 'Perhaps the Plant children are better behaved than mine, but the idea of a ten-year-old being in bed and asleep at half-past seven doesn't ring true to me. Mine are both younger than that and they'd both probably still be up and about later than that.'

'She's right,' Peter agreed. 'Lucy doesn't usually go to bed until gone eight, either, and then she reads in her room after that, so it'd be decidedly risky to sneak out assuming she wouldn't notice.'

'Hmm,' Jonah thought back to when his own children had been younger. 'I see what you mean … and of course, even if Geoffrey Plant did go to see Fellowes, as he says he did, that doesn't explain the woman that your down-and-out saw getting out of the boat that evening. If she exists – and we have no particular reason to assume that he was making it up – she must either be the killer or else have gone in after Fellowes was already dead. In which case, why didn't she report it?'

'If it was Martina, she was probably afraid of being accused of killing him herself,' Peter pointed out.

'Or, she may have gone there knowing that her husband was planning to do him some harm,' Anna suggested. 'She could have been hoping to stop him, but arrived too late.'

'Yes,' Jonah agreed, 'that makes a lot of sense. Whether or not Geoffrey killed him, if she thought that he had, she might well lie in order to protect him. I think it's time we talked to her, don't you?'

'Better not let her know that Geoffrey's admitted to the murder,' Peter warned. 'The last thing we want is to have both of them confessing in order to shield the other.'

Jonah and Peter entered the interview room, leaving Anna to type up a report of the day's proceedings so far. Martina looked up as they entered, appeared to be about to speak and then changed her mind. She looked tired and there were lines showing on her face that Peter had not noticed before. She watched the police officers warily as they took their seats and began the interview.

'Mrs Plant,' Jonah began. 'I think you haven't been completely frank with us when you told us what you were doing last Tuesday night.'

'What do you mean? I was at the hospital – you can ask the staff there if you don't believe me.'

'We have – and none of them could be sure that you didn't slip away for a while during the period from, say, quarter past seven to nine o'clock.'

'I was there,' Martina repeated emphatically, but Jonah noticed her colour rise as her heart started beating faster, and he pressed his advantage.

'We have a witness that saw you leaving the *Maid of Saxony* round about eight that night. Your face is well-known. He's unlikely to have been mistaken.'

Martina looked round wildly as if trying to think what to say. Then she took a deep breath and appeared calmer. She looked back defiantly and, for a moment, Jonah thought that she was going to deny having been there, but then suddenly her resolve weakened and she nodded miserably.

'Yes,' she admitted,' staring down at the table in front of her, reluctant to meet Jonah's gaze. 'Amber was sleeping and they said there was nothing I could do for her until the morning. I wondered whether to go home, but then I thought – why not have one last go at persuading Martin to drop his stupid story. I thought that even he might listen to me if I told him about Amber's overdose and how upset she'd be if she thought everyone was talking about her. So I drove over to Oxford and went to see him on that boat that Martin Riess had let him have.'

'Thank you. That's better,' Jonah treated Martina to one of his lop-sided smiles. 'And did you manage to persuade Fellowes to change his mind about publishing the story?'

'I didn't get the chance to try – he was already dead when I got there.'

'Really? And can you tell me what time that would have been?'

'Eight-ish, I think. I didn't look at my watch. I just got out as quickly as I could and went back to the hospital.'

'Without reporting that you'd found a man, apparently bludgeoned to death?'

Martina looked round at the two police officers but did not reply.

'Did you know that your husband also went to visit Martin Fellowes?' Peter asked gently.

'On the Sunday? Yes – he told me that Martin just laughed at him. Amber came into the room, just as he was finishing telling me. Afterwards, I wondered if that could have been what pushed her over the edge. We hadn't told her about the article, obviously, but she may have heard enough to draw her own conclusions and get upset about it.'

'So your husband may have drawn a direct connection between Fellowes' article and your daughter's suicide?' Peter suggested.

'Yes – you could put it like that.'

'Which would make it understandable if he decided that the article had to be stopped at all costs,' Jonah commented quietly. 'Do you think he could have killed Fellowes?'

'No. He was at home with Harry and Zoe all evening.'

'How do you know?'

'He must have been. He wouldn't leave them in the house on their own. Look, what is this?' Martina looked alarmed and gazed round at Peter and Jonah as if trying to read their faces. 'What makes you think Geoffrey did it?'

'Well,' Jonah said slowly, 'however you look at it, the people with the most to gain from Fellowes' death are you, your sister and your husband. You all now admit to having visited him on the boat between two and eight last Tuesday afternoon. So, I think we can be forgiven for thinking that in all probability one of you – or possibly more than one – was responsible for his death.'

Martina sat silently for a few moments, taking this in. Then she appeared to brace herself before looking up and addressing Jonah in a business-like manner.

'Where's Geoffrey?' she asked briskly. 'I want to see him.'

Jonah hesitated momentarily. Then he smiled at her again and told Peter to fetch Mr Plant.

Geoffrey came in, looking rather sheepish and confused. He sat down next to Jonah while Peter remained standing. His wife looked across the table at him, alert now and looking more at ease than at any time since the start of the investigation. She smiled at Geoffrey as she often did when welcoming a nervous interviewee to her television programme.

'Geoffrey,' she began gently, 'these officers having been telling me a very surprising story about you leaving Harry and Zoe alone and coming over to Oxford to see Martin. Do you have any idea what could have made them think that?'

'Yes,' Geoffrey said gruffly, avoiding his wife's eye. 'I told them. They'd found out about you going over there and finding the body and they thought it meant that you'd killed him, so I thought I'd better come clean. It'll be bad enough for the kids as it is – far worse if their mother was convicted of something she didn't do.'

'It's very sweet of you to lie to protect me,' Martina said tenderly, 'but don't you think it would be better to trust the police to find the person who really did it?'

'But, but…' Geoffrey stared at his wife with an expression of disbelief on his face. 'Don't you get it?' he said at last. 'I really did do it. I killed Martin – with the hammer from the tool box. You have a look for it, if you like. I got rid of it after I'd used it on Arthur.'

'Are you saying that you killed Martin and Arthur?' Martina asked, her disbelief turning into horror. 'How could you?'

'It was the only way I could think of to stop them writing about poor Amber and driving her to kill herself. The way I saw it, it was them or her. I'm sorry, Marty, I was only trying to do my best for Amber.'

'But, what about Harry and Zoe? You must have left them on their own in the house.'

'I left them watching a film in Harry's room, and got them to promise not to say anything about it. I told them it was one that you wouldn't approve of them seeing, so we'd all be in trouble if they said anything. I told them that I had to go out for a few minutes, but I'd be back before the film was over – and I was. I suppose I'd better change my statement,' he added, turning to Peter. 'I told you they were in bed when I left, because I didn't want you to question them about what happened. I thought that if you thought they were both asleep you'd leave them alone. You won't need to interview them, will you?'

'No, of course not,' Peter said quickly. 'At least,' he added, realising that the children might have important evidence to give, 'we'll do our best to avoid it being necessary. You can help by telling us the truth, so that we don't have to go round testing everything you say.'

'I suppose that's fair enough,' Geoffrey agreed, appearing more relieved at the promise to keep his children out of the investigation than concerned at being charged with a double murder. 'I'll tell you everything. There's no point trying to hold anything back now, is there?'

EPILOGUE

A week later, the monthly meeting of the University of Oxford Intercollegiate Widening Participation Committee drew to a close. As its members prepared to leave, Bernie hurried over to speak to Martin Riess before he could make his exit.

'Do you have time to come over to St Luke's for lunch?' she asked. 'They do a dead tasty cheese and onion pie on a Thursday.'

'That sounds like an offer I can't refuse,' Martin replied, smiling back at her. 'And maybe you'll be able to fill me in on what really happened to Martin and Arthur – or is that still off-limits?'

'I'm not sure that I can tell you much more than has already been reported in the press,' Bernie said, as they walked through the narrow streets on the way to her college. 'Geoffrey's confession stands up under rigorous scrutiny. If he *is* shielding someone else – Martina, say – then she must have filled him in on all the details, such as where to find the murder weapon, the exact times of both murders and how she gained entry to the Finches' house. So the case is closed and Geoffrey has been charged with both murders.'

'Will he plead guilty, do you think?'

'Probably – to minimise the publicity, because of the impact it will have on the kids.'

'So he won't be able to try to get it reduced to manslaughter?'

'I don't think so.'

'That's going to be hard on the family.'

'I know,' Bernie sighed. 'The whole thing is a dreadful mess! Peter's frantic about what effect it'll all have on Amber Plant, and frustrated that he can't do anything to keep a lid on the media frenzy that's only going to get worse when the case comes to court.'

'It makes me wonder if I ought to have kept quiet about Geoffrey threatening Martin,' Martin murmured.

'It wouldn't have made any difference,' Bernie assured him. 'Once they had evidence that Martina was there just before the body was found, it was inevitable that everything would come out – unless somehow they managed to convict Martina instead, which would have been even worse for the kids.'

They walked on in silence, turning in at the porters' lodge of St Luke's college and crossing the quadrangle to the hall. Once they were seated, facing one another across one of the long bench tables, Martin decided to broach a new topic.

'Tell me about Stephen,' he said, unexpectedly.

'Stephen?'

'The man you were going to get married to – way back when.'

'How do you know about him?'

'Lucy told me – while we were out in the boat last Saturday – she seemed to think that being blighted in love was something that the two of us had in common.'

'How did she make that one out?'

'She wanted to know whether I was still in love with Edwina …'

'Did she, indeed? The little madam! I'd better have

words with her about asking personal questions.'

'Yes. I asked her whether she was always that forward on a first date, but she just giggled.'

'If that's how you put it, I'm not surprised. But, getting back to the subject in hand, what has that got to do with me and Stephen?'

'Lucy told me that it was because you were still in love with Stephen after he died that it was so long before you got married, and she wanted to know if I was still single for the same reason.'

'And what did you tell her?'

'I said that I didn't think so.'

'I don't think that was the reason for me either,' Bernie said, after a pause. 'I think it was probably more that I was afraid of making a commitment in case it all went wrong again.'

They continued in silence for several minutes.

'Did Lucy tell you what happened to Stephen?' Bernie said at last.

'No. She just said that he died.'

'He killed himself,' Bernie said bluntly, 'two weeks before we were due to get married.'

'That's awful! Why did he do it?'

'Since he didn't have the consideration to leave a note behind, we can only speculate, but the consensus was that he probably thought he'd messed up in finals ... but when you're only twenty and the person who told you he wanted to spend the rest of his life with you goes out of his way to ensure that the rest of his life is a short as it could possibly be,' Bernie went on, speaking rather quickly in a low voice, 'you can't help wondering if maybe you weren't the sort of person that someone would want to spend the rest of their life with, after all.'

'That's ridiculous!' Martin said heartily. 'I know at least two people who want to spend the rest of their lives with you – unfortunately one of them managed to miss the boat!'

Bernie laughed.

'Peter told me about that,' she said. 'I can't think what came over him, throwing down the gauntlet to you like that. I warn you – you won't succeed!'

'We'll see about that,' Martin smiled. 'You do realise that, having accepted the challenge, I feel honour-bound to do my best to inveigle myself into your affections?'

'Naturally. And I'll be very interested in observing your technique. I'm just warning you not to get your hopes up, that's all.'

'Just so long as you don't intend to banish me from your lives – I've promised Lucy she can come out in the boat again next week.'

'I know – so she told me. And you mother has offered to give her music lessons, so that she'll be able to play her father's piano. I hope you both know what you're letting yourselves in for, getting involved in our family!'

'Oh, I think I'll cope. After the way the Martians seem to have turned out, I think a police inspector, a mad Scouser and a budding pathologist are rather run-of-the-mill by comparison with my usual company!'

THANK YOU

Thank you for taking the time to read MURDER OF A MARTIAN. If you enjoyed it, please consider telling your friends or posting a short review. Word of mouth is an author's best friend and much appreciated. Thank you,

Judy.

MORE ABOUT BERNIE AND HER FRIENDS

Bernie features in six other full-length books.

- Changing Scenes of Life: Jonah Porter's life story, told through the medium of his favourite hymns.
- Awayday: a traditional 'whodunnit' set amongst the dons of an Oxford college.
- Two Little Dickie Birds: a murder mystery for DI Peter Johns and his Sergeant, Paul Godwin.
- Despise not thy Mother: Bernie's quest to discover the truth about her first husband's early life.
- Death on the Algarve: a mystery for Bernie and her friends to tackle while on holiday in Portugal.
- My Life of Crime: the collected memoirs of DI Peter Johns.

Read more about Bernie Fazakerley and her friends and family at https://sites.google.com/site/llanwrdafamily/

See her latest news on Facebook here: https://www.facebook.com/Bernie.Fazakerley.Publications?

Follow Bernie on Twitter: https://twitter.com/BernieFaz.

ABOUT THE AUTHOR

Like her main character, Bernie Fazakerley, Judy Ford is an Oxford graduate and a mathematician. Unlike Bernie, Judy grew up in a middle-class family in the South London stockbroker belt. After moving to the North West and working in Liverpool, Judy fell in love with the Scouse people and created Bernie to reflect their unique qualities.

As a Methodist Local Preacher, Judy often tells her congregation, "I see my role as asking the questions and leaving you to think out your own answers." She carries this philosophy forward into her writing and she hopes that readers will find themselves challenged to think as well as being entertained.